LAURA

Vivian Schurfranz

SCHOLASTIC INC.
New York Toronto London Auckland Sydney

To The Millers: Fred-Flo-Jennie-John

ISBN 0-590-33381-X

12 11 10 9 8 7 6 5 4   8 9/8 0/9

Printed in the U.S.A.   01

LAURA

A SUNFIRE Book

SUNFIRE

Chapter One

LAURA Mitchell gazed out the classroom window at the snow-laden branches and the spirals of gray smoke that drifted upward from the brick chimney on a roof and into the bright blue sky. A few wet snowflakes gently descended on the iron fire escape. Laura's thoughts strayed from Mr. Blair's boring lecture on the Civil War to Joe Menotti. Darling Joe, the love of her life! To think he didn't even know she was alive! How she yearned for him to see her as a mature young woman, instead of a freckled-faced youngster. After all, on March 10, 1918, she would be sixteen and next fall a senior at Jefferson High.

With a pang she wondered if the war would still be raging and if Joe would be sent overseas. She hoped that Joe, who was so good and kind, would be spared. She knew that his enrollment in medical school would help, but more and more young men were being sent overseas to fight the Germans. The war, which had been going on for four years, surely couldn't last much longer.

Suddenly Joe's handsome image danced across the frosty windowpane. In the lacy pattern she could trace his dark head and his finely chiseled profile with the strong chin and straight nose. Gradually her own face materialized. All at once his head moved down to touch her lips. As she visualized his sparkling dark eyes and slow grin, she smiled and a wave of love swept over her. Yes, *she* knew she was a woman, but now she had to convince Joe of that fact. At least she had Friday night at the movies to look forward to.

Every Friday night since she had been nine, and Joe thirteen, he had faithfully taken her to the movies. Well, one of these Friday nights he would see her in a new light. After all, she was beginning to notice that a transformation was taking place in her. Only last night she had stood before the mirror and examined her changing features. She *was* growing up! Her freckles were dwindling, and her big green eyes had taken on a deep, rich emerald glow, especially when contrasted with her deep brown hair surrounding her pure oval face. Her nose, though short, was well formed, and her cheeks had traded their roundness for hollow valleys. Her figure, too, she realized, was maturing. She smiled as she thought of how she had preened and pranced around the room, dressed only in her "teddy bear," her silky one-piece underwear.

Her mother, pillar of the war effort, would have thought her frivolous. Maude Mitchell was always involved in activities to help her community and society, so she would not have been amused at Laura's preening. She would no doubt have laid down stronger guidelines for Laura to follow, so her excess energy would have a more proper outlet. It seemed to Laura that *she*, rather than her older sister, Sarah, received the brunt of new guidelines and ground rules in the Mitchell household.

Laura's thoughts returned to her new look and the way it could help her gain Joe's attention. She promised herself that at one of these Friday night movies he would *see* the new Laura Mitchell. She tucked an unruly curl back from her cheeks, pondering how she could accomplish this mission without appearing like a flirt. Quietly she tapped her pen against the inkwell. There must be some sort of solution to this problem.

"Laura?"

"Y-yes?" she stammered, pulling her thoughts back to the chalky classroom.

"We'd like an answer," said Mr. Blair, her history instructor. He was a young man in his thirties who was always impeccably dressed from his spats to his high, stiff collar. With arched eyebrows he now waited, holding the map pointer against his left leg, much as a Prussian general might hold his swagger stick. His blond hair was oiled to perfection and combed back from his high forehead, accentuating the ice-blue eyes that now bored into hers. He looked like a mannequin as he stood rigidly poised, awaiting her answer.

"I-I'm sorry, but I didn't hear the question." She felt the warmth creep into her cheeks. No matter what she had done this semester, she had never been able to please Mr. Blair.

"Of course you didn't," he said softly. "You've been daydreaming again. I asked you to describe Pickett's Charge for the Confederacy." His smile was smug, certain she wouldn't be able to answer.

Just last night, however, Laura had read about the charge of the Southerners as they tried to break the Union line at Gettysburg. She vividly recalled every detail as she cleared her throat and began to recite, "Pickett's force of about fifteen thousand men attacked the Union center. Heavy artillery was used on both sides, and Pickett's cavalry crumpled but re-formed and pressed forward." She paused, enjoying Mr. Blair's widening eyes. She could have sworn his blond mustache twitched, as she went on,

"When the Confederate troops approached closer, the Northern sharpshooters opened fire, General Pickett was forced to retreat to Seminary Ridge." She ended her response with a sweet smile at her teacher.

Running his fingers up and down his watch chain, which dangled between two vest pockets, Mr. Blair observed her for a moment. Reluctantly he nodded and muttered, "Not bad for a girl."

Laura supposed she should have been pleased at his backhanded compliment, but she only flushed angrily. Why was he always surprised that a girl could grasp history as well as a boy? Seething, she watched as he turned and drew a map of the battlefield on the blackboard, showing the various positions of the generals.

"Gettysburg, Pennsylvania, is only about one hundred miles from Washington, D.C., but our city wasn't threatened." His monotonous voice continued, and Laura was no longer interested in the Civil War. She wished he would discuss current news and what was happening along the western front. Thousands of Americans were pouring into France and filling the gaps in the Allied line. How many of General "Black Jack" Pershing's troops, including her brother, Michael, were in France? If only this wretched war would end and Michael would come home again. She missed him. Her older sister, Sarah, had a double reason to wish the war were over, for besides Michael, her fiancé, Frank, was in northwestern France. Frank was a flyer with the Lafayette Escadrille. Poor Sarah. She didn't talk much about Frank . . . the experts predicted that the average life of a pilot was only three weeks. Frank had been a flyer in France for three months, one of the lucky ones. But luck had a way of running out. He wrote to Sarah often, and she knew their letters were filled with wedding plans. As soon as he came back to Washington they would marry. Please, God, she prayed, let Frank come back safe and sound.

"Cassandra." Mr. Blair called out the name of Laura's closest friend. "What was the result of Lee's retreat at Gettysburg? Did General Meade pursue him?"

Laura glanced over at Cassie, whose large brown eyes stared at Mr. Blair. Cassie finally lowered her long lashes and studied her folded hands. It was obvious she didn't know the answer.

Laura's hand shot up in the air, waving it eagerly back and forth, trying to save her friend. But Mr. Blair wouldn't be side-tracked. He studiously ignored Laura.

"Have you read the material, Cassandra?" he asked with a resigned expression on his face. He glanced at Olaf Jorgensen, his prize history student, and a brief smile flickered between them.

Cassie looked up, her elegant long neck

accentuating her short, wavy hair. Her delicate face was impassive as she said quietly, "No, sir, I didn't have time for my schoolwork last night."

"You didn't have *time*?" he mused. "How very odd. Perhaps we should take *class* time to read our assignments." His lopsided smile mocked his unsmiling eyes.

Cassandra said nothing, but her cheeks reddened. Mr. Blair continued, "Did you have more pressing matters to attend to rather than your history?"

"Yes, sir, I did," she said, as her lovely chin rose a notch and she looked straight into Mr. Blair's eyes.

Mr. Blair was obviously enjoying this confrontation, knowing he had the upper hand. Laura was astonished at Cassie's bold reply. What was she thinking of? It was bad enough that she, Laura, and Mr. Blair were always sparring, but if Cassandra got on his bad side, too, there would be constant battles.

Mr. Blair tapped the pointer against his leg. "What may I ask was this other urgent matter?"

"I'd rather not say," Cassandra answered calmly.

Laura studied Cassandra's perfectly formed nose and mouth, envying her friend's beauty. Her gentle, but firm, stand against Mr. Blair reminded Laura of Joan of Arc facing her inquisitors.

"Very well," Mr. Blair snapped. "Come in

before school in the morning for additional work." He dismissed Cassandra Adams as if she were a bothersome gnat. "I see it's almost time for the bell." He paged through his textbook. "For tomorrow, read pages 201 to 230 and answer the questions at the end of the chapter." He glanced around the room and spotted Laura, who was not writing. "Jot the assignment down, Laura," he admonished sternly.

Dutifully she opened her hardcovered notebook and wrote in the page numbers, wondering why Mr. Blair's assignments were always the same. Read and answer questions. Read and answer questions. She never missed an assignment, though, for she loved history, despite Mr. Blair's attitude.

When the bell shrilled, she gathered her books and hurried to Cassandra, who was already halfway down the hall. Breathless, she came alongside her friend. "What made you say that, Cassie? Mr. Blair will loathe you forever."

Cassie shrugged her slim shoulders and looked over at Laura, giving her an enigmatic smile.

"Well?" Laura questioned, consumed with curiosity. Even though she was of medium height, she still had to look up to Cassie, who was taller. "Are you going to tell me about your mysterious doings last night?"

Cassie hesitated, then slowly moved her head sideways. "Not yet, but perhaps one day soon, Laura." Her expensive gray-and-black-plaid dress was cinched at her small waist with a wide black belt, and she moved gracefully. Every time Laura walked beside her she felt like an energetic, disheveled child with her long hair in disarray and her jacket flung over her shoulder.

"All right," she said, respecting Cassie's secret. "When you're ready to confide in me, I know you will. I just hope you don't antagonize Mr. Blair any further. I know how vindictive he can be." She halted before the English classroom. "No matter what I do, he pokes fun at me or drips sarcasm." Her tone was one of bewilderment as she tried to fathom Mr. Blair's reasons for disliking her.

"Don't you see?" Cassie said soberly. "He's upset by women and what they're doing now. Look at your mother . . . a trolley car conductor, and your sister, Sarah, who's taken over a man's factory job. You're a threat to him, too, Laura. You stand up to him. A man like Mr. Blair can't tolerate that."

"I'd say you do a good defiance number, too." She looked at Cassandra in amazement though, for in a few sentences she had analyzed Mr. Blair's treatment of women and his female students in particular. She turned the knob on the door. "Just be careful you don't push him too far," she warned.

"Oh, I won't," Cassie promised.

Laura was doubtful. "Your reply in class wasn't very diplomatic." She saw Miss Emerson, her short, vibrant English teacher, coming to close the door.

"Don't worry," Cassie said with a laugh. "My father is Mr. Blair's doctor. Mr. Blair will treat me as well as he treats any girl. As long as I don't get *too* uppity I'll stay out of trouble."

"You were pretty uppity today," Laura teased.

"Come, come," Miss Emerson said in her gravelly voice. "It's time for Shakespeare, Laura. Don't dawdle. Hurry to your seat."

Laura liked Miss Emerson and gave her a broad smile. Miss Emerson was dressed in the latest hobble skirt and plunging neckline blouse. A bond had grown between them ever since they had talked about Mr. Blair last month. She wondered if Miss Emerson had suffered from the "slings and arrows" that Mr. Blair threw out so frequently. She couldn't imagine Miss Emerson's facile tongue letting Mr. Blair get the best of her. Maybe that was why she was so understanding of the problems of students.

"Skedaddle to your desk," Miss Emerson hissed in Laura's ear, shooing her away from Cassie. Miss Emerson pulled a pencil out of her black hair, piled on top of her head with loose tendrils drooping around her ears, and pointed it in Laura's direction. "I'll have to mark you late." But her stern tone didn't mean much with the smile that was at each corner of her mouth.

Cassie waved and hurried down the corridor to domestic science.

English class was pleasant, and the period passed quickly in a discussion of Mark Antony's funeral oration from *Julius Caesar*.

After school, in the girls' locker room, Laura reached for her motorcade uniform nestled behind her middy blouse and bloomers. She hurriedly changed into her khaki skirt and matching blouse, laced up her boots, and set her khaki wide-brimmed hat firmly on her heavy head of hair.

On the way to the parade grounds she walked along E Street and thought of Cassie's secret. What could it be? What was her friend up to that she didn't know about? She and Cassandra had shared secrets with one another since kindergarten days, and now Laura felt shut out.

Chapter Two

COMING closer to the Washington Monument where her motorcade unit met every Tuesday and Thursday, she stopped to survey the towering obelisk. The granite shaft, stark against the blue sky, never ceased to awe her. In the distance she could see the motorcade women in line formation, all dressed alike in their brown skirts, boots, heavy overcoats, and wide hats. They stood at attention in front of their vehicles.

Today they were practicing putting their cars in reverse and then driving them between a row of white pegs. Laura hurried to stand before her open car, feeling pride in her ambulance and the way she could maneuver it.

Miss Proctor, their instructor, a large woman with a stern face, marched to the middle of the field. "Attention!" she ordered in her booming voice, glowering at the women in line. Her thin hair peeked from beneath the brim of her hat, which was lowered almost to her eyebrows. Her chin strap held back her outthrust jaw. "Places!" she ordered, surveying the twenty women before her. "Start engines!" she bellowed.

Laura spun about and took the crank from beneath the dashboard. Connecting it to the crankshaft in front of the car, she vigorously turned the handle to spark the four-cylinder engine, and when it finally sputtered to life, she raced to climb onto the front seat. She sat, bouncing from the motor's vibrations behind the wheel until the command came to move forward.

"Proceed!" shouted Miss Proctor, pointing her finger at the field. "Drive between the pegs!"

Laura skillfully maneuvered her Ford between the stakes and zigzagged through the maze, neatly cutting the corners. She wished she could open up the throttle and drive on a straight road. The Ford could do forty miles an hour!

Laura was an expert at driving, but if Miss Proctor knew her age, she would be thrown out of the corps. To be eligible to train as a driver, one had to be eighteen, but Laura figured one little white lie in the service of one's country wouldn't hurt anyone, particularly when she was such a good driver and could aid the war effort with her expertise.

She smiled when she remembered first reporting to Miss Proctor last July. The unit commander had been extremely suspicious, but when Laura demonstrated her driving ability, Miss Proctor was so impressed that she hadn't questioned her further.

Laura knew she could drive better than most women, or men for that matter, for her brother had been an excellent teacher. Michael had taken her in hand when she was fourteen, and she had driven their car all over Washington. Their poor Tin Lizzie! The old Ford hadn't had a run for over a year because Michael had put it up on blocks before he had been sent overseas. The priority to save gas was uppermost in his mind. Even though the country had imposed gasless Sundays, Laura's mother had said that every day would be gasless for them, so they'd have to take public transportation or walk.

"Turn right!" Miss Proctor blared, pointing with an unswerving thumb.

Laura jammed on the brakes and veered to the right.

"Reverse!" shouted Miss Proctor.

Concentrating, Laura stepped on the foot pedal, putting the car in reverse.

A woman's cry and a brake squeal caught her up short. One of the women driving a truck had almost backed into her. Quickly Laura pressed her foot on the accelerator and flew forward, averting an accident.

After an hour's drill they drove their cars in formation down the avenue to the garage where Miss Proctor dismissed them. Laura bade several women good night, for it was already becoming dark. Four of the older women were slated to go overseas the following week to serve as ambulance drivers. She wished she were eligible, but one had to have at least a year's training and be twenty-one.

She could never look like twenty-one, but she would keep training and hopefully be used as a driver here in the city. It was important to her mother that she finish high school, and with only her senior year left, it would be foolish not to stay. Nonetheless, if she had to suffer through many more classes with teachers like Mr. Blair, it would be tempting to leave school.

Since it was late, she got on a trolley that ran almost the length of Virginia Avenue until she reached H Street, then she walked the rest of the way home. It was a clear night, and the streetlights formed strange shadowed patterns across the brick sidewalks. As she approached Washington Circle, she noticed a crowd with several mounted policemen shouting as they tried to hold their rearing horses in check. When Laura came closer, she could see that they were disbanding a group of women. She caught and held her breath. What was happening? Why were they hurting these women?

All at once a patrol wagon, with siren blaring, pulled up and came to a screeching halt in the center of the melee. Several policemen leaped out and pushed their way into the crowd, hitting women at random. One man knocked a thin woman to the ground while another officer stood over her with his billy club raised. Laura stifled a scream. She wanted to run to help the prostrate woman, but her knees shook beneath her. Three policemen surrounded the poor woman, yanked her to her feet, and half-dragged, half-carried her semiconscious form over to the closed van. It was horrible, and all she could do was stand and tremble.

The sound of the neighing horses, cursing police, and screaming women unnerved Laura. She was so helpless, almost paralyzed, as she watched a woman who had chained herself to a lamp post being taunted by a policeman, attempting to open the padlock on the chain.

The women began to run, scattering in every direction, so that the whistle-blowing officers, both on foot and on horseback, couldn't grab them.

A small woman in black, with a yellow ribbon across her breast, darted in Laura's direction, shrieking all the while. Her hat was askew, and one long braid dangled free.

Instinctively Laura ducked behind a hedge but peered at the scene through the branches. The woman, hoisting a placard high in the air, dashed to the statue of Washington. Her hat flew off, and she spun around to fling her sign at the pursuing horseman. As the policeman dismounted she huddled at the base of the statue. Then, as she tried to scramble away, he grabbed her by the loose braid. With his nightstick waving above her, he pulled her along like a reluctant, leashed dog. Despite the woman's frantic struggle, she was hustled to the waiting van, handcuffed, and thrust inside.

Terrified that she might be arrested, too, Laura watched in agony as each of the women was captured and forcibly thrown into the van. One suffragist fought with a police officer, beating him on the head with her sign, but he furiously jerked it from her hands, threw it in the gutter, and stomped on it.

Laura placed her fist against her mouth, not daring to utter the moan that threatened to escape. What had these women done? Of what were they accused? She knew they were suffragists by the yellow ribbons across their chests, and she knew they were demanding the right to vote, but what terrible deeds had they really done? They certainly weren't threatening the security of the Capitol; they weren't carrying guns to assassinate the President.

The woman chained to the lamp post spoke softly to one of the officers, but he paid no attention. Several others joined him, and they roughly pried her loose from the tangled chain links.

"Oh, no, no," Laura whispered, seeing the woman's bloody wrists. Her stomach heaved, and her hands were clammy. "Why?"

After the van had been jammed to capacity, it rattled away with its horn honking triumphantly. The mounted police followed while Laura stood numbly watching them leave the violent scene.

Washington Circle, deserted and tranquil, appeared as if nothing had happened.

The moonlight cast a silver glow over the circle, empty except for a marble George Washington, who perused all before him with a calm, but resolute, face. For one hysterical moment Laura felt a laugh bubble up in her throat. What would the "father of her country" think of the scene he had just witnessed? If only he could have stepped down and thundered a command to the police.

The laugh never materialized, and Laura quickly sobered as she stepped lightly to the place where such angry activity had taken place only minutes before. With the women's cries still hanging in the air, Laura picked up a placard from the wet snow and read the words aloud: EQUALITY FOR WOMEN. Why were men afraid of this sentiment? Her heart hammered as the image of the courageous women danced before her eyes. Why were they arresting defenseless women and trampling their signs?

Laura moved forward and reached for a torn banner, staring at the slogan: GIVE US THE VOTE. The women only wanted to cast a ballot and were willing to risk their lives for it!

Strewn over the ground were pamphlets and tiny American flags, which fluttered in the wind like dead butterflies. Laura, tears filling her eyes, slowly gathered several pamphlets, all the while thinking of the brave suffragists and their cause. She stooped for a tiny flag and stuck it in her lapel.

Chapter Three

SHAKEN and upset, Laura relived the arrest scene as she opened the brightly painted blue door of their Federal house with its three apartments. She wished someone were home. After seeing the suffragists brutally hauled to jail she didn't want to be alone. However, her mother and Sarah were attending their Red Cross meeting tonight, and she doubted if Otto Detler, their janitor, who lived in the basement apartment, was in, or if the Menottis, who lived directly above them, were home. The Menottis were probably still working in their grocery store. How she wished she could talk to Joe, their son, for he would have understood what was happening and why she was in such a turmoil. He, too, would have been sickened at the treatment of the women. That was one reason she loved him — because of his gentle nature and the care he felt for all human beings. He had chosen a good profession for his career, too, for he'd make a wonderful doctor. She longed to tell him about the awful beatings and arrests, but knowing how hard Joe worked, he was no doubt unpacking fruit and vegetables for the next day's trade. Either that or he was studying for one of his science courses at Georgetown University, where he was enrolled as a second-year medical student.

She sighed and removed her coat. She didn't know when her spirits had been this low, and all she wanted now was comfort and solace. Why did her mother and Sarah have to be at the Red Cross again? They must have each knit a dozen sweaters, and who knew how many socks, for the soldiers overseas.

After a late supper of scrambled eggs and sausage, Laura soaked in the bathtub, then wriggled into her nightgown and wrapped a flannel robe around herself. She felt refreshed and not quite as heartsick, but the vision of the suffragists kept haunting her.

Just as she picked up one of the suffragist's pamphlets to read, the front door opened, and she flew downstairs to welcome her mother and Sarah.

As she helped her mother off with her coat, she shook off the snow.

"Ah, thank you, Laura. It's beginning to snow harder." Her mother lifted the veil of her feathered hat and removed her metal-rimmed spectacles. The angular lines of her strong face were pink from the frosty air. "I can't see," she complained with a smile as she wiped off the steam-coated lens. There was little doubt where Laura had inherited her lovely brown hair, although her mother's, pulled back in a twisted knot, was now streaked with gray.

"Wait until you hear what I saw tonight," Laura said, pleased to have them home at last. "I'll put on the teakettle so we can talk."

"Wonderful, Laura," Sarah said, unclasping her cape and draping it over the clothes tree in the hall.

Leading the way into the kitchen, Laura excitedly talked about the women and police in Washington Circle. She could feel her blood rise as the replayed scene created a flurry of images in her mind.

Sipping her tea, she ended the story in a low, emotion-charged voice. "It was terrible, the way the police herded the suffragists into the van as if they were cattle. No one should be treated like that!" Laura glanced from her mother to Sarah, expecting to see horrified expressions, but they remained impassive. Her voice rose a notch. "The women hadn't done a *thing*! All they want is the right to vote. We need to help them!"

At these words her mother stirred her tea faster and frowned slightly. "Laura, don't fly to their defense so easily. These women are zealous over a cause that should wait. Right now they should use their energy for the war effort."

Laura gazed at her in disbelief. Was this the Maude Mitchell who was noted for her civic work? Was this the Maude Mitchell who was noted for her strong-mindedness? How could her mother condemn the suffragists' cause?

Maude reached over, patted her daughter's hand, and offered an explanation. "Yes, someday I want the vote, too, but until the Germans surrender, there are more important issues to consider."

Laura couldn't swallow away the disappointment she felt. She turned to Sarah, but her sister studied Laura with troubled blue eyes and shook her head. "You mustn't think of becoming involved in a group that provokes such violence. I agree with Mother."

Laura carefully set down her cup. "When don't you?" she murmured, miserable at Sarah's lack of sympathy.

Sarah gave her a sharp look; that is, as sharp a look as she could muster. Sarah seldom frowned or criticized and always tried to find something positive to say, which annoyed Laura no end. Laura observed her older sister's plump, round face with its rosy cheeks and cherubic smile. Sarah's blonde, waved hair, short and stylishly cut, her crisp, white blouse so carefully ironed, all were signs of her meticulous nature. It was hard to imagine Sarah as a suffragist and carrying a placard, yet Laura had seen women just as well dressed in the fight tonight.

"Hmmm," her mother said, breaking the silence. "On such a cold night this tea tastes marvelous." She was adroit at changing the subject.

But Laura, pouring more boiling water into her cup, didn't intend to be put off. "These women have as much backbone as a regiment of men. All they want is equality!" She glanced at Sarah. "That affects you, too, Sarah. You know very well that your factory job was held by a man for fifty cents an hour, and you're doing the same work for only twenty-five cents. Doesn't that make you angry?"

"I'm glad to do my part for the war," Sarah said calmly.

"Girls, please," Mrs. Mitchell said wearily.

"Well, why is Sarah so dense?" Laura inquired. "Why can't she understand what I'm saying?"

"Laura," Sarah said in her best older sister voice. "There's nothing more important right now than winning the war."

"It's not as if these women are plotting

to blow up the White House! And they aren't interfering with the war effort, either," Laura snapped. She gulped her tea and glared at Sarah.

The two sisters gave each other a long look. Then Sarah said, condescendingly, "I declare, Laura, you'd defend Mata Hari if she were alive today."

Mata Hari! Laura bridled at Sarah's words. The glamorous German spy who had been caught and executed by the French was hardly her idea of a heroine. Laura pressed her lips together and refused to dignify Sarah's reproach with an answer. But she silently vowed to read every word of the pamphlets she had brought home.

Maude Mitchell rose, turned, and set her teacup on the countertop. "I'm going to bed." She kissed the top of her daughters' heads.

"Mother, I'm so tired of Sarah's prim and proper attitude," Laura said defensively, trying to reason with her mother, so that she'd see that Sarah wasn't always right.

Her mother sighed. "*Please* don't argue anymore."

"But, Mother," Laura began, then stopped. Maude Mitchell looked so tired. The dark circles under her eyes meant she was worried and not sleeping well. Laura knew it was because she was deeply concerned about Michael, since they had not heard from him in weeks. "All right, Mother," she agreed. "No more arguments." She managed a small smile.

However, after Mrs. Mitchell left, Laura glared at Sarah. "You're living in the wrong century, Sarah. Don't you realize it's *1918*, not *1818*?"

Sarah's little laugh tinkled throughout the kitchen. "Your freckles are dancing right off the tip of your nose!"

Laura couldn't help grinning. Her affection for Sarah was always there, no matter how much their views differed. Despite the fact that Sarah was nineteen, only four years her senior, she might as well have been forty. Instinctively her sister always did the correct thing. Well, that was fine for Sarah but not for her. There were just some ideas you had to respect and stand up for. Impulsively she reached over and squeezed Sarah's hand. "I didn't mean to snap at you."

"I know you didn't." Sarah touched Laura's cheek with her hand. "You look tired, Laura. Your motorcade drill must have been strenuous today. Why don't you go to bed?"

"If you will, I will," Laura retorted smartly.

"I'll be right there. Just as soon as I put out the bottles for the milkman."

"Good night, dear Sarah," she said in mocking affection. She gave her a quick hug, turned, and ran upstairs.

As she turned down her bed she could hear the Menottis' record player above her. No doubt Joe had come home from work.

Slipping off her camisole, she paused and listened to the strains of the song, "Over There." The stirring refrain made everyone a patriot. As the tune permeated the wall she softly sang, "Over there, over there. . . ."

Her fight with Sarah was forgotten as she thought of a line from the song: "The Yanks are coming." Her brother was a Yank who had gone over there. When the Germans saw the number of Americans pouring into France, she thought, perhaps they'd surrender.

She flung her robe across the bed. If only the war would end and Michael would come back to his job at the American Institute of Architects. He was respected for his creative designs, and it was little wonder that he'd won awards, for he'd had the best teachers in the world. He had studied under Frederick Law Olmsted, Jr., the famous city planner whose designs even now were making sweeping changes throughout the city. Her father had helped him, too. Like father, like son, she mused. Her heart lurched at the memory of her dad. He, too, had been a famous architect, until his heart attack two years before.

When he had died, Laura had lost a portion of herself. For a year she had moped in her room, losing herself in the fantasy world of books. How she had missed him! She could still hear his booming laugh, see his black beard and impish eyes. He had believed in her and promised that she, too, should become an architect. He had been so proud of her designs, and she had kept them under her bed until his death. Then, one night, she took them out in the backyard and burned each one, watching the blueprints catch fire, curl up, and become ashes. She would never become an architect. One in the family was enough.

Now she had no idea what she wanted to do. Her father had told her she could become anything she wanted to. She had brains and energy, and just because she was a girl didn't mean a thing. "Do you want to be a doctor? Lawyer? Indian chief? You can!" he had said firmly.

A tear slipped down her cheek. She would never forget him, but she thought she was all through with tears. She sniffled. She had adored him. He had called her "his Sun Ray" because she was such a bright and warm daughter. She blew her nose and smiled at the picture of them dancing together on her thirteenth birthday. He had waltzed her around the parlor, not only because it was her birthday, but also because she had brought home a report card of straight As. Now, however, she had no one who had such a deep faith in her. Her mother loved her and believed in her, but her mother's horizons were more limited than her father's had been.

In a fury she stood before the mirror and

touched her toes twenty-five times. A few more exercises and she jumped in bed and slipped down beneath the quilt, reaching for a pamphlet — anything to take her mind off the past.

She began to read about the women's movement and Miss Alice Paul, the leader of the National Women's Organization. Miss Paul, who had come over from England to help her American sisters get the right to vote, had been arrested last June and kept in prison for seven months. She had been released only last month. One of the women with her described their ordeal and how they had been force-fed with tubes up their noses. Laura shuddered at the graphic description. How could these ugly things happen in a free United States? She continued to read about the history of the movement and the way it had started in the early 1800s, but she was too sleepy to continue. She reached over, switched off the light, and snuggled beneath the covers, thankful she was in a soft bed rather than on a prison cot.

Abruptly the record player stopped. Was Joe getting ready for bed, too? She could hear his footsteps moving back and forth. Darling Joe! Little did he know what future plans she had in store for him. She stared into the dark for a long time. Maybe tomorrow night at the movies he would notice her, but she knew there was not much chance that this Friday would be any different from last Friday. She sighed and rolled over, punching the pillow. What a farfetched dream — to think Joe would see her as a grown-up overnight. She curled up and closed her eyes, hoping to dream of Joe, but when she slept, instead of sweet dreams she had nightmares of running, screaming women.

Chapter Four

THE next morning when the alarm sounded, Laura groaned and pulled the blankets over her head. Six o'clock, Friday morning, the last day of school before the weekend. She didn't know if she could face Mr. Blair this morning. Obviously her views baffled and frustrated him, and she, in turn, could not fathom his attitude.

Reluctantly she threw back the quilt and dashed into the bathroom, filling the sink with water and splashing her sleepy eyes awake.

She dressed quickly, but fastening the cuff links on her starched striped blouse and buttoning the high collar slowed her. "Devils and hobgoblins," she muttered as she hooked up the side of her full skirt.

Next she used the buttonhook to fasten her

high-buttoned shoes and was finally ready, except for catching her thick curls with a large black taffeta ribbon, which stood out at the nape of her neck like two miniature bat wings.

She hurried to the kitchen where she cut a slice of bread, drank a cup of black coffee, and listened to the house's silence. Her mother and Sarah had left for work, the Menottis were at their grocery store, and the only sound was the swish, swish of Otto's broom. What would they do without Otto Detler, she thought, scraping the dishes before washing them. Since her father had died and left them this house, they had worked very hard to maintain it. Otto had lived in the basement apartment for twenty years. He was not only an excellent tenant but also a fine handyman, and he took as much pride in their eighty-year-old house as they did. Otto had come from Hamburg, Germany, and though his English could be understood, he still spoke with a heavy accent.

It was not easy to keep the house and yard immaculate, but they managed. Her father had designed the back porch and helped plan the landscaped, terraced backyard with the two large elms and the array of flowers along the fence. The trees were bare now, but in the spring all the blossoms throughout Washington would be wonderful to see. This whole house was a source of pride, but it was also back-breaking work.

Now, of course, they no longer had the flower garden, for it was replaced by a vegetable patch, a "Victory Garden." It was more evidence of the war effort. She glanced about the large but cozy kitchen with such bright touches as the yellow canisters, the red bowl holding fresh fruit, and the green rug. She knew little of the history of this house and enjoyed thinking of who had once occupied 314 Cherry Alley.

The house on Cherry Alley had welcomed a number of families. Laura wondered who would follow them. Not that the Mitchells wouldn't live here a good long while. A smile twitched at the corners of her mouth. The future was rich with promise. The war would soon be over, and she would become Mrs. Joseph Menotti, wife of a noted surgeon. Her smile disappeared. But she wanted to become known for herself, too, not only as a doctor's *wife*. Maybe she would become a doctor herself . . . or a lawyer . . . or even go back to her original dream of being an architect.

As she dried the last dish and gazed out the bay window at their snow-covered small lawn, the graceful trees with their snow-laden branches, and the white picket fence, a wave of sad nostalgia swept over her. It was such a pretty picture, and she, herself, was growing pretty, too. She wished her father could be there to see how well they were all doing.

She loved Washington and their home, but it was so ironic to live in the capital of the world's greatest democracy and yet have women denied the right to vote, especially when at least sixteen states had granted women the ballot. The facts in the pamphlet had made more of an impression than she had thought. She frowned grimly as she folded her apron and put it into the drawer. How could any congressman dare to look a woman in the eye? But now was no time to reflect on the stodginess of Washington, D.C. She hurried to the hall and flung her cape around her shoulders. She had more important things on her mind — like Mr. Blair.

In a flurry and a swirl of her cape she locked the front door and ran down the curving stairs of the front stoop to the brick sidewalk. The iceman waved to her from his horse-drawn car, which trundled down the narrow street, dripping water over the cobblestones. He, too, was helping the war by conserving gas.

Breathless, she raced into school and down the corridor to history class, where Mr. Blair had already closed the door. She could hear the Pledge of Allegiance being recited. Her pulse picked up a beat when she opened the door and walked as unobtrusively as she could to her desk. Remaining standing, she held out her hand to the forty-eight-star flag and finished the last line, "with liberty and justice for all."

"Be seated," ordered Mr. Blair.

As she slid into the seat and lifted her desktop to take out her notebook and U.S. history text, she noticed Mr. Blair's dark suit with a miniature American flag in his lapel. The memory of the broken little flags left fluttering on the ground after the women had been arrested caused her to flinch. Unconsciously the desktop slipped from her fingers and banged down noisily. Silently she groaned. If Mr. Blair wasn't going to mention her lateness before, he would now.

Her heart sank when he said disdainfully, "You disrupt the class, Laura, by coming late! You must leave yourself extra time in the morning." His sharp face, with its constant frown, looked even more fierce. His quick blue eyes became pale ice.

"Yes, Mr. Blair," she answered, as a matter of course. Cassandra turned her head, winked, and smiled; Laura smiled back with her eyes. Then she looked again into Mr. Blair's eyes, bracing herself for a tongue-lashing.

For once, however, Mr. Blair ignored her. He had more important things on his mind than tormenting Laura Mitchell. He launched into an explanation of the theme that would be due next week.

Laura mulled over the topic, "What Democracy Means to Me," and a germ of an idea began to take shape. The pamphlets she had read last night had given a new direction to her thoughts. The subject of her paper might annoy Mr. Blair, but the contents would be so good he'd have to give her an A. She would be certain that her writing would be so forceful that he wouldn't forget the suffragists and their struggle. She intended to write about the arrest of the women who were carrying placards and emphasize their innocence. Was this a democratic country that advocated free speech, or wasn't it? At any rate, she knew Mr. Blair would be purple when he finished reading her paper, but it would be so well written that he couldn't give her a bad grade.

Later that evening at the local movie house, the theme and Mr. Blair were forgotten as Laura watched the new Charlie Chaplin film. He was such a funny man, yet she wasn't terribly absorbed in the short comedian's antics because she was too aware of Joe sitting next to her. He was so relaxed. She loved to hear his low chuckle, but she wished he'd forget Charlie Chaplin long enough to reach over and take her hand. The scent of soap and lemon lotion made her aware of his every move. Had he noticed the jasmine perfume she had dabbed behind her ears? She leaned closer to him, but he was too absorbed in the movie to pay any attention to her.

Afterwards they stopped for a soda.

"Well," Joe said, leaning his tall frame back against the booth and surveying her.

"Only one semester and Laura Mitchell finishes her junior year. My little friend is growing up!" He flashed a grin, and his dark, handsome face lit up from an inner glow. His thick, straight, shiny black hair was complemented by his ebony-coal eyes with their ever-present twinkle. "What are you going to do this summer?"

"Do? You should know my summer is packed with plans. I've got the Women's Motor Corps, the vegetable garden, and I'm volunteering for Red Cross work two days a week." She stopped for breath. "And if that isn't enough for you, I'll find a job!"

"Whoa! Enough already!" Joe threw back his head and laughed, showing straight white teeth. "How are you doing at the motorcade?"

"Top-notch," she answered without any false modesty, for she knew Michael had been a good teacher. "I can drive better than most of the women there. I wish I could show you on your Tin Lizzie, but mother insists we take public transportation for the duration of the war."

"Could it be because she's a conductor on the trolley line?"

"Could be," responded Laura, laughing, "but it isn't. Mom is just doing her bit for the war."

"I guess you're right, Laura." Joe paused, gazing at her from beneath thick, heavy brows. "Speaking of cars, has your instructor at the Motorcade Corps discovered your real age?"

"No, she still thinks I'm eighteen. That's the only way I could inveigle my way in. In case you haven't noticed, Joe Menotti, I'm going to be sixteen March tenth, and I look older than I am." She gave him a demure smile and lowered her long lashes.

There was a moment of silence.

Joe cleared his throat. "You have grown up, Laura," he said slowly. He studied her as a slow smile spread across his face. "Yes, you've become quite a young lady."

Her eyes widened. Had he at last noticed that she was no longer a child? Her heart beat rapidly, and she sipped her soda to hide her nervousness.

Joe said, half-mockingly, "Where's that baby face and those plump cheeks?" His tone was light and teasing, but his eyes, dark inkwells, never left her eyes.

Not daring to break his attention, for once focused on her, she replied pertly, "My plump cheeks are gone forever. And most of my freckles." She held her breath at the look in his eyes and then furiously drew up her soda through the straw. She was basking in his admiring look, trying to keep his concentration from straying. She wanted to show him that she was a sixteen-year-old woman — well, almost sixteen — and that he'd be a fool to let her slip away.

Joe gave that low, delightful chuckle and reached over, pinching her cheek. "Laura, don't lose all your freckles. They remind me of an energetic little imp who trustingly took my hand when we crossed Connecticut Avenue to go to the zoo. Remember?"

Laura giggled, relaxing with Joe again. She was too much at home with him to be nervous or demure or to try to captivate him. "Oh, I remember, all right. How patient you were with a little girl who ran ahead of you and hid behind the lion cage."

He shook his head, still smiling. "You were a pretty good kid, though. You obeyed me then, but look at you now. You're a young woman with a mind of her own. What makes you so independent, Laura? Is it your Irish blood?"

She lifted her shoulder. "I don't know, Joe. I think it's a combination of my mother's strength and my father's compassion. I know that lately I've been feeling deeply about injustice, and I've been reading about the injustices women suffer every day."

"I agree with you," Joe said, nodding. "Look at Mrs. O'Shaughnessy. I see her come into the store with a baby in her arms and three-year-old Erin tugging at her skirts. Her husband drinks, while she works in the laundry, keeping the family together." Joe snorted in disgust. "And she can't vote but Tom can! Laura, there are many men who see the injustices done to women."

She smiled. "I only wish you were in the legislature." She shook a finger under his nose. "But our day is coming, Joe. You just wait and see."

He extended his hand, and his long fingers touched her beneath the chin. Her throat went dry at his touch, which was as gentle and soft as a feather. "With such strength of purpose as I see in you, Laura, the women won't have long to wait." He withdrew his hand.

"I know our day is just around the corner." Her smile disappeared as she stared into his soft eyes. "I just don't want your day to come," she told him. "The day when you'll be called into the army." She twisted the straw, not daring to look at him anymore. If she did, he would see how much she cared. "If you do go," she said softly, "I'll write, bake cookies, knit sweaters for you." She hesitated. Their eyes locked. "If you like," she added lamely.

"That would be wonderful." He patted her hand and flashed a grin once more, severing the magic moment. "But don't ship me over-seas yet. The army has deferred me until next November, so that I'll have another semester of medical school under my belt. The recruitment officer said I'd be a bigger help to them that way, even if I don't have my medical degree, for I'd be eligible for the Medic Corps."

"You'll be a doctor soon." She lifted her

eyes and stared at him with affection. Surely he must see the love shining in her eyes. She pushed her empty glass to one side and said, "I'm scared. Scared for you, Joe."

He laughed. "Now, Laura, don't worry about me. Next fall is a long way off. And as for my becoming a doctor, you'll remember I've had only two years of medical school. It's difficult attending school part-time and working." He shrugged. "But Dad needs me to help in the store. He and Mom work too hard, anyway. I'd like to see them quit and take life easy in their old age."

"And they will, Joe. You've been a wonderful son to them." Her eyes sparkled. "They dote on you." She shook her head. "I don't know why," she teased, "but they're so proud of you that they could shout it from the rooftops."

He didn't respond to her banter but said soberly, "I'm plenty proud of them, too."

No wonder she loved him and, when he was near, felt such a warm glow. At a time when foreigners were suspect, and anyone with an accent was often made fun of, Joe wasn't ashamed of his Italian parents. She'd heard of factory workers with an accent who had been forced to crawl across the floor and kiss the American flag. Things could have been much worse for the Menottis if Italy had honored the Triple Alliance they had signed with Germany. Instead, at the last minute, Italy had sided with the Allies.

Joe paid the check. "Finished?" he asked.

"Hmm," she answered as he held her cape and wrapped it around her shoulders. She longed to lean back into his arms, but instead she lifted her hair so it would fall outside her cape, and walked into the brisk night through the door he held open.

Walking along Wisconsin Avenue, not speaking much, they passed rows of shuttered houses. A snowflake or two elicited a brief comment from Joe, but on the whole, they walked in companionable silence. Laura felt a tingle in the air, sort of like electricity. Joe kept glancing her way, as if she had changed into a wonderful woman before his very eyes. His admiration made her step lighter and hold her head higher and her spine straighter. He made her feel beautiful and desirable. She knew her long hair, curling softly about her face, fell gently over her shoulders like a mantle. She was glad she had traced her lips with lip rouge and that the frosty air had brought color to her cheeks. She felt lovely every time Joe's eyes swept over her.

When they crossed the street to Cherry Alley, he took her arm, and his touch lingered a little longer than necessary, but he didn't take her hand. Not yet. That would come later, she was sure of it!

Later, in bed, she was buoyantly happy, sure of Joe's blossoming love.

Chapter Five

THE next morning, humming "Oh, How I Hate to Get Up in the Morning," the tune which was the hit of the army, Laura went into the kitchen in her robe and slippers. As she yawned and stretched she thought how lovely Saturdays were and that today she felt particularly vibrant.

Her mother, wearing a checked apron as long as her ankle-length skirt, was scraping carrots while the aroma of beef chunks and onions browning in the cast-iron skillet permeated the large room.

Impulsively Laura nuzzled her mother's neck, where a thick bun at the nape smelled of antiseptic soap.

Pleased, Maude turned and smiled, peering above her small glasses at her daughter. "You're in a good mood, young lady. Any reason?"

"Hmmm," Laura murmured noncommittally. "Just happy to be alive." Her mind flickered briefly over last night and the walk with Joe. There had been a closeness between them that she had never experienced before. Joe had really noticed her at last. Now it was only a matter of time before he took her in his arms and smothered her with kisses. The delicious thought caused her to wrap her arms around herself and sway back and forth. It was wonderful to see such a bright day; to be in love and to be loved.

"I like to see you this happy," her mother said, returning to her carrot scraping. "The more energy you have, the more work we'll get done around here." She turned and lifted her brows teasingly.

"Okay, Mother. What's on your mind? What do you want me to do?"

"Will you run to the Menottis' store and buy a bunch of celery after you've had your breakfast?"

"Sure, anything else?"

Slicing the carrot into a bowl, her mother frowned. "Seems like I'm forgetting something." She hesitated. "Oh, yes! I need a package of chocolate. I'm packing a box for Michael, so I'm baking cookies. I just hope it gets to him."

"How wonderful!" Laura took a deep breath. "I wish the war would end. I'm weary of heatless Mondays, wheatless Mondays and Wednesdays, meatless Tuesdays, and porkless Thursdays and Saturdays." She wrinkled her nose. "To ask us to substitute whale meat for beefsteak is downright *heartless*!"

"Laura, it's the least we can do for our boys. Mr. Hoover, the food administrator, knows what he's doing." Her mother moved to the stove, turned down the flame, and put a lid on the skillet. "As long as we follow his directions, it's not that much of a sacrifice."

"You're right, as usual, I guess. I just get tired of hearing about our belt-tightening 'Hooverizing' programs." She poured a cup of coffee, buttered a slice of brown bread, and sat down at the kitchen table. "Maybe we'll hear from Michael today. It's been over a month."

"I know," Mrs. Mitchell said softly, stopping to gaze out the window. "I worry about him in the trenches, always waiting to fight."

"Michael can take care of himself," Laura answered confidently. "Besides, he's in the Fighting Sixty-Ninth, one of the crack regiments in the army."

"No matter how good the soldiers are, it's hard to fight against machine-gun fire or mustard gas." Her voice quivered as she dumped the carrots into the frying pan. Laura knew she voiced the concern that was on all their minds. Mustard gas was one of the worst weapons of war. When the insidious vapor filled the trenches, the men didn't stand a chance unless they had a gas mask.

"Speaking of mustard gas," Laura said, jumping to her feet, trying to forget the soldiers in the trenches. "How many peach pits have we saved?"

Her mother shrugged. "Check the jar."

Laura pulled back the curtain and lifted from the shelf a jar half-filled with dried peach pits. "About a quarter of a pound, I'd guess." She shook her head. "And it takes seven pounds to make a filter for one gas mask! We've got a long way to go."

Maude Mitchell wiped her hands on her apron. "I'm going to the Red Cross office this afternoon."

"Red Cross office! Mother, can't you relax, even on Saturday?"

Her mother smiled, and her well-scrubbed face shone. "I'll only go for an hour or so to finish a sweater I'm knitting. Besides, I enjoy the women at the office." She studied her daughter and said stiffly, "Almost as much as you enjoy your motorcade friends."

Laura's mother had always disapproved of her lying about her age to get into the corps, even if it meant that she was helping on the home front. A small smile emerged, and her mother said dryly, "Better the motorcade, I suppose, than these suffragists you've been admiring."

Laura swallowed her last bite of bread and said quickly, "I'd better start on my errands." No arguments, she thought, on such a glorious day. The pleasant sun's brightness warmed her back as she drained her cup.

"That would be nice, dear," her mother murmured. It seemed she, too, was not interested in an argument as she dragged out a sack of flour and emptied part of the contents into the tin canister.

For a moment Laura watched her energetic mother, then rose. "I'll run to the store and be right back to make my bed and dust."

Pulling on her galoshes, she wondered why her mother and Sarah were so far from her way of thinking. *Well, that's supposed to be what makes the world interesting. If it weren't for differences of opinion, there would be a sameness in the country, and that would be boring,* she thought as she flung her cloak around her.

At the Menottis' grocery, Joe greeted her warmly. "How are you, Laura?" His eyes and smile were admiring, and the look on his face was new and oh, so marvelous. Her heart leaped when she knew that he hadn't forgotten last night.

Joe dipped into the pickle vat, offering her a large dill. His hand brushed hers, and she was sure it was deliberate.

"Thanks," she said shyly, taking the pickle. What was the matter with her? Every time she was around Joe now she became flustered. "Mother needs a bunch of celery and some chocolate." When Joe left to fill the order, she perched on top of a cracker barrel

47

and nibbled on the sour pickle.

Upon his return Joe handed her a brown bag and began arranging a display of apples and oranges.

His movements were so graceful, she thought. Whatever action he performed, she observed it in a new light. Every once in a while he would glance in her direction and she would blush and think, *Here I am with a silly pickle in my hand, instead of looking mature.*

"Did you enjoy the movie last night?" he asked. There was a hint of tenderness behind his words, or did she imagine that?

She nodded. "It was fun, but I enjoyed our talk afterward even more." There! She had been courageous and said what was on her mind to get his reaction.

Before she could find out, however, Aldo Menotti, Joe's burly father, entered from the back room with a slab of beef slung over his massive shoulder. He was whistling, but when he spied Laura, he stopped and his eyes opened wider. He knowingly looked first at her, then at his son. "Laura Mitchell! What you do? Eat up my profits, eh?" He laughed good-naturedly, and his wide mouth curved up to touch the edges of his bushy mustache. He flung the side of beef down onto the wooden block table and, with hefty strokes, began to chop it into pieces. "My profits fly out the window!" His huge hands reached to the roof in supplication.

"We're not doing too bad, Papa," Joe said, winking at Laura. "The account books are in the black."

"Not bad? I say, not good!" Whack! Another slice of meat was cut from the bone: "The army wants fifty pounds of beef a week! Salting and wrapping for export is big job!" He wiped his hands on his leather apron, which was so long that it almost touched the sawdust on the floor, and so snug that it stretched tightly across his ample stomach.

"The army pays well," Joe countered.

"Santa Maria! Ten cents a pound? For all my work?"

"Doesn't Joe help you?" Laura asked innocently, knowing well that Joe often stayed at the store until after midnight, getting the army shipments ready.

"Ah, Joe!" Aldo threw out his hands, but the sharp jibe died on his lips, and his brown eyes softened as he glanced in his son's direction. "Joe is a good boy," he said gently. "Good boy."

"Hey, Papa! I'm no saint," Joe said, scooping up an orange that had rolled across the floor.

Aldo let out a bellow. "I agree. Saint you are not!"

Bertina, Aldo's wife, bustled in with a tray of freshly baked cookies. Her face lit up when she noticed Laura. "Good morning, Laura. How fresh and pretty you look. By all the saints, Joe, what you give Laura? A pickle?" The plump, short woman chuckled. "I can do better than that!" She reached over and encircled Laura's upper arm with pudgy fingers. "We need to fatten you up. Here's a warm *biscotti*."

Laura bit into the Italian sweet. "Delicious," she said. It tasted doubly sweet after the dill pickle. It was such fun coming to the Menottis' store. She needed to go home, however, as her mother was waiting. "I must go," she said reluctantly, slipping down from the barrel.

Joe, hands on hips, surveyed her and then spoke hesitantly. "You liked the Charlie Chaplin movie so well, would you like to go again tonight?"

She opened her eyes in astonishment. "Joe Menotti!" she exclaimed. "Two movies in two nights? Whatever has come over you?"

He grinned, tossing the orange in the air and catching it. "Sure, why not?"

"Sorry, Joe." She felt wretched, hating to refuse him. "I promised Sarah I'd go with her to the Liberty Bond Rally." She glanced at Joe wistfully. "I have to go. Sarah's been talking about it for weeks. Douglas Fairbanks and Mary Pickford are going to be there. Sarah wouldn't miss dashing Douglas or 'America's Sweetheart' for anything!"

"Oh," Joe said, his smile disappearing. "It's just as well you can't go tonight, anyway. I should stay home and dive into the books. I'd better know all about the digestive system for an exam on Monday."

Bertina arranged the cookies on the counter, muttering the whole time. "You two work all day . . . study . . . bond meetings . . . If they had their way they'd turn the world around, wouldn't they, Aldo?" A wisp of her raven-black hair, pulled back from her face, spiraled down over a gold loop earring.

With a loud snort Aldo sharpened his butcher knife on a whetstone, then began to trim away the fat on a large roast. "The two of them run here and there like a chicken before my hatchet. Too much activity!"

Pretending not to notice Aldo's reaction, Laura turned to Joe. His disappointment was evident. Was he that upset that she couldn't go to the movies again? "Why don't you come along, Joe? The bond rally will be fun!"

Joe's grin reappeared. "I just might do that. Are you certain Sarah wouldn't mind?"

"She'd love it." Laura reached out and touched his arm. "Do come with us, please."

"When you put it that way, how can I refuse?"

"Seven, then?"

"I'll be there!" His pleasure was as evident as his disappointment had been a minute ago.

As Laura crossed Cherry Alley she was pleased that Joe had wanted to go with her to the movies again. This was the first time he'd asked her for both Friday and Saturday nights. Now that Joe would be along, tonight would be twice as much fun.

As she walked along the sycamore-lined street with the charming rows of brick-red homes, she met Clara Jurowski, a large-boned woman in an ill-fitting postal uniform who had taken over Mr. McKay's route.

"Any mail?" Laura called.

Clara's long face lengthened. "Sorry," she said, knowing how much the Mitchells were all waiting for a letter from Michael. "The only thing is the Sears Roebuck catalogue."

She handed the heavy book to Laura, who took it reluctantly. Usually she was over-joyed to see it, but now the only mail she wanted was from Michael. What was wrong? Why didn't he write?

Dejectedly she walked into the house and was surprised to hear voices in the parlor. She took off her galoshes, threw her cape on the clothes tree, and hurried in to see who was there. When she entered the room, one of the handsomest young soldiers she had ever seen leaped to his feet.

Laura's mother motioned her forward to meet him. "Laura, come in and meet a friend of Michael's. They were in training camp together at Fort Sheridan. Shawn, this is my daughter, Laura. Laura, Shawn O'Brien." Laura held out her hand, and immediately he dismissed a handshake, lifting her fingers to his lips. "Hello, Laura. I can see quite a resemblance between you and Michael." His blue-gray eyes glittered, and the rakish smile on his face was warm and appealing. He had broad shoulders and a lean waist, which was emphasized by his neatly pressed uniform. His look was cool and appraising as his eyes swept over her from the top of her hair to the shoes on her feet.

Flustered, all she could utter was, "Oh, please, sit down." Then she smiled and said graciously, "Any friend of Michael's is welcome in our home." Her hand inadvertently strayed to her shining hair, poking back a few unruly curls.

"I understand you haven't heard from Michael yet." Shawn sat on the horsehair sofa, leaning back nonchalantly. "You should receive a letter any day, because I heard from him about two weeks ago." His jacket had a number of ribbons. "Michael and I were best friends," he said.

"We're so pleased to have you here," Sarah said. "You don't know how we've longed to hear from Michael. It's been over a month since we received his last letter."

"Oh, yes," Laura said excitedly. "Tell us all about Michael."

Shawn beamed, his eyes once again boldly sweeping over her. Laura almost expected a low whistle. Embarrassed, she could only stare, fascinated by this beautiful stranger.

"I'll be happy to tell you about Michael, but I haven't seen him in a long time," he said, enjoying the fact that he had flustered her.

It was as if he'd seen this reaction many times before.

"Please," Mrs. Mitchell said, rising, "let me bring you a cup of coffee."

Shawn held up his hand. "Thank you, but I can only stay a few minutes. I need to report at noon for my first briefing." He casually threw his arms across the sofa's back. "Michael has told me so much about the Mitchell family that I feel I know you. The only thing he didn't mention was how pretty each of you is!"

Sarah flushed. Even Maude Mitchell's pink cheeks turned a deeper red as she sank back down in her chair. Laura smiled, relishing the compliment. If only Joe could hear Shawn. Maybe it would take something like a Shawn O'Brien for Joe to become more aware of her new maturity. She couldn't keep her eyes off this good-looking boy with his Irish charm and easy manner. His smile never left his face, and his confident air bordered on cockiness, but not quite.

"Shawn," Maude Mitchell asked, "how long has it been since you last saw Michael?"

"Hmmm"—he squinted up at the crystal light fixture—"about six months. He was shipped overseas in August, and I was kept at Fort Sheridan for more training."

"Have you been in Washington long?" Laura asked.

"Three days." He picked up his hat, which was next to him, twirling it around in his hands. "I'll be an aide-de-camp to General Long at the White House." He winked. "That's a fancy name for messenger boy."

"Oh, but what a fantastic opportunity," Laura burst out. "You'll be able to see the president, his wife, and all the important people of the world that come calling on the Wilsons."

Shawn cocked a brow in her direction. "It could be an interesting assignment."

"It's certainly better than being sent overseas," Sarah said softly. Her delicate pink blouse made her look like a rose with her lovely gold hair, pink cheeks, and porcelain complexion.

Shawn turned his head, observing her. "I know, and believe me, I'm not complaining. Poor Michael."

"Oh"—Sarah's hand flew to her mouth— "I didn't mean . . ."

"I know you didn't, Sarah." There was an awkward pause in the room as Shawn looked at each of them with a smile. "Yes, siree," he said, glancing about the cozy room. "It's good to be in a home again. A barracks doesn't have many comforts."

"Michael told us you're a New Yorker," Mrs. Mitchell said. "What part?"

"Manhattan, Seventieth and Madison. My folks live in a brownstone there." He tilted his head and grinned. "I'm an only child."

"Are you spoiled and willful?" Laura teased.

"Oh, no," he assured her. "Dad put me to work when I was only ten in his photography studio. In fact, I still take pictures as a hobby." He reached in his back pocket and pulled out his billfold. "In fact, I've a picture right here that you'd be interested in." He extracted a snapshot and passed it around.

The picture was of Michael and Shawn standing in front of an army truck. They were in their khaki uniforms, hatless, arms draped carelessly around one another's shoulders, with grins that threatened to split their faces.

"Michael looks wonderful," Laura's mother said gently. Laura knew the same thought crossed both their minds. Michael was so happy on this sunlit day in the photo, and now he was in the mud of French trenches.

"This is a picture of my mom and dad on their twentieth anniversary," Shawn said, handing them the snapshot.

Shawn's parents were an attractive couple. His mother was in a flowered chiffon dress and had a shy little smile on her oval face, while Mr. O'Brien had the same grin Laura saw on Shawn's face.

Laura handed the photo back, noticing that Shawn hastily tucked two snapshots back in the billfold, no doubt a girlfriend or two.

Shawn caught Laura watching his action. Quickly he stuffed the wallet in his pocket and jumped to his feet. "Sorry, but I've got to run."

"Could you come to dinner about six o'clock next Saturday evening?" Mrs. Mitchell said, standing also. "I'll prepare corned beef and cabbage. Any Irishman should like that!"

"The dinner sounds swell!" he exclaimed. "I'll be here." He turned to Sarah. "Goodbye, Sarah." He bent over Maude Mitchell's hand and brushed it with his lips. "Mrs. Mitchell." He bowed politely to her and turned to face Laura. "I'm looking forward to seeing *you* again," he said meaningfully.

Laura walked with him to the front door where Shawn settled his wide hat on his wavy hair. As he slipped into his great overcoat he half-turned and asked bluntly, "Will you go dancing with me one night soon, Laura?" He reached for her hand as if to shake it but held it instead.

She caught her breath. She blushed and gradually pulled her hand free. She answered his brashness with her own. "If you don't mind having your boots stepped on."

He touched her hair, letting his fingers slide down her cheek, then he laughed and said, "Oh, Laura, you and I are going to get along just fine." With a flick of his finger to his wide brim, he sprinted down the front steps and was gone.

Laura stared at the closed door for several moments. She had never met anyone like Shawn O'Brien before.

Thoughtful, she went upstairs.

As she made her bed, cleaned the bathroom, and mopped the floors, she kept thinking of Shawn. She was glad he was coming next Saturday night for dinner. She began to plan the salad and dessert and what she would need to do, such as polish the silver candelabra and iron the Irish linen tablecloth. With a guilt pang she thought of Joe. What if he asked her to the movies next Saturday? Her happy spirit was dampened. She would simply have to tell him the truth. After all, there was no harm in entertaining a friend of Michael's. What a ninny she was to be dreaming of Shawn O'Brien with such a flutter in her heart. She had only just met the boy. Joe was the one she loved, had for years, and would forever! She smiled. She was, after all, only fifteen. How could she predict what her future held? She wanted to get out and see the world. As much as she wanted Joe to notice her, she had to admit it was nice when someone else like Shawn admired her right away. Shawn was from New York, and she'd never visited the largest city in America. Someday she would see New York, she vowed. She might even go out with a boy from New York!

Chapter Six

AFTER Laura finished her Saturday morning chores she soaked in a hot tub and thought of Shawn and his flashy style. She had never met anyone quite as gregarious and daring, and it was pleasant to have such a dashing soldier want to take her dancing. Humming, she soaped her arms and scrubbed her neck, wetting a fallen tendril of hair.

While drying herself she wondered how Shawn would adapt to his White House assignment. Knowing Shawn with his cocky smile and charming manners, she knew he'd feel right at home.

Dressing in her middy blouse and wool skirt, she settled down to read a pamphlet on Alice Paul, the leader of the Women's National Organization in Washington, and then to write her history theme. She decided to start with a poem that Miss Fisher, a suffragist, had written about Alice Paul. The more Laura read about Alice Paul, the more she wanted to meet her, for Miss Paul was the type of woman she would be proud to be like.

The work on her history essay progressed well, and she was pleased with the flow and the idea. She hoped Mr. Blair would be, too. The paper was a fervent appeal for equality for every citizen. Who could argue with such a concept? Certainly not Mr. Blair, who was an American history teacher. Nonetheless, there was a nagging doubt in her mind that perhaps she had gone too far and that he'd find her pro-suffragists' viewpoint indefensible. Perhaps she would only further antagonize him and he would become angrier with her.

At seven o'clock, when she had finished recopying her essay, the doorbell rang and she dashed downstairs to greet Joe. She was always impressed with his tall, slender frame and the way he moved with such grace.

"Hello, Laura," he said. "It's a beautiful evening for the rally. Fifty-seven degrees, which isn't bad for February." He talked about the weather, but his eyes said he wanted to talk of other things.

Laura wondered if she and Joe were going to go through life being so shy with one another that they would never touch or kiss. She smiled at the idea. "Joe," she said brightly, "you look wonderful." And he did, too, dressed in knickers and a heavy navy sweater, belted in back.

He grinned, white teeth flashing against dark skin. He was so good-looking and sweet, she had the mad impulse to give him a hug.

"You don't look bad yourself, Laura." He reached for her coat. "Let me help you."

Fastening her coat at the neck, she went into the parlor for Sarah. "We're ready to leave."

Putting aside her sewing, Sarah rose and slipped into her brown suit jacket. "Laura," she said, her rosy cheeks shining and taking away her matronly look, "my bedspread is almost finished."

"Your hope chest must be bulging," Laura said, chuckling. "Frank will be overwhelmed." She handed Sarah her hat. "Come on, the rally will begin, and you'll be too late to see your idols, Douglas Fairbanks and Mary Pickford."

Lafayette Square was thronged with thousands of people. It was true that Washington had almost doubled in population in wartime, but Laura didn't think they would all be at the rally tonight.

Joe, holding both sisters' arms, maneuvered them through the crowd and nearer the platform.

Sarah clutched Laura's hand when the announcer came out and told the audience that Mary Pickford was ill and had to cancel her appearance. "Oh, no," she whispered. "I so wanted to see her!"

"But ladies and gentlemen," the announcer continued loudly, "Douglas Fairbanks will be on stage as promised, and as an added attraction, Al Jolson will sing for us!" He leaned down and winked broadly. "Wait until you see these two silver screen stars, ladies. I hope you have your smelling salts handy!"

Then, in the midst of his introduction, Douglas Fairbanks dashed onto the stage and stood before the flag-draped grandstand, blowing a kiss first to the row of Red Cross girls standing at attention behind him and then to the audience. His exuberance and smile seemed to reach out and embrace the crowd. It was little wonder he was so popular.

Joe leaned down and asked Sarah, "What do you think of your handsome movie star? Does he fulfill your expectations?"

"Oh, yes," she breathed. "Look at him. He's so slender and agile. No wonder he's able to do all his own stunts in the movies." Then her face clouded. "I did want to see Mary Pickford, though."

Just then Douglas Fairbanks, megaphone in hand, exhorted the crowd to buy Liberty Bonds. "Raise your hand if you'll buy a ten-dollar bond!" he shouted. Sarah raised her hand, caught up in the excitement of the banner waving and the band playing Sousa's "Stars and Stripes Forever."

Knowing how Joe scrimped and saved for medical school, Laura was surprised that he, too, bought a bond. She wished she could afford to buy one; however, she had filled five twenty-five-cent Liberty Stamp books. The popular phrase "Lick a Stamp and Lick the Kaiser" flashed through her mind, and she pledged that she'd fill another book before the month of February was over.

The Red Cross girls passed through the crowd and collected more money and more pledge cards.

As the people dispersed Laura thought that the evening must have been a huge success for the government. It was as if a momentum was building to give Germany a knockout blow — and soon. America was on the march!

When they reached home, Laura started to go in, but Joe reached for her hand. "Stay a minute," he urged.

Amazed and pleased, Laura walked to the back of the house with Joe, where they paused in front of the outside stairs leading to the Menottis' apartment.

Joe, still holding her hand, said with a broad smile, "I'm glad you invited me tonight, but I still want to take you out on a Saturday night. How about next Saturday?"

Inwardly she groaned. "Oh, Joe, I'd love

to, but we're entertaining one of Michael's army buddies."

"Oh?" Joe's eyebrows shot up. "Who is he?"

His eyes were too difficult to fathom in the dark, but she hoped they showed disappointment. "His name is Shawn O'Brien; he's from New York. He and Michael were in boot camp together at Fort Sheridan."

"Is Shawn passing through Washington on his way overseas?" Joe asked casually.

"No, he'll be stationed at the White House as an aide to General Long."

"Hmmm, I see," Joe said thoughtfully. His thick brows descended into a brief frown, then his smile flashed again. "Well, I don't want to keep you out in the cold night air any longer."

"I'm sorry, Joe." Of all times not to be able to go with him! This is what she had wanted for a long time, and now she couldn't go. Why did things always come in bunches? she thought.

"Don't look so sad, little one." He cupped her face between his mittened hands and kissed her lightly on the lips. "Sleep tight." He opened the back door for her, then turned on his heels and mounted the wooden steps to his own home.

She looked longingly after him. Joe had kissed her, actually kissed her! She touched her mouth. True, it wasn't a very romantic kiss. In fact, it was more of a big brother-kid sister kiss, but it was a sign of affection, and it was a sign she meant to encourage in future meetings with Joe. Perhaps she could have done this next Saturday night, but she would be busy entertaining Shawn. Again she felt a twinge of disloyalty. Joe was the one she loved, she reminded herself.

When she entered her bedroom and turned on the light, Shawn's image loomed before her. Shawn of the dancing eyes and confident air. She felt a little shiver of anticipation when she thought of him.

That night she was so tired, she slept a dreamless sleep, not once dreaming of handsome Irish boys filled with blarney.

Although the week passed quickly in a flurry of classes, motor drills, and Red Cross meetings, she had expected Shawn to phone. There were no calls; however, he rang the doorbell at six-thirty Saturday evening.

Her pulse raced as she ran to answer the door. There was Shawn, just as jaunty and good-looking as she remembered.

"Laura!" he exclaimed, a beaming smile spreading across his face. "I've thought of you all week."

But not enough to call me, she thought silently.

As if reading her thoughts, he hastily explained, "It's been a busy week. I didn't have time to write to my parents or to telephone you, but I wanted to. Every time I even looked at the phone it seemed General Long gave me another errand to run."

"Why does General Long keep you so busy?" she asked, hanging up his coat.

"The White House has been hectic ever since the rumor hit about the Russians pulling out of the war and signing a separate peace with the Germans."

"Oh, no!" Laura felt her heart dip. "If the eastern front is no longer a threat, the Germans will be able to concentrate all their forces in the west."

Shawn gazed at her with new respect. "You understand what's happening perfectly."

"It's been in all the newspapers," she said, wondering why he wouldn't expect her to be aware of what was happening.

"Bravo!" He chuckled. "I didn't know girls read the news."

She felt a flash of anger, but she tried to keep her voice light. "Oh, women not only read the news, they can even digest it." She would have continued with a discussion of the Russian Revolution just to show him, but her mother and Sarah entered the room.

The dinner was a great success and the corned beef and cabbage was delicious. Laura had prepared lentil soup and green salad, which Shawn loved, too. When she began to clear the dishes, Shawn jumped up, insisting on helping her. No one was quite as attentive as Shawn. Every time she looked in his direction his eyes were fastened on her, and every time she moved he followed. It was a wonderful feeling to have him constantly at her side, as if he were totally under her spell. If she wasn't careful, she'd forget Joe and his mild advances. She frowned, feeling a prick of conscience. What a silly goose she was! She was the one becoming smitten with Shawn. Here she was — an intelligent girl being taken in by a little charm and attention. She would never forsake Joe and his quiet, solid ways for all the compliments and blandishments that Shawn tossed in her direction.

Shawn smiled at Maude. "That was the best corned beef and cabbage I've ever tasted." He gallantly rose and held the chair for Maude, who looked very attractive in her lace blouse and slit skirt.

"And now, Mrs. Mitchell and Sarah," Shawn said jovially, "you two relax in the parlor while Laura and I finish clearing the dishes, and then we'll serve you coffee."

"And cake," added Laura.

"How nice," Maude said, folding her napkin alongside her plate. "I'm ready to be waited on. How about you, Sarah?"

Sarah giggled. "Laura will make a good waitress. One sugar in my coffee, remember?"

"I remember," Laura said. "Now scoot, before we change our minds."

After they left the dining room Laura stacked a few dishes and carried them into the kitchen with Shawn following, although she noticed he had forgotten to bring any dishes with him.

"Before we serve the dessert, let's scrape the plates," Laura said.

Shawn wrinkled his nose, then gave her his most engaging grin. "That's woman's work, my dear Laura." He perched on the kitchen stool. "I'll watch you, which is always a pleasure. You're beautiful, and yet you don't seem to know what a beauty you are. Those long eyelashes fringe the biggest, greenest eyes I've ever seen!"

Blushing, she stacked the last plate and began to cut the cake. Although she enjoyed his wonderful compliments, she was upset that he didn't follow through on his offer to help. Women's work, indeed!

Standing, Shawn approached her and whispered in her ear. "I have something to ask you, little Laura."

His nearness caused her to stop slicing the cake. She liked feeling him so close. His head was so near that if she turned ever so slightly, his mouth would press against hers.

"What do you want to ask?" she said brightly, masking the flutter in her heart.

He slipped his arm around her waist. "Will you go to the dance with me a week from Saturday?"

Taking a deep breath, she nodded. "I'd like to, but I need to ask Mother." Then she deliberately turned, allowing his lips to brush against hers.

"Oh, Laura, what an enchantress you are. We'll have such fun at the dance," he promised in a low voice.

She was confident her mother would say yes, for she, too, had fallen for Shawn's charm, and he could do no wrong in her eyes.

"I'll be the envy of everyone at the dance, with the most gorgeous girl in Washington on my arm."

Stepping back from his encircling arm, she shakily handed him two plates, each with a generous slice of cake.

"Angel food! My favorite cake," he said, licking his lips with relish.

She laughed. "I hope the 'angel' food will take some of the devil out of you."

He chuckled. "You can't tell me you don't like a little devil in me."

She pointed to the door. "Mother and Sarah are waiting," she said sternly, but she wasn't able to control the smile that lit her face. He was right. His ways intrigued and flattered her.

After their ice cream and cake Shawn set up his equipment to take photos. Michael, he said, would appreciate a recent family picture. Shawn's sense of humor was all too evident when he regaled them with tales of his first week at the White House. He had helped the second Mrs. Wilson out of a limousine and taken a guided tour of the President's residence, which was almost a disaster. When he walked through the Blue Room with a guide, he had upset an eighteenth-century vase that Napoleon had presented to Dolly Madison, catching it just before it could topple off the pedestal. It seemed that even this debonair New York boy was awed by the White House and all its treasures.

When Shawn said good night, Maude Mitchell had indeed come over and given him permission to take Laura dancing.

It had been a wonderful evening, and Laura practically danced her way upstairs. Before she went to bed, she practiced the fox trot step in preparation for next Saturday.

Monday, on the way home from school, Laura was still euphoric over the weekend. She relived the kisses Joe and Shawn had given her. Delight swept over her at the idea of all at once having two beaux at her feet. Suddenly the feeling of delight was replaced by puzzlement. How could she like both Joe and Shawn so very much and so equally? Weren't you supposed to fall head over heels in love with one boy at a time? Leave it to her to have two!

As she turned onto Cherry Alley she saw Clara coming down their neighbor's steps. Her mailbag must have been particularly heavy today, for she was very late.

When Clara spied Laura she waved a

letter over her head. "Here's what you've been waiting for, Laura!"

Her heart racing, she dashed to Clara's side and snatched the envelope from her hand. Michael's letter was, indeed, what they had been waiting for. She hugged the precious letter to her heart. "Oh, Clara, thanks — Mom and Sarah will be so happy!"

"And how about you?" Clara said, and gave a booming laugh.

"I'm ecstatic!" Laura said, laughing. "Thank you, Clara, thank you a million times!"

"Enjoy it!" Clara chuckled and went on her way.

Flying into the kitchen, Laura shouted, "Here it is! Michael's letter!"

"At last!" Her mother wiped her floured hands across her apron. A broad smile spread across her sharp features. "Read it aloud, Laura, will you?" She sank down at the table, looking at her daughter in eager anticipation.

Sarah, working at the sink, had spun around and lifted the percolator from the stove. "This calls for a cup of coffee!" She poured three steaming cups and sat across from Laura, eagerly awaiting Michael's words.

With nervous fingers Laura ripped open the flap and began to read:

Somewhere in France
January 1, 1918

Dear Mom, Sarah, and Laura,

It's New Year's Day, and the Allies are starting the fourth year of this lousy war. I shouldn't complain. The Americans have only lived in the trenches for a few months, while the British and French have for three years. You should see these trenches. Hundreds of miles all along the western front. It's a maze of interlocking dugout ditches; The Sixty-Ninth has been slogging through mud for two days, but Father Duffy and Captain "Wild Bill" Donovan are with us every step of the way — always with a joke or a word of encouragement. Really swell officers.

We left Paris last week and have been marching ever since. I hated to leave "Gay Paree." They gave the American soldiers a terrific reception!

We've stopped along the Marne River and settled in. They say the Germans are getting ready for a big offensive under General von Ludendorff. We're ready for him! Our cannon is aimed directly at them, and when they go over the top, we'll give 'em a reception they won't forget. They can't hurt us. We're snug behind sandbags and barbed wire, which is strung all along the parapets. The most dangerous thing is the flu — we've lost one hundred and twenty men in our unit, but I seem to be immune.

When I was in boot training at Fort Sheridan, one of my good buddies was Shawn O'Brien. He's going to be stationed in Washington, D.C., as an honor guard at the White House. I asked him to pay you a visit. I even told him you'd give him a home-cooked meal. He'd love your cooking, Mom. He's from New York ... in fact, my whole regiment are New Yorkers, but a great bunch of guys. Shawn is special, so be kind to him.

By the way, Sarah, I'd better warn you that there's a bit of the devil in Shawn. Be careful you don't fall for his blarney and leave poor Frank out in the cold.

Laura paused for a second. Little did Michael know that Shawn had already been here. It was obvious her brother thought she was still much too young for any romantic entanglements. Well, she'd like Michael to see the attention Shawn O'Brien was showering on her. *She* could fall in love, too. With a secret smile she returned to read the conclusion:

Well, the firing has begun again, so I need to leave my cozy dugout and man my rifle post.
                    Love and hugs, How I miss you!
                                  Mike

Laura glanced at Sarah's flushed face. "Beware of Shawn, big sister," she teased, knowing that Sarah would never be interested.

Sarah drew herself up straight. Her lovely eyes threw out blue sparks, and her mouth formed a small Cupid's bow. "As if I'd ever love anyone besides Frank Wexler!" she said indignantly, reaching for the letter. "Just think, it took over a month for Michael's letter to arrive," she said, deftly changing the subject.

"Somewhere along the Marne River," Mrs. Mitchell mused. She reached for the atlas on the kitchen countertop and opened it to the well-worn map of France. With her finger she traced the Marne River. "Look, he's north of Paris, but it could be anywhere along this river." Her gray eyes were worried. "The Germans' big offensive sounds dangerous for Mike, and now the flu. If it's an epidemic in Europe it could spread to America — that would be a catastrophe! I've heard of a few cases in New York. We need to pray for Mike's safety."

How lucky Shawn and Joe were to be here in Washington. It would take lots of prayers and luck for Michael to come home.

Chapter Seven

FOR the rest of the week the war, the influenza epidemic, and Michael occupied Laura's mind. That is, until Thursday when she was sitting in Mr. Blair's history class, and he announced that their themes were graded. Then all other thoughts flew out the window. She watched anxiously as he pulled a sheaf of papers from his desk drawer. Her heart began to thump. Had she gotten an A? She had worked hard, writing and rewriting, and knew it was an excellent paper, but would he? One thing was sure, and that was that when he read it, he would be aware of what women were going through.

Mr. Blair, holding the themes, cleared his throat and ran a finger along the rim of his high, starched collar. "Your papers, for the most part, showed understanding of the topic: 'What Democracy Means to Me.' You seem appreciative of this great nation in which we live.

"A few of your papers brought in our country's background and our forefathers' work on the Constitution, and some of you used quotes very well."

He turned to Olaf Jorgensen in the front seat and smiled. "Olaf, I particularly liked your quotations from the Declaration of Independence." The large, raw-boned boy blushed furiously. Mr. Blair hesitated, then rushed ahead with the rest of his speech.

"Some of you, however, were sidetracked from the topic." He glanced at Laura, shaking his head in sad reproach as he tossed her paper on her desk. "Your essay, Laura, is an example of what one shouldn't do." His eyes narrowed, and he watched as she looked at her grade.

There, emblazoned across the top, was a large red D. She was stunned. She could feel her face redden, but she tried to remain calm and not let Mr. Blair see the frustration and anger welling up inside her. Calmly she stared at the paper, not daring to meet Mr. Blair's eyes. Why, she thought, couldn't she write the syrupy drivel she knew he craved? Why couldn't she dish out every platitude about democracy that she'd heard since the first grade? But she couldn't. The memory of the woman chained to the lamp post made it plain that democracy wasn't for everyone.

Mr. Blair stopped at her desk. "Well, you evidently didn't grasp the topic."

She bit her lip, trying to keep it from trembling. She swallowed before speaking. "It's a subject that should give me some freedom to express my own ideas." She bitterly repeated the title: " 'What Democracy Means to Me.' As long as I'm a second-class citizen, that subject doesn't mean very much."

Titters were heard throughout the classroom after her daring reply.

Cassandra leaned over and whispered loudly, "I agree."

"No talking!" Mr. Blair snapped. He paused for a moment as if trying to be fair. "Perhaps rewriting your paper will shed a new understanding on the question, and this time, Laura, try not to be so negative."

"I understand the question, sir," Laura persisted. "It's just that you don't understand any view that differs from yours."

The class, accustomed to their exchanges, laughed aloud.

"Silence." Mr. Blair rapped on her desk. "Laura, I'll see you after class. Perhaps your low mark will make you rethink your views, especially since we're in a war. I would expect each and every one of you to think twice before you criticize our wonderful country. How would you like to live under the iron rule of the Kaiser?" He pressed his lips together in a thin line. "Laura even dared call our illustrious congressmen a 'bunch of muddleheads.' This is no time to carp against America when our soldiers are dying along the western front!"

Laura's sharp retort died on her lips. She resented being called unpatriotic. She *was* patriotic! Patriotic to the core! The memory of the jingle found on posters all around town played its little refrain in her head and brought a smile to her lips:

Do not permit your child to take a bite or two from an apple and throw the rest away; nowadays even children must be taught to be patriotic to the core.

"I'm glad you can smile about your theme, Laura." Mr. Blair lightly tapped the long map pointer against the palm of his left hand and said coolly, "I would suggest a change in attitude and work habits or you may be repeating History 101." He frowned at her as if trying to understand her strange reasoning.

She gazed coolly at this martinet before her, silently labeling him a "blind ostrich with its head stuck in the sand." Another year in this class would be insufferable. She had one more semester in her junior year, and she hoped she could hold her temper and tongue long enough to pass. "I'll try, Mr. Blair. Perhaps I should give up my motorcade training." *There!* she thought. *That should answer your unpatriotic slur.*

Mr. Blair drew himself up to his full height. "I pity the poor soldier that is chauffeured by the likes of you. You'd always be late and would need help cranking up the car. But enough about you, Laura." His cold smile reappeared. "It's just that every day you give me fresh reminders of what a student ought not to be."

"Really!" Her eyes widened in all innocence. "That's strange, Mr. Blair, because I've tried so hard to pattern my behavior after your advice."

This time loud guffaws broke out.

Rapping his pointer sharply on the desk, he glared at Laura. The scorn that emanated from his blue eyes skipped over the heads of the students in front of her and swooped down on her, as if she were a mouse and he an avenging hawk.

Laura opened her book without another word, realizing that too much goading of this narrow-minded, intolerant teacher could only hurt her chances of promotion. She had seen that same look of contempt on a policeman's face before he shoved one of the suffragists into the police van. Soberly Laura studied the map in her textbook, warning herself to tread lightly where Mr. Blair was concerned.

Mr. Blair asked Olaf to read his theme as an example of what the essay should contain.

Olaf Jorgensen lumbered to his feet and

ambled up to the podium where he shifted uneasily behind the stand. His theme praised the United States and equality for all. Laura had to admit it was organized well, and Olaf had used specific examples to emphasize his major thesis.

The day crawled by, and her heart was as heavy as the books she carried. If she could only make Mr. Blair see that she also had some good examples in her paper and that she could write, too. The awful part of it was that she couldn't even go in and talk to him about it, because he had such a closed mind. She vowed to show her paper to Miss Emerson and get her opinion. If it really was a bad paper, she could then accept Mr. Blair's grade more gracefully.

After school she hurried to see Miss Emerson, who was grading papers. Laura always liked coming into her colorful classroom with its posters and portraits of Shakespeare, John Milton, Charles Dickens, and the Brönte sisters.

Unlike Mr. Blair's barren desk, Miss Emerson's was cluttered with papers, a framed class picture, and a coffee cup near her books.

Her English teacher looked up and smiled. "What can I do for you, Laura?"

Suddenly tears sprang to her eyes. "It's Mr. Blair. He gave me a D on my theme." She gulped. "Do you have time to read it and give me your opinion?"

"I'm certain I'll like it better than Mr.

Blair, but that will be small consolation," she said ruefully.

"It would console me," Laura said. "If it's a rotten essay, then I can accept his D." She wiped away a tear, composed herself, and offered her the theme. "Would you read it?"

"Of course, I'll read it," Miss Emerson said sympathetically, taking the paper that Laura held out to her.

After ten minutes Miss Emerson looked up from the theme, tapped the paper with her pencil, and said, "This is good. Oh, there are a few minor flaws in syntax and verb agreement, but that's minor compared to your powerful subject. The suffragists are a movement that can't and won't be ignored, despite Mr. Blair's attitude. I myself go to the suffragist meetings, but that's beside the point." She leaned back in her armless desk chair, swiveling back and forth. "You realize I can't interfere with another teacher's grade."

Laura breathed deeply with relief. "I value your opinion, Miss Emerson. It's so unfair being stuck in his class. Not only does he make history boring, but he hates me," She fingered a button on her blouse. "You don't know how I dread going into his class."

"Stick it out, my dear. You have only a semester left of Mr. Blair, and you must realize that all through life you're going to encounter men like him. Most are not quite as open in their dislike of any form of emancipation of women as Mr. Blair, but you'll encounter his attitude in many ways and from many individuals. Some women are just as bad." Her gray eyes flashed. "Set yourself a goal. Do you have a goal in life, Laura?"

Laura shrugged, hating to admit that her career goal of being an architect had gone up in smoke. "I — I don't really have anything in mind," she stammered, and managed a smile. "If I set my sights too high, my sister and mother bring me down to earth in a hurry."

"Nonsense," Miss Emerson snapped. "You can be anything you want to be, and no one can hold you back. I've been watching you, Laura Mitchell, and you've got style, ambition, and fire. Go to college and don't let anything hold you back. It's different now than it was in 1898 when I attended college. Then there was a set curriculum for 'young ladies.' Now there are many fields open: science, law, medicine, the arts," she said, ticking them off. "Oh! It's four o'clock and I have a meeting." Abruptly she stood. "Come in and talk anytime, Laura, but I can't run interference between you and Mr. Blair. That's something you'll need to solve yourself."

"Thanks for listening," Laura said. "I can deal with a low grade on my paper, knowing what you think of it." She smiled as she tucked her essay in her notebook. "I should have guessed that you'd be a suffragist."

Miss Emerson grinned. "You'd be an asset to the cause yourself!" She closed her classroom door behind them.

"Thanks, Miss Emerson, I'll see you tomorrow." She waved. "Cassie's waiting for me, and she probably thinks I've deserted her." She raced down the hall to her locker, hoping Cassie hadn't grown tired of waiting. She was relieved when she rounded the corner and saw her.

"What kept you?" Cassie asked, but she wasn't angry.

"I saw Miss Emerson. She read my paper and gave me her opinion." Laura opened her locker and put in her math book, taking out her history book.

"Ah, Mr. Blair's grade. No wonder you're so glum." Cassie shook her head. "He's so awful."

"Did you get a bad grade, too?" Laura said.

Cassie laughed. "No, my topic was safer than yours. I wrote about the wave of German immigrants in 1848. I managed a B."

Laura closed her locker, and they walked down the corridor. "It's one thing to write a bad paper and get a D, but to write a good one, that's what hurts." She opened the front door. "Even Miss Emerson agrees it was good. I know what made Mr. Blair angry. It was the part about women and voting that set his teeth on edge."

Cassie's carefully plucked eyebrows shot

skyward. "I didn't know you wrote about women's rights."

"Well, sort of," Laura admitted. "The other night, when I was coming home from my motorcade training, I saw a group of women being arrested. I couldn't believe my eyes." She glanced at Cassie and was surprised at how absorbed she looked. "What's wrong, Cassie? Is it a crime to sympathize with the suffragists?"

"Not at all," Cassie responded quietly.

As they walked past the linden and elm trees, Cassie looked elegant in her beaver hat, matching muff, and leather boots. She cleared her throat and took a deep breath, facing her friend. "Laura, I think you're ready to hear my secret."

Surprised, Laura stopped walking. "I won't tell a soul," she promised, waiting patiently for Cassie's next words.

"I'm a suffragist," Cassie said clearly, the words ringing in the cold afternoon air.

Amazed, Laura sank back against the trunk of a tall elm. "You?" She gasped, staring at her sophisticated classmate. "A suffragist?" Not Cassandra Whiting, she thought. All at once she reached out and grasped Cassie's gloved hand. "Oh, Cassie, that's so exciting. So daring!" Her thoughts returned to that day in class. "No wonder you wouldn't tell Mr. Blair why your homework wasn't completed."

"Yes," Cassie said dryly. "I didn't feel like being yelled at that day."

Laura laughed. "Cassie, you astonish me! I can't believe someone as rich and glamorous as you is involved in the women's movement."

Cassie smiled. "You'd be surprised how many prominent women are at our meetings."

"Miss Emerson is a suffragist, too," Laura said in wonder.

"I know," Cassie said. She paused, then asked, "Would you like to go with me to a meeting?"

"I don't know," Laura said slowly. "My mother doesn't exactly approve of the suffragists, and I'm involved in a lot of things now."

"Few people *do* approve of our activities," Cassie countered. "Anyway, on Sunday night there's a meeting at the Women's National Headquarters. Miss Paul, the leader, is speaking." Cassie's eyes were bright. "I wish you'd come."

"Maybe . . ." Laura still wasn't convinced. She didn't know why. Perhaps she knew that if she became involved with this organization it could become an all-consuming passion.

"Don't you see, Laura?" Cassie persisted. "We can make a difference. You and I. President Wilson has just issued a statement in support of our cause. Now is the time to push for our rights. If we don't, time will pass us by."

Suddenly Laura wanted to know more about what made these women such fervent believers. What made them stand up in the face of arrest and vilification? What made Cassie's eyes shine? She made a decision. "I'll go, Cassie!" She squeezed her friend's hand, knowing it was the right decision.

Chapter Eight

SATURDAY night the dance at the armory was every bit as exciting as her wonderful hopes had been all week. The glittering lights and the garlands of flowers made the large hall an enchantment. Here she was swirling around in Shawn's arms wishing the evening would never end.

Shawn drew her closer as they danced the fox trot. "You know you're a natural-born dancer, Laura." He held her at arm's length, gazing into her eyes. "You're agile and light as a butterfly. Ah, Laura, I love to hold you in my arms." The music soared. Laughing, he swept her around in a giant arc and they glided over the shiny floor swiftly and gracefully. She felt like a fairy princess in her prince's arms.

"That lavender dress does something for

you, sweetness. In these twinkling lights your hair looks beautiful." He touched her hair and she felt a wave of delight. He did make her feel so feminine, as if she were the only girl on the floor. She did feel pretty in her soft chiffon dress, which reached to mid-calf. The bodice had a rounded neckline and cap sleeves, and the dress was encircled with a taffeta sash with tiny rosebuds around her small waist. She nestled in Shawn's arms, enjoying the texture of his rough wool uniform beneath her hand.

After the latest jazz steps, the band played her favorite music to the "Castle Gavotte," which was initiated by Vernon and Irene Castle, the best dance team in America, and the dance she loved above all others. With arms outstretched and hands touching, they rocked forward two beats, back two beats, then facing one another, she took Shawn's hand, and, to the heavy drum beat, danced completely around him to his sheer delight.

Dum-de-de-dum-de-de-dum-dum.

Shawn clapped out the rhythm as she swayed back and forth. She felt heady with the throbbing music and Shawn's admiring glances.

"Laura, you're gorgeous," Shawn said, eyes twinkling. "If I had my camera I'd capture that sparkle in those green eyes. I swear they're brighter than two emeralds."

As they wended their way back to their table, she glowed at his compliment and for a moment thought of Joe, who had never been quite so eloquent or appreciative of her.

Sitting down, she looked up to thank Shawn, but before she could say anything, he leaned over and kissed her.

Blushing, she glanced around, but the other couples were oblivious of her happiness.

"Will you be my girl, Laura?" he whispered in her ear.

"I-I . . ." She didn't know what to reply. Was he serious?

Shawn chuckled. "You will. You just need a little time to get to know me."

Secretly she wondered if he was right. Despite her wish, the special evening did come to an end, and although they said very little on the ride home, nonetheless the silence between them radiated a warm rapport.

The next evening, as Laura walked down the brick sidewalk, past the small clapboard houses on the way to Cassie's house, her mind wasn't on the suffragist meeting they would attend but on last night's dance. She looked up between the elm branches at the star-filled sky and saw herself dancing with Shawn. It had been a marvelously romantic evening, and what was even better was that they were going dancing next Saturday, too. But the most thrilling part of the dance was that Shawn had kissed her and asked her to be his girl.

With a brief frown she snapped off a small

twig of an overhanging branch and wondered if perhaps Shawn O'Brien was only charm and sweet words. However, she dismissed the unpleasant thought, wishing that Joe had more of Shawn's lighthearted banter and appreciation of her.

As she turned off N Street onto Fishing Lane, she glimpsed the Whiting home in the distance. The gaslight lantern at the entrance of the red-brick house and the green ivy entwining the turquoise-painted double doors looked so inviting. For a moment she could almost hear the night watchman of Colonial times going up and down the street on his nightly rounds calling out, "Seven o'clock. A fair, bright night . . . all's well!"

As she neared the front steps she could see the chandelier's sparkling crystal teardrops twinkling over the Whitings' dining room table. Her mind came back to the reason she was going with Cassie, and she remembered the pamphlet she had read, written by Alice Paul. Tonight she would actually hear her speak. A twinge of doubt assailed Laura, and she wondered if she should really involve herself in the Women's Movement. If her time was so taken up now, how could she squeeze another activity into her schedule?

As she lifted the heavy brass door knocker, she smiled. Just because she was attending a suffragist meeting, it didn't mean she would have to become one.

Cassie, tall and striking in her coat and

high boots, answered the door. "Let's go," she said quickly, fitting her fur hat over her dark hair. The white fox fur was a stunning frame for her lovely oval face. "We mustn't be late, because Miss Paul will start her speech at the stroke of seven-thirty."

The two girls hurried to catch the trolley that would carry them to the Women's Headquarters in Lafayette Park, just across from the gates of the White House.

When they entered the warm hall filled with banners and posters, Laura estimated that there were about five hundred women there. Some were seated in the rows of chairs; others, in small groups, were in animated discussion. Laura caught a few of their words as she and Cassie moved toward their seats: ". . . the vote . . . President Wilson . . . workhouse . . . jail . . . force-feeding." She could feel the energy and vitality pulsate in this room. Her anticipation heightened.

They sat close to the front of the stage, and while Cassie chatted with a suffragist behind her, Laura sat studying the poster on the wall. However, when a small woman entered, accompanied by a stout younger companion, she sat straight up in her chair. Laura would recognize Miss Paul anywhere. Her thin face was dominated by metal-rimmed spectacles, and her dark hair was piled on top of her head. She looked smaller than in the photograph she had seen. Despite being a tiny woman, Miss Paul radiated confidence and zeal. It was evident, too, that all her energy was focused on one thing — the Women's Movement.

As Laura watched this woman take a chair in back of the rostrum, her pulse picked up a beat, and she waited eagerly for Miss Paul's first words. Laura marveled at this woman, a veteran of the English suffrage campaign, who had sailed to the United States to help her fellow sisters in their vote crusade and who had climbed to be the head of the National Women's Party. She was amazed that Miss Paul was such a fighter. She was not only an activist, but a militant one as well. Laura wondered how many parades and cross-country motor cavalcades she had organized since 1913, and how many White House pickets since 1917.

Everyone quieted as a stout lady stood behind the speaker's podium and waited for a few stragglers to find their places. Laura's eyes returned to Alice Paul, the diminutive woman seated calmly with her hands folded on her lap. Her square chin was just as determined as the eyes that snapped with intelligence and fire. She wore a simple blue serge suit that was a good background for the brilliant yellow "Votes for Women" sash across her chest.

The first speaker, her round face aglow with fervor, began to speak. Immediately a hush came over the hall. "As most of you know, I'm Miss Logan, and it's my great pleasure to introduce Miss Paul. It is so good to have Alice back in our midst again, for this is her first appearance since her release from prison. While in the workhouse, Alice demanded to be treated as a political prisoner and was able to win this privilege for all suffragists."

Applause burst upon the room, but Miss Logan held up her hand. "Alice went on a twenty-two-day hunger strike, and at one point was force-fed, but the antisuffragists still couldn't elicit a promise from her that she wouldn't come back to us and organize more picket lines in front of the White House. Our work will continue!" Miss Logan turned slightly and bowed her head at Alice. "She came out of prison a heroine. Even the House Rules Committee, which for years has bottled up the suffrage amendment, has brought it to the floor for debate."

A cheer broke out, and although Miss Paul inclined her head and gazed around the room, she didn't smile. Her cool demeanor was to be admired. Laura wondered how she could remain so serene in this warm room with the exhilaration rising from each word.

"I leave you with a statement of the prison doctor," Miss Logan said in a louder voice, "who said of our leader, Miss Paul, 'This is a spirit like Joan of Arc, and it is useless to try to change it. She will die, but she will never give up!' "

Briefly the words from a pamphlet she had

read about Alice Paul's imprisonment flickered through Laura's head: ". . . the meal of soup, rye bread, and water was not palatable. We all tried to be sensible and eat enough to keep up our strength. One of the worst problems was the enforced silence. . . ." A slight shiver vibrated up Laura's spine when she recalled the description of the force-feeding, but just then, Miss Logan resumed speaking.

"As you can see," the rotund woman said, "Alice is very much alive and back with us to carry on our struggle." Her voice rose to a shrill tone. "I present to you, Miss Alice Paul!"

The applause and cheers were deafening, and Laura's blood surged with each wave of applause.

Miss Paul stepped to the podium, shook Miss Logan's hand, and looked out over the audience. It was surprising that such a slightly built woman could command this militant organization. Her belted long jacket, with a gray squirrel collar and cuffs, reached almost to her skirt hem, which came just above her buckled shoes. Her hand touched her hair in a quick, nervous gesture, and she showed the ravages of her seven-month stint at Occoquan, a workhouse for women prisoners in Virginia. Laura's heart twisted in an agony of sympathy for Miss Paul's ordeal. It was difficult to fathom how she could return to the cause with such indomitable courage.

Miss Paul cleared her throat and drew herself up to her full height. "Our picketing has resumed and will continue until women have the right to vote! For the first time last month, President Wilson has acknowledged that he will support our amendment, but until it has passed both houses of Congress, we mustn't relax for a moment. The twelve suffragists who stand their hourly vigils before 1600 Pennsylvania Avenue are the backbone of the women's cause. They don't falter . . . they stand through rain, snow, and sleet. You are the ones that should be cheered. I salute you. Don't give up until we win!" She held up her clenched fist.

Laura listened with every fiber of her being as Miss Paul's clear, ardent tones rang throughout the hall. There was no faltering in her speech or in her plan. The plan was simple. To picket. To go to jail if necessary and not to stop until the goal was achieved. Laura felt a resolve growing within her that was close to bursting. She wanted to be part of this wonderful organization, and she made up her mind to become a member. She realized that she could make a difference. On impulse she reached over and grabbed Cassie's hand.

Cassie turned to Laura. "Isn't she marvelous?"

"Oh, yes," Laura whispered. "I'd follow her anywhere."

Cassie laughed. "I knew you couldn't resist our cause. I only had to get you here in order for you to realize what we stood for."

Miss Paul finished her short speech, and while the women clapped and cheered, she hoisted a sign above her head, which read: EQUALITY FOR ALL.

Soon engulfed by women who wanted to shake her hand and say a few words to her, Miss Paul could no longer be seen.

"Come on," Cassie said, pulling Laura to her feet. "I want you to meet her."

They waited for their turn to speak to Miss Paul, and when they did, she was gracious and quite perceptive. "We need young women in the Movement, Laura. I'm glad you want to be part of the National Women's Party."

A thrill of pride swept over her as she pumped Miss Paul's hand. "I'm ready to take my turn on the picket line," she offered enthusiastically, hoping Miss Paul wouldn't find her too forward.

A slight smile crossed Miss Paul's features as she shook her head. "I'm sorry, my dear, but you must be twenty-one to stand in the line, for there's a strong chance you'll be arrested." She inclined her head. "How old are you, Laura?"

"I'll be sixteen next month," she said defensively, and almost told her of her deception in the motorcade but thought better of it.

"You can help, though," Miss Paul explained quietly. "Cassie is an aide in the organization. We can use more. How would you like to start tomorrow after school, Laura?"

Her heart jumped. "I'd like to help in any way I can."

Miss Paul nodded slowly, appraising Laura. "The women on the line need encouragement and such things as coffee, umbrellas, and shawls. Whatever the women need, it will be your job to bring them. Would you like to do your bit in this way?"

"Oh, yes," Laura breathed, already under the spell of this powerful, charismatic leader. "I'd love it!" Laura silently thought that it would only be a short time from running errands to actually taking her place in the line.

However, in the next two weeks Laura found Miss Paul exceedingly strict, and she was not allowed to picket. She didn't mind, however, as she loved just being around these dedicated women, some of whom had spent the last fifty years fighting for equality. She and Cassie had become even closer, sharing the meetings and discussions later. Mr. Blair had noticed their closeness and made several remarks about studying instead of engaging in silly gossip. Little did he know!

She had become so immersed in the movement that she turned down Joe twice and Shawn once, when they had asked her out. Her meetings with Miss Paul came before all else. She remembered her reluctance to become involved in the Women's Movement for fear it would become an all-consuming passion. She had been right. Several times she had tried to explain to her mother and Sarah the importance of her job in running errands, but it was useless, for they always gave her the old argument of using her time and energy for Frank and Mike and the boys overseas.

One night she came in from a meeting later than usual and quietly opened the front door, carefully closing it behind her. She unclasped her cape and tossed it over the coat tree, shivering a little from the March chill. Creeping toward the stairs, she winced as one of the wide planks in the oak floor creaked.

"Laura? Is that you?"

Laura's heart sank. Her sister's hearing was as acute as a forest deer's.

Sarah entered from the kitchen, wiping her hands on her long apron. A lock of her blonde, waved hair fell forward, and she brushed it back with long, slender fingers. She arched her brows. "Have you been helping the pickets again?"

Defiantly Laura lifted her chin. "Yes. Haven't you heard? They're plotting to blow up the White House."

Sarah's lips thinned. "Don't even joke about such a thing. Picketing the White House is bad enough! Calling yourselves the 'Sentinels of Liberty,' indeed!" She snorted. "The suffragists go too far!" Sarah untied her apron and wearily slipped it over her head. Her clear blue eyes softened as she looked wistfully at Laura. "Why do you insist on joining these women? Do you think you'll save the world at fifteen?"

"Sixteen!" Laura snapped. "I had my sixteenth birthday last week, remember?"

"Then you should know better," Sarah answered sharply. A brief frown creased her forehead, and she shook her head in disbelief.

"You don't understand, Sarah," Laura said in measured tones. "You never will. You and Mother are always against me. The women's platform is so simple. Why can't you comprehend it? We want the vote and equal pay for equal work!" She glared at Sarah, whose eyes seemed tired. She shouldn't argue with her, but it was difficult to hold her tongue when she yearned to have Sarah understand the Movement and be on her side. If only she could convince her earthbound sister to sprout wings — at least small ones — in order to soar above her everyday existence.

Attempting to clarify her position, she explained, "Sarah, if you'd go with me to one of the meetings you'd realize what we're fighting for. I wish you could hear Miss Paul just once."

"I have no desire to be associated with a group of subversives!"

"It's women like you who hold back anything the suffragists try to do!" She angrily shook a finger beneath Sarah's nose. "We're fighting for you, and you don't appreciate it!" Her cheeks were hot, partly from trying to show Sarah what the suffragists believed and partly from the exhilaration of the speech she'd heard at tonight's meeting. She had made a circle to the White House gates and could still see the women pickets standing in the rain. How she longed to take her place with them, but in the meantime she would fulfill her assignment cheerfully and bring coffee for the pickets.

"Did you hear me?" Sarah questioned.

"What?" Laura pulled her thoughts back to Sarah.

"I said, try not to wake Mother. She went to bed early. She had to do an extra run. She didn't return her trolley car to the barn until after nine-thirty."

Laura lowered her voice. "All right. Sorry." She shifted the stack of pamphlets she was carrying from one hip to the other and prepared to go upstairs.

"What do you have there?" Sarah asked uneasily.

Laura gave a little shrug. "Pamphlets. Want one?" She handed the top one to her sister. "Read it, you might learn something." She smiled, anticipating Sarah's reaction.

Sarah glanced quickly at the writing. "Democracy Begins at Home, Kaiser Wilson!" she shouted. "How can you call our president by that German title?"

Laura impishly put her finger across her lips. "Shh. You'll wake Mother."

Sarah waved the pamphlet under Laura's chin and said in a low voice, "This is traitorous in wartime!"

"Woodrow Wilson must recognize women as first-class citizens." Laura planted her fists on her hips, daring her sister to argue further.

For a moment they stared stonily at one another, then Laura flounced up the stairs, muttering, "What's the use."

As she raced into her room she hated herself for becoming angry, but she wanted to shake people when they refused to understand.

Flinging herself across the bed, tears came to her eyes. Not a person in this house believed in her and her cause. If only her father were alive. With him she had felt like a small sailboat skimming over the waves, and he acted as the breeze that scooted her along. Now she felt more like a lumbering rowboat with her mother and Sarah acting as the mooring post that kept her tied.

Chapter Nine

TODAY Laura felt like a sailboat again, happily flying before the wind, for she and Joe were going to the Smithsonian Institution to see the Wright Brothers' plane that had recently been placed in the museum. She loved to go to the Smithsonian. Then, too, she hadn't really seen Joe for weeks. Even their Friday night movie had been canceled, once by her, and once by Joe, so this Saturday was a special treat for both of them. Joe didn't have to work, and her mother had told her to run along and have a good time.

As they walked down the steps and onto the sidewalk in front of her house, Joe stopped, took hold of her shoulders, and turned her to face him. "Well, Laura, let me take a look at you. It's been a long time since I've seen my girl." His dark, sparkling eyes swept over her with pleasure.

His girl! Her heart soared at those words. Was she at last his girl? Did he at last realize he loved her? She wrinkled her nose. Joe's words were no doubt merely an expression. He still thought of her as his "little girl."

Hiding a smile, she spun around, causing her full skirt to swirl around her ankles. Her red sweater and plaid scarf gave her the casual look she liked. "Do I meet with your approval?" she asked in cheerful mockery.

"Oh, indeed, you do, fair maiden," he answered with a bow.

They both laughed. Then his serious gaze sought and held hers. "I've barely seen you since you joined the suffragists." In the familiar gesture she loved, he rakishly scooped back a shock of hair that touched his heavy black brows.

She put her arm through his, and they moved on.

"I've missed you at the store," he said lightly.

"And I've missed you, Joe Menotti." She was surprised at just how much she had missed him, despite her seeing Shawn.

Then, not able to contain what had been foremost in her thoughts for the past weeks, she said excitedly, "Joe, I'm learning so much in the Women's Party, and we're so close to pushing the nineteenth amendment through Congress." She stooped and picked up a fallen branch on the bricks and tossed it to the side of the walk. "Just think, I'll be able to vote in a few years."

"I know. I've been keeping up with Alice Paul and her followers' activities in the newspapers. The senators and representatives are beginning to respond to the women's demands, and even their speeches are becoming favorable." His tone was admiring; so was his glance.

The early spring breeze ruffled her hair. Her hand tightened on Joe's arm as they crossed Independence Avenue. "It's a good feeling to have the president and the Congress on our side at last."

"Only some of them, Laura. Don't become overconfident," Joe murmured, his lips firm and straight. "Be careful, too. The arrests, despite your favorable publicity, are becoming more frequent, and you could be thrown in jail."

She snorted in derision. "I wish they would arrest me. I'd welcome prison, but I'm not allowed on the picket line. Only the women over twenty-one can stand hourly shifts, and they are the only ones arrested. I can bring them coffee, but that's all a sixteen-year-old dare do! I'd like to be able to make a statement by going to prison, too!" Her chin jutted forward. "Why do you think the public's jeers have changed to cheers? It's because of the suffragists' courage in the face of vicious treatment and their willingness to serve out their jail terms."

"You're right, Laura," Joe agreed. "I admire them — and you, too. I always knew you had grit, ever since you were five years old. Remember Christmas Day? I gave you a ride on our old buckboard, and the horse shied at a barking dog."

"Remember!" she exclaimed. "I'll never forget. That was the wildest ride down New York Avenue I've ever taken and I hope I ever will again! A runaway horse on an icy street. . . ."

"You didn't scream once; you just clung to my hand, and the faster we flew and slid down the avenue, the tighter you squeezed. By the time we came to Blair House I had gained control. You were scared, but you never uttered a sound." He looked at her fondly. "Your face was as white as ashes, and your freckles stood out like measle spots!"

She chuckled softly at the memory of how she had tagged after him. "Joe, we've been through some good times and bad times together."

"And knowing you, Laura, we'll go through a lot more," he assured her.

She gave him a quick glance and a smile. *Indeed we will,* she pledged silently.

Joe continued, a nagging anxiety in his voice. "The suffragists are going through some bad times right now, and I don't want to see you hauled off in the police wagon." His tone changed, and he said dryly, "Even though I admire what you're doing, I hardly relish visiting you in jail."

She was pleased by Joe's praise and concern as they approached the red Victorian-style museum with all its turrets and spires. "I'll be careful," she vowed solemnly, but her spirits were high and she believed too much in the cause to be swayed by Joe's caution. Why, she'd volunteer tomorrow to go to prison if they'd let her.

"Come on," Joe said with a short laugh, and ushered her into a large, domed room. "For once, Laura, forget the Party. Remember, I'm on your side, and your defense of what you're doing or what Miss Paul is doing is unnecessary."

He paused, staring straight ahead at a huge double-winged plane. "There it is!" he exclaimed. "That plane of the Wright Brothers is a slice of history, Laura."

"I know," she agreed, observing the Winton aircraft that seemed poised and ready for takeoff. "Fifteen years ago Orville flew that plane and launched an industry. Now the sky is filled with German Fokkers, English Sopwith Camels, and French Spads."

Joe looked at her in wonder. "You always amaze me — now it's planes you know about."

She shrugged. "I could tell you about Manfred von Richthofen, the German ace and his 'Flying Circus,' but I don't feel like giving a lecture right now." She smiled mischievously.

Joe grinned and circled the fragile aircraft. "Look how delicate those struts are supporting the wings."

She peered at the space where Orville had lain full-length and wobbily flown low over the ground while Wilbur ran alongside. "I don't think I'd fly into the clouds in this machine," said Laura. "It looks like it would burst apart in the least gust of wind."

Chuckling, Joe said, "You wouldn't have to worry about soaring too high. Listen to this," and he read from a plaque. "On December 17, 1903, at Kitty Hawk, North Carolina, the longest flight by the Wright Brothers was undertaken. The plane flew 852 feet and stayed aloft for 59 seconds."

Laughing, they wandered off, spending some time viewing First Ladies' dresses.

After three hours they went outside on the mall, past the Library of Congress and the National Archives, then stopped briefly to observe the White House. By the gates they could see several of the faithful suffragists in the distance. *They're always there, no matter what the weather*, Laura thought.

As they walked down Pennsylvania Avenue Joe reached for her hand. They hadn't gone a block, however, when a long, black Ford pulled up by the curb and her happiness vanished.

"Laura," Shawn called. "What are you doing on the mall?"

"Hi, Shawn," she called, trying to be casual. She should have realized they might bump into Shawn, for this was his post, squiring the general between the Capitol and the White House. "We've been visiting the Smithsonian." She darted a glance at Joe. She hadn't intended for her two boyfriends to meet like this.

Tentatively she took Joe's arm and pulled him forward. Why was she so fearful? She had told Joe about Shawn and Shawn about Joe. Now they were going to meet, that was all. "Joe, I'd like to introduce you to Shawn O'Brien. If you recall, I told you he was a friend of Michael's."

Joe stepped forward, extending his hand.

"Shawn," she said, "this is Joe Menotti."

She watched apprehensively as the two shook hands.

"So this is the grocery boy," Shawn said insultingly.

She drew in a quick breath. How dare Shawn say such a thing! She glanced at Joe and recognized the sparks of anger in his black eyes.

Shawn grinned. "Glad to meet you, Joe. I'm on my way to meet the general at the Capitol," Shawn explained, placing his hands on his hips and appraising Joe's appearance. "But I'm in no rush. You know how long these committee reports can last. Besides, if

I'm a few minutes late, it won't matter."

Laura shook her head in amazement. "Shawn, only you would dare risk your elite post here in Washington by being late."

Shawn shrugged. "General Long likes me. My post is safe. I'll admit it's a good army job to have. The only thing better would be not to wear a uniform and to be back in civvies again." He stared pointedly at Joe's plaid jacket.

Puzzled, Laura stared round-eyed at Shawn. It wasn't like him to be snide. She had told him about Joe being deferred because of medical school. However, it was obvious he chose to ignore that by calling him a grocery boy.

Shawn continued smoothly. "I understand you've been Laura's guide. You've squired her around since she's been a little girl. I must say, Joe, you've done a good job" — he winked broadly — "all except in the area of dance. I've had to teach her the latest steps, but it's been fun teaching her a few things." He paused, and Laura's heart leaped in her throat.

"Things like the fox-trot, right, Laura?" He gave Joe a sidelong glance; then his eyes swept back to Laura. "We had fun, didn't we, sweetness?" He flashed her a smile.

The faint pink that spread across her face announced her embarrassment. Why did Shawn have to flaunt their dancing and call her "sweetness" in front of Joe? Glancing at

Joe, she noticed he was calm and even wore a small smile, although there was fire flickering in his eyes and his jaw was rigid.

"I'm glad to have met you, Shawn. Perhaps we'll meet again." Joe stepped back. It was plain he wanted to end the conversation.

"I'm certain we will," Shawn said with confidence as he hopped back in the open car. "See you next Saturday night, Laura," and his Ford jerked forward, heading in the direction of the Capitol.

For a moment they stood in silence until the shiny black car was out of sight, then Joe turned to her and said deliberately, "Well, Laura, you have yourself a good-looking boyfriend there. Be careful," he warned. "Shawn looks like he's broken a few hearts."

Her temperature rose ten degrees. How quickly Joe reverted to his role of tutor, giving cautionary advice where it wasn't needed or wanted.

"I can take care of myself," she retorted with a calm equal to his.

"I'm not so sure," Joe said. "You'd better watch your step."

"Oh, I will," she promised with frigid politeness. "But I can assure you that Shawn is a perfect gentleman, although it's nice to have you do my worrying for me."

Joe stopped, confronting her. "Look, Laura, I only want what's best for you. I always have." He hesitated, and their eyes locked. "You above anyone else should know that."

She knew that Joe cared, and she wouldn't belittle his advice. She just wished he would act more like a jealous suitor than a big brother who was only looking out for her welfare.

Later, as she climbed the stairs to her room, Laura frowned. The day had started out so light and airy and had ended dark and stifling. What had caused it? Certainly not Joe and Shawn, at last meeting one another face-to-face. What was it, then? Perhaps, Laura conceded, it was herself. She was confused and muddled. One day she was in love with Joe and the next day with Shawn. How could that be? Could you be in love with two men at the same time? She knew, though, that her Saturday night dances with Shawn were more romantic than the Friday night movies with Joe. But Joe was so kind and so steady. Although Joe held her hand and brushed her lips with a kiss, he still treated her like a kid sister. Her anger flared again. Watch her step with Shawn, indeed! She was sixteen, and her mother had been married at seventeen.

Chapter
Ten

THE dance hall was lit by colored lanterns, and the overhead fans gently wafted the streamers trimmed with silver stars back and forth. The army dance was one of the most beautiful and festive that Laura had ever attended. She knew her beaded emerald dress enhanced her wide green eyes, and as she went back to the table after doing the two-step with Shawn, she felt as light as the plume that swung in her headband. She had chosen not to pin her hair back but let it fall over her shoulders.

Suddenly Shawn rose on tiptoe, plucked a sparkling star from a streamer, and tucked the piece of glitter in her hair. "Your eyes shimmer more than the star," he said as he held out her chair.

Breathless, she sank down while Shawn

ordered two colas. "Oh," she said, fanning herself with her lace hanky, "that was fun. You're a wonderful dance teacher, Shawn."

He reached over and stroked her cheek. "And you're a wonderful student — quick, agile, and graceful. What's more, I'm the envy of the regiment." Jerking a thumb over his shoulder he said, "Did you see the captain back there? He's been watching you all evening!"

She glanced in the direction Shawn indicated and noticed a tall soldier, with many ribbons across his chest, staring at her. Hastily she averted her eyes.

"You make the war recede in the distance," she said, laughing. "Every time I'm with you I forget everything. It's hard to believe that on Monday the routine will start all over again and I'll go back to drills, knitting, and suffragists' meetings.

"The suffragists." Shawn snorted, shooting an eyebrow upward. "They certainly aren't helping the war effort." He took her hand. "They are the laughingstock of the guards at the White House. What do those women hope to accomplish?" He leaned back, his blue eyes glittering but with a grin splashing across his face. "They'd be better off staying at home, keeping a good man happy." The blue of his eyes darkened while he lightly caressed the inside of her wrist.

As his fingers slid up her arm, she felt her blood tingle, longing for those firm lips to kiss her. But she wouldn't let Shawn sway her into denying the suffragists and belittling what Miss Paul was trying to do. She knew better than to discuss the suffragists with him, because he always mocked their activities, refusing to see what they stood for. She had tried before to explain, and unconsciously, she lifted a shoulder, realizing it was useless. Gently she withdrew her hand. It was necessary to show him that she wouldn't be influenced by his touch, although every time he came near, her knees weakened. She mustn't let her feelings for Shawn block out her beliefs.

Clearing her throat, she switched to another topic. "I've read that the flu has reached a few army camps in Massachusetts. I hope Washington will be isolated from it."

Abruptly Shawn leaped up. "Hear that music? No more talk of suffragists or influenza." He offered her his arm. "Let's see how well you remember the steps to the foxtrot."

Forgetting how Shawn closed his mind to unpleasant subjects and how much it annoyed her, she rose and, laughing, followed him onto the dance floor. The fast-paced number sent her feet flying to keep up with him. The thumping rhythm matched her racing blood.

Twirling her out and back, they danced apart, and she kept her eyes glued to Shawn's. His wide smile and flashing white teeth entranced her. How trimly his dress uniform fit his muscled, lean body. If he thought she was the prettiest girl here, she was positive he was the handsomest soldier.

On the way home she thought that April was her favorite month, for she loved cherry blossom time when the small trees burst into thousands of snowy white blossoms. Tonight, in the moonlight, the sight was particularly spectacular.

"Shall we stop and take a walk?" Shawn asked, slowing the car.

"I can't," she said reluctantly. "It's almost midnight and Mom will be waiting for me."

Groaning, Shawn pressed his boot to the accelerator and sped forward. When they reached home, a light in the parlor indicated that her mother was indeed sitting up. The tower clock at the university chimed twelve bells, and she grinned with satisfaction. "Right on time."

On the steps Shawn brushed her cheek lightly, then firmly pulled her to him, kissing her lips. With a motion she couldn't stop, her arms twined around Shawn's neck. His desires were her desires, and she couldn't obtain enough of his warmth and love.

All at once an upstairs window banged closed and she guiltily stepped back. Was it Joe at the window above? Had he seen their embrace?

Taking a shaky breath she whispered, "Good night, Shawn."

"Good night, sweetheart." He pulled her back and his gaze pinned her to him, but he didn't kiss her again. Instead he said in a husky voice, "Next Saturday?"

"I'm not sure," she lied, knowing that there was a suffragist meeting scheduled. "Call me." She didn't want to start another argument.

He studied her face, then brushed back a fallen lock of hair. "Be careful, darling. There will be a lot of suffragist arrests during the month of May. The rumor is out that President Wilson is tired of having his limousine flanked by fanatical women every time he drives through the gates."

She stiffened, turning to open the door. "Thanks for the warning, but I hope I *am* arrested!" she retorted tersely.

"Don't be ridiculous," he snapped, grabbing her wrist and holding it in a viselike grip.

With one hand on the doorknob she tried to twist free but was no match for his strength. Confronting him, she said coldly, "Please let me go!"

He dropped her wrist and said gently, "Oh, Laura, please. I only told you for your own good."

"I know," she said, unable to remain angry with Shawn. His advice was meant for her own well-being, so why should she resent it?

"I'll call you this week." His grin reappeared, and the old bravado crept back into his voice as he stood with his head cocked to one side and a hand on his hip.

She blew him a kiss to show that all was forgiven . . . as if he didn't know it, she thought with a smile.

Closing the door, she wondered how many times Shawn had laughed at Joe, and the suffragists, and the motorcade unit. Why did she put up with him? But when her fingertips touched her lips, she knew why. His charm more than outweighed his attitude about other things. Besides, she meant to change his viewpoint on a few topics.

When Shawn called on Tuesday, there did seem to be a change in his attitude, for he was understanding about the meeting on Saturday night. It was as if there had been no animosity between them about the suffragists. Perhaps he was being *too* understanding, she thought, knowing how he loved to dance. Was he seeing another girl? She dreaded the thought, but at present her work with the Women's Party was too important to be dismissed over jealousy.

Saturday night didn't disappoint her — it was an important meeting. Miss Paul knew all about the picket arrests targeted for May. Not that there hadn't been arrests during March and April. But the courts were very sympathetic to the Women's Movement ever since Alice Paul and Lucy Burns had been released from prison last month, and it looked as if all arrests would be invalidated.

However, that hadn't happened yet, and it was rumored that the police chief in the capital city wanted to make an example of pickets being photographed in front of the White House. He wanted to sweep them from Pennsylvania Avenue and give the president a rest from their constant demands and insistent presence on his front doorstep. So, despite the court's attitude, the chief intended to step up the suffragists' arrests and teach these women "their places."

The hall at national headquarters was packed, and it was warm despite the open windows and the crisp spring breeze that blew in.

Cassie, seated beside Laura, was tight-lipped as she whispered in her ear, "If only we could picket, too."

Laura nodded glumly. "I know, but since we can't, we'll at least deliver black coffee and a cheery word."

"Hmmpf," Cassie retorted. "Small comfort when banners are ripped out of the pickets' hands and they're kicked and shoved."

"It's difficult to watch," conceded Laura.

"Shhh," Cassie said, "Miss Paul is going to speak."

A hush fell over the hall when Miss Paul stepped briskly to the podium. She wore a large black hat, which framed her indomitable face, and a plain black suit with the Votes-for-Women banner making a striking yellow splash across her chest.

Laura listened intently to her brief but fervent speech.

". . . and so," concluded Alice Paul, "now is the time to show this country the mettle women are made of. Be dignified when you're arrested . . . and make no mistake, you *will* be hauled off to jail. Be prepared to suffer indignities with a serene silence." Her alert eyes scanned the hall. "If you do not want to stand your posts this next week, I'll understand. My seven-month sentence at Occoquan Workhouse was unpleasant. It's possible you'll be force-fed if you choose to go on a hunger strike, and you won't be able to communicate with one another, which is perhaps one of the worst aspects of being imprisoned. I'd like a show of hands to see how many are willing to chance arrest and stand their vigil."

There wasn't a woman there who didn't raise her hand and cheer.

"We're with you, Alice!"

"We'll stand at the White House till we drop!"

"We'll win the vote!"

Cheers and foot stomping followed Alice Paul as she stepped down from the platform and went down the rows shaking hands and offering words of encouragement.

Miss Logan returned to the podium, waiting for the pandemonium to recede. Finally, when all was quiet, she spoke. "It won't be easy. Alice's hunger strike lasted twenty-two days, and she wasn't alone in the terrible force-feeding that followed. The prison officials even declared Alice insane and forced her to undergo a medical examination."

A deep hush fell over the audience. Miss Logan continued in a louder, firmer voice. "Through Alice's arrest and others like her, the suffragists have become heroines. Many are now on our side, but we mustn't falter when we're so close to victory, for there are still a few, including our Police Chief Bentley, who are determined to break our spirit. Monday morning will be a test. Everyone is to be at the White House gates at eight o'clock for a huge rally. At nine o'clock we will disband, leaving our pickets in their usual places." She paused; then her reedy voice rose again. "Remember. Be firm."

Laura's heartbeat accelerated. She would have to miss school, but the Women's Party came first. Hang Mr. Blair and his vengefulness.

"Laura and Cassie." Miss Logan looked straight at them, the youngest members of the group. "Are you ready to help?"

"The coffee cups will be filled and extra banners provided if the pickets have theirs destroyed," Laura responded resolutely.

Cassie nodded her agreement vigorously.

"That's the spirit," Miss Logan said.

When she came home from the meeting, Laura still was elated and confident. There would be an ordeal ahead for the women, but in the end they would have the vote!

Closing the door, she walked into the parlor. Why had her mother sat up again tonight? Was she waiting for her again? It wasn't eleven o'clock yet.

Maude Mitchell and Sarah, talking and knitting, looked up when Laura entered the room. She stood surveying them. "Hello, why are you still up?" she asked suspiciously. It probably meant another lecture.

"Come here, Laura." Her mother stood, leaving the rocking chair still moving. "We received two letters today. One from Michael and one from Frank!"

Laura's elation came, and a sense of relief washed over her. Their two military men were still alive. She ran to Sarah, hugging her. "I'm so glad you heard from him. It's been a long time."

"Six weeks," Sarah answered.

"What did Frank have to say?" Laura knew better than to ask to read his letter. Sarah never shared Frank's words with anyone, but she did tell them a few general things.

Sarah's face beamed. "He shot down two German Fokkers and was awarded the Croix de Guerre." She added happily, "Frank has only two more missions to fly and he'll be given an honorable discharge and sent home!"

Laura, thrilled, took Sarah's hands and

twirled her around the floor. "How wonderful!" When she stopped, she stood with her arm around Sarah's waist, then her mother joined them, slipping an arm around Laura. Laura's happiness knew no bounds. She was fortunate to have a mother and sister that were so wonderfully loving. With a stab of remembrance she wished her father could be there with his arms around them, too. Then her world would be completely happy.

"Here's Michael's letter. We've been waiting all evening for you so you could read it with us." She held out the unopened envelope.

"Sorry," Laura mumbled. "The meeting was a little long." She didn't go into a further explanation because, if she mentioned the planned Monday rally and picketing, both her mother and Sarah would be upset. Besides, if it came to light that she was planning on staying out of school, Maude Mitchell would get Aldo Menotti or someone equally brawny to drag her, if necessary, into Jefferson High. She had no intention of divulging her secret plans.

With steady fingers she took the envelope and sat in the rocking chair by the Tiffany lamp so she could read Michael's words without faltering. How sweet of them to wait for her.

Laura read the letter in a clear, steady voice:

165th U.S. Infantry,
42nd Division
March 22, 1918

Dear Mom, Sarah, and Laura,

I received the package. Thanks. Sarah, I'm wearing the socks you knitted, and Laura, I appreciate Booth Tarkington's *Seventeen*, and even if it's too young for me, for some of the boys it's just the right level.

The Germans started their big offensive yesterday, and we were bombarded all day. The "Big Berthas," their largest cannon, has a range of seventy-five miles and shoots one-ton shells, but it's not too accurate. This morning all is calm again, but Battery B, about twelve miles west of here, is being shelled.

I've seen a lot of gassed soldiers being carried to the rear. We've been lucky and only used our gas masks once.

Last week we were singing songs with the Germans across No Man's Land, the area between the trenches. But this week we're out to kill one another. It's a crazy world! Don't worry, though. The Allies are holding every inch of ground, and the Germans won't get past the Marne River to capture Paris, which is what old General Ludendorff has in mind! Our commander, Brigadier-General Douglas MacArthur, is a young soldier, but every inch the commander that Ludendorff is! All the soldiers here have great faith in him!

More and more Americans are pouring in, but I have to hand it to the French soldiers and the British, for they're good fighters. Right now, though, they're exhausted after so many years in combat and welcome us Yanks with open arms!

I see it's chow time — more hardtack and mutton, so will stop for now. Keep your letters, photos, and socks coming.

> Love to you all,
> Mike

P.S. I knew you'd like Shawn — he's a fine fellow.

When Laura stopped reading, she dropped the letter in her lap, tears stinging her eyes. If only her brother could come home from the horrors he described.

Here she was, in a beautiful home, and the biggest problem she faced was whether to go out with Joe or Shawn. A wave of despair washed over her. And poor Michael was being shelled and constantly surrounded by mud, blood, and death.

She held her hand over her eyes, wondering if Michael would approve of Miss Paul and her meetings. Yes, she thought. She was sure of it. Michael, just like Father, would applaud her suffragist activities.

Chapter Eleven

MONDAY morning, May 1, 1918, was to be an extra-special day for the suffragists. The morning dew sparkled on the tulips along the iron fence in front of the Women's Headquarters at 14 Jackson Place, and the smell of cherry blossoms filled the air. Something else was in the air, too; a sense of excitement and exuberance swept through the women in the crowd. It was as if this rally were the last hurdle to jump before they reached the finish line.

Laura swelled with pride as she joined the ranks of women in Lafayette Square, where they gathered in front of the door of their cream-colored tiled mansion in anticipation of Alice Paul's speech. Laura wished Cassie were here, but she had foolishly told her parents about the rally, and Dr. Whiting forbade his daughter to miss school. He even personally had chauffeured her to the steps of Jefferson High.

Laura's excitement heightened as she observed the hall's facade. A red, white, and blue banner was draped dramatically on one side of the door, while on the other was the purple, white, and gold banner, the tricolor of the Women's Party.

When Miss Paul emerged, a loud cheer greeted her as the slight woman waved. Her voice carried throughout the hushed audience. "The pickets need everyone's support," she exhorted. "This week will be grim, with prison staring us in the face again, but remember, we will gain more and more Americans' sympathy. Police Chief Bentley will find that if he arrests us, the climate is very different from when I went to prison last October!" She stopped to study her audience, then smiled. "I have deep faith in every one of you and want you to know your efforts are appreciated.

"Now," she said, adjusting her spectacles, "for our strategy. We will keep our same pattern, six pickets at the east gate and six pickets at the west gate. Again I must remind you that it will not be easy, and anyone that desires to drop out is free to do so with no censure whatsoever."

The women stirred restlessly, obviously with no intention of dropping out, eager only to begin their show of strength in front of the White House.

Miss Paul went on. "I've asked fifty of you to accompany me to the Senate today, to lobby for our amendment." She paused, searching the crowd in front of her, then, pointing a finger at a striking brunette, she called, "Miss Younger, please come forward."

A young woman in the audience modestly walked to a place by Miss Paul's side. "I give you Miss Younger," Miss Paul said loudly. "The woman responsible for organizing our lobby efforts. Since she took over the Lobbying Committee, twenty-two senators have changed their minds about the suffragist amendment, and they, in turn, are persuading their fellow congressmen to vote the right way! Please, a round of applause for Miss Younger!"

The clapping sounded sharp and loud in the early-morning air. Miss Younger held her arms above her head, smiling broadly.

Miss Paul signaled for silence and continued. "Never give up hope. I leave you with the same words I spoke a year ago. 'If a creditor stands before a man's house all day long, demanding payment of his bill, the man must either remove the creditor or pay the bill.' Well, Mr. Wilson has tried to remove us and failed. It's time now that he pay the bill. Our asking price is only the ballot!"

Laura felt a thrill shiver through her as

the hurrahs went up from all sides. Although most of the women were young, their ages ranged all the way up to the eighties. Lavinia Dock, standing beside her, was sixty, and Mary Nolan, near Miss Paul, was seventy. The Reverend Olympia Brown was eighty-four. Despite their ages, they were young in spirit and leaders in the movement, serving prison terms and taking part in parades and rallies.

When Miss Paul left, most of the women disbanded, going to their jobs or back to their homes, while the twelve pickets that were to stand their hourly vigil marched proudly and slowly forward, a banner's length apart. Four of them carried a lettered banner: HOW LONG MUST WOMEN WAIT FOR LIBERTY? Eight of them carried the purple, gold, and white colors. The suffragist colors fluttered brightly in the sunlight. Laura couldn't wait to serve these faithful women who showed such courage and determination. How she longed to be one of them!

Giving the dignified banner carriers one last, admiring glance, Laura moved into the house.

She poured coffee into six mugs for the east gate pickets, and as she went outside with the steaming cups on a tray, the sun suddenly dipped behind dark clouds and the light blue sky changed to an overcast gray. Thunder rolled in the east, and a flash of lightning sparked across the clouds.

She noticed that several boys had entered the square. Their belligerent attitude signaled trouble.

A few raindrops splattered her face, and realizing that the women wouldn't want coffee in the rain, she retreated to get umbrellas from the supply room. She remembered that Refna Slocum, one of the pickets, had a history of colds, so Laura wanted to be certain she was kept as dry and comfortable as possible.

Back outside with umbrellas, she maneuvered her way through the mushrooming groups of young boys, clutching the six umbrellas tightly under her arm. Her heart hammered, for she didn't much relish running the gauntlet of these sneering anti-suffragists.

Though the rain-splattered cobblestones were slick, she hurried toward the pickets at the White House gates. However, she slipped on one of the raised stones and went sprawling on all fours, hitting the sides of her face, the umbrellas flying before her. She touched her cheek and saw some blood on her fingers. Her cheeks burned fiery red from her humiliation, not from blood.

One young man pointed at her prostrate figure and hooted, "There's a suffragist for you. Can't even stand on her own two legs and she wants the right to vote! Boys, have you ever heard of anything so dumb?" He turned to his fellow hecklers and chortled,

"She wouldn't know what to do with the ballot if she got one . . . which she ain't gonna!"

With their jeering laughter ringing in her ears, Laura rose painfully. There was no gallant Joe or Shawn in this mob to dash forward and help her to her feet. She brushed at her white blouse and gray skirt, but it was hopeless. The dirty rainwater had soiled her school outfit. Her hair, too, loosened from its clasp, tumbled down around her shoulders, and the loud catcalls unnerved her.

Stooping, she picked up the umbrellas with shaky hands. Very much aware of her disheveled appearance, she hurried past the smirking faces surrounding her, stumbling once. She kept her eyes resolutely fastened on the women holding the placards while the thought flickered through her head that these boys were her own age — between fourteen and sixteen. Young enough to be rowdies, yet old enough to know better. Where were the police? she wondered. No doubt, as so many times in the past, they were staying discreetly away. Chief Bentley didn't want to do any favors for the pickets. If the public wanted to harass them that was too bad, but it was none of his affair.

One of the boys dashed up to Refna, tore the sign from her hands, and threw it to one of his companions, who commenced to rip it to pieces.

Laura, dropping all the umbrellas except

one, rushed at the skinny, grimacing boy, swinging the black umbrella like a bat. "Stop it, you bully! Leave her alone!" she shouted.

"Catch me if you can," crowed the hoodlum, darting just beyond the range of the umbrella's spiked top.

Dismissing him, she turned her attention to Refna, rushing to her side. "Are you all right?" she asked, opening the umbrella and holding it over the gaunt woman's head.

Refna's eyes gleamed with determination. "I'm fine. Just bring me another placard, Laura." Holding the umbrella high overhead, Refna stared straight ahead as her shoulders shifted slightly in her canvas coat. There were tiny white lines around her thin lips. Why, she's afraid, thought Laura, afraid of these young hooligans! She wanted to cry for her, to take her place, not to let her suffer alone amidst the taunts and the pelting rain.

"Hurry, Laura," Refna said between chattering teeth.

"I wish I could take your place," Laura offered sympathetically.

Refna nodded, smiling briefly. "Run back and find a bigger sign. President Wilson goes to the Senate this morning, and we want him to be sure to see our message."

Laura nodded grimly. The president must realize that these women would continue to picket just as long as it took to obtain their demands. With her chin firm and her head high, she didn't hear or see the hecklers as she went back to the mansion.

The next day at school, Mr. Blair noticed Laura's skinned cheekbone but said nothing.

Laura, quiet and subdued, kept her eyes on her history book. The section on U. S. Grant's presidency was boring, and she'd be glad when they came to Theodore Roosevelt. She much preferred recent history to what they were studying now.

"Laura, tell the class what mistakes U. S. Grant made during his presidency."

Oh, no, she groaned to herself, still staring at the blurred page before her. Why would he call on her, knowing that she was absent yesterday and hadn't read the assignment?

"Laura?" His voice rose in irritation.

"I don't know, sir," she answered evenly.

He sniffed and tapped his forefinger on his text. "I thought as much." Staring disdainfully at her for a few seconds, he finally said, "See me after class."

"Yes, sir," she mumbled. If he found out what she had done yesterday, there was no telling what he might do.

She rubbed her bruised cheek ruefully. He had certainly observed her appearance. It was all she could do this morning to keep her mother and Sarah from seeing the bruise, but the generous rouge she applied had hidden it from eyes that were busy with morning chores. However, she couldn't hide it forever. Besides, she had no excuse for missing school, and her mother would never be dishonest and write a note for her.

After class her pounding heart proved justified when Mr. Blair pointed an accusing finger at her cheek. "Did you get that bruise at the suffragist rally yesterday?"

Her hand involuntarily flew to her cheekbone, too flabbergasted to reply.

"Oh, you needn't look so surprised that I've discovered your secret. Dr. Whiting and I had an interesting chat yesterday when he told me that he wouldn't allow Cassandra to attend the rally." He directed a thoughtful frown in her direction. "But you, Laura, being a headstrong, obstinate, unthinking young girl, decided you didn't need to abide by the rules. So you played hooky from school and evidently were involved in a brawl while listening to that radical, Alice Paul."

His last words were said with a sneer; "Well, Laura, you are not going to get away with flagrant disobedience this time! I intend to see that you're punished." He coughed slightly, holding his fist near his mouth. "I have tended to overlook your transgressions in the past but not anymore!"

Openmouthed, she stared at this opinionated, prim viper. When had Mr. Blair ever overlooked anything she had done?

"I'm recommending to Mr. Cole, the principal, that you be expelled from school," he said harshly as he turned on his heels. "You can go. By Friday Mr. Cole and the Board of

Education will act upon my recommendation."

Stunned, Laura could only glare at Mr. Blair's rigid back. Her face flamed with shame and fury. Expulsion from Jefferson High! How could she leave her high school in disgrace? How could she tell her mother?

Chapter Twelve

STUMBLING out of the classroom door, Laura moved through the morning in a daze. How could Mr. Blair do such a thing! Just because she missed one day of school! Tears stung her eyes, and she had to blink hard to keep them from spilling down her cheeks as she sat through each class like an automaton. In English Miss Emerson gave her a strange look, but Laura wasn't ready to talk to her yet.

At the end of the day she piled her books in her locker, taking only her history book home. She would at least have her homework finished so Mr. Blair couldn't criticize her on that score.

Rushing down the hall to leave school, she didn't want to see anyone, not even Cassie. Still, she felt the need to confide in someone, and making a decision, she knew exactly whom she must see.

As she hurried down Cherry Alley, she turned into the Menottis' store, hardly able to wait to speak to Joe. He was the only one who would understand and offer her advice. Shawn was fun to be with but dismissed her problems as inconsequential.

Threading her way between the cracker barrels and flour sacks, she wiped away the teardrops and looked around for Joe. Bertina, alone in the store, was packing up potatoes for an old man.

After the customer left Laura asked in a thin, little voice that she tried to keep from cracking, "Where's Joe?"

Bertina's forehead creased in concern at the sight of Laura. "He and Aldo go to fruit market to get load of bananas. They be back in very quick time." The heavyset woman watched Laura with narrowed eyes. "You cry, Laura. What is wrong?" Her jovial face was transformed into a caring, sober one.

Laura moved her shoulders in a gesture of despair, and before she knew what had happened, tears spilled over again. "It's — it's Mr. Blair, my teacher. He's going to have me expelled from school!"

"Santo Cristo! What is this 'expelled'?" Bertina asked, wiping her hands on her half-apron and holding wide her fleshy arms.

Laura moved into Mrs. Menotti's welcoming arms, sagging against her ample breasts with relief. "Expelled," she snuffled, "means that I will be forced to leave Jefferson High."

"Leave school?" Bertina echoed, dumbfounded. "But this is free country . . . education for everyone."

"Yes, but if you do something bad. . . ." Laura couldn't finish and wept bitterly against Bertina's shoulder.

"There, there," Bertina comforted, patting Laura's back. "Here." She stepped back, fumbled in her apron pocket, and pulled out a clean handkerchief. "You dry eyes. Bertina give you a cannoli, which I baked one hour ago." Winking, she grabbed Laura's hand and pulled the young girl from behind her to the pastry counter. Laura smiled in spite of herself. She had come to the right place. But, unlike Bertina, she didn't believe food would solve all problems.

As she ate the Italian pastry with the delicious ricotta cheese filling, Joe and Aldo entered, each carrying two huge bunches of bananas.

When Aldo spied Laura, his booming laughter resounded throughout the store, and he lifted the bananas off his broad back, setting them on the counter. "Ha! There is Laura, my *tressora*!"

My treasure. She liked the sound of it and she smiled, wiping a crumb from her mouth.

"Laura in trouble," Bertina said with a

137

clicking tongue. She puckered up her mouth and shook her head, offering Laura a second cannoli.

Laura declined, holding up her hand.

"Trouble?" Aldo pulled up a crate and sank his hefty frame on top. "What trouble?" He indicated with a huge hand that Joe should sit, too.

Joe, leaning against the counter, looked at Laura with a bemused expression, knowing she probably wanted to be alone with him.

Laura once more told her story, glad to be with people who loved her and wanted to help. At one point she faltered when she realized with a pang that she'd have to repeat her story to her mother and Sarah. How upset they'd be! If only they wouldn't be ashamed of her. She knew her father would have been proud of her activities with the suffragists and would fight to keep her in school. With her mother, however, she had her doubts. Maude Mitchell would probably survey her with a steely eye and say the punishment was well deserved. Laura dragged her attention back to the warm circle of the Menottis.

"Joe!" Aldo exclaimed, pointing at Laura. "I know nothing about this school business. You take our girl for a walk, eh? You work enough today." He shooed them out the door. *"Vai! Vai!"*

Grinning, Joe took Laura's hand as they

sauntered down the walk, past the home of the von Hindens, a German family who had a large American flag flying at all times by their front door.

"That flag means different things to different groups," she said acidly. "I'm just finding out what it takes to be an American these days. You mustn't deviate from the path our president has set for us. If you do you're suspect of betraying this great republic!"

Joe shrugged. "That's wartime for you. Times are not the same, and everyone had better be a patriot or else."

"How true that is," she said, following his lead as they cut through a back lane and headed for H Street. "The conflict with Mr. Blair and me erupted after my theme. Up until then we'd had sort of a sparring feud, but the essay really angered him, and he's been after me ever since!" Viciously she kicked at a pebble before her. "Now it looks like he's trapped me and can get rid of me for good!"

Joe's hand tightened around hers, but he said nothing as Laura poured out the whole story. "I feel so awful, Joe. Everything I do is wrong. I'm too young to be a picket or go overseas with the motorcade, yet I'm old enough to be condemned because I associate with the suffragists, and I can be kicked out of school for it. Why is life so unfair?"

"Don't worry, Laura," Joe reassured her

in his strong, level voice. "The first thing you should do is have your mother go to school with you."

Her heart plummeted. "She won't go with me, Joe," she said raggedly. "Mother disapproves of Miss Paul's tactics, and I know she won't help me."

"You might be surprised," Joe said. "Next you need to see Mr. Cole and Miss Emerson. Gather your forces. You, yourself, can plead a good case and head Mr. Blair off before he can take this hearing to the Board."

She looked into his black eyes, sparkling with understanding, and felt her confidence resurfacing. "Good advice, Joe. I'll see Miss Emerson first."

As they walked past show windows Laura noticed a crowd in front of a butcher shop. A large flag hung outside. "Must be another German-American displaying his loyalty for everyone to see," she said. Craning her neck for a better view, she wondered what everyone was looking at. "What do you think is going on, Joe?"

"Looks like more vandalism," Joe said grimly. "If you're a German it's hard to stay in business these days."

When they joined the crowd, she could see the smashed window and the angry, sullen people milling about.

"Go back to Germany!" one man yelled, and heaved a brick at the remaining pane of glass. "We don't need traitors in this neighborhood."

"Get out, get out," chanted the crowd.

Inside was an old man, stoically sweeping the glass and debris that littered the floor.

"Most of these German-Americans are loyal to the United States government, but that doesn't make any difference to this mob." With his hand on her elbow Joe ushered her through the crowd. "Americans are trying to stamp out anything or anyone that's from Germany."

"I know," she responded, remembering all the name changes that had been made. "Sauerkraut is called 'Liberty cabbage,' and I heard an Iowa town, Berlin, was renamed Lincoln, and German measles are now Liberty measles!"

Joe nodded as they left the crowd behind. "Some of these renamings are pretty ridiculous. The other day I untied tin cans that some boys had tied to a dachshund's tail or 'Liberty pup,' as they call these German dogs now." He shook his head. "Poor little pooch. He didn't know what was happening. He was so low-slung, anyway, and when I came near, he slunk so low that his belly touched the sidewalk!"

"Well," Laura said, "they do say there are German spies lurking everywhere."

Joe snorted. "Yes, and if you believe that, I'm Kaiser Wilhelm."

"I don't know," she said doubtfully. "You know Otto Detler is German."

"Yes, and a better handyman and a better person couldn't be found. You've caught 'war jitters,' just like everyone in Washington," Joe said. "Let's hope this war ends, so America can get back on an even keel. You can bet your shoe tops that the Germans here hope so, too."

She felt better after her walk with Joe, and although her problem still remained a big one, it didn't seem quite so insurmountable anymore. When he brought her home, she gazed into his eyes. "Thanks for being a good listener," she said, tweaking his ear. "Ah," she said laughing, "your ear is still there. I thought I might have talked it off."

He reached up and pulled her hand to his lips. "Any time you want to talk, you know where you can find me." He shuffled his feet and smoothed back the unruly shock of hair on his forehead. Finally he said, "Our Friday nights have sort of come to a standstill, haven't they?"

"Yes, between Mr. Blair and the suffragists, I'm kept hopping."

"How about Saturday?" he asked, never taking his dark, questioning eyes from hers.

"Saturday?" she asked lamely. "Saturday I'm busy."

"Is 'busy' another word for Shawn O'Brien?"

"Yes, I — I promised to go out with him."

"I see," Joe said evenly.

"Joe," she said, "he's my brother's best friend. He's in the army, and this is his home away from home." Her words fairly tripped over one another. "Shawn is lonely and —"

Holding up his hand, Joe cut in, "Spare me. There will be other Friday nights." For a moment he studied her oval face. "Go slow, Laura. You're a sixteen-year-old beauty, and Shawn is an attractive soldier, but he's not the type to go with only one girl."

"That's fine with me!" she snapped. Joe's advice on school problems was one thing, but on social problems — that was something else again.

"I'm just telling you to be sensible and to see Shawn for what he is. He likes girls and he couldn't help but like you, but just remember you're not the only one." He looked at her and laughed. "Stop glowering. Your eyes are shooting green-gold rays." He smoothed her sweater collar, then touched her hair. She held her breath. Pulling her to him, he leaned down, his mouth pressing against hers.

Astonished, she allowed his sweet lips to linger on hers longer than she should, encircling his neck with her arms.

At last Joe gently disentangled her arms and kissed her with the old familiar peck on the nose. "Good night, Laura. And good luck tomorrow."

Her hand moved in a limp wave after his

retreating back. Her heart pumped wildly at the memory of his kiss. How long she had yearned for a kiss like that! Now that she was going out with Shawn, why did Joe have to change, to treat her more like a sweetheart than a kid sister? Her confusion was bittersweet as she opened the door. Joe's kiss had almost pushed the expulsion problem from her mind — almost, but not quite!

When she came in, her mother and Sarah were in the parlor, knitting as usual. Wondering how to approach her mother, she swallowed hard and decided the best way was to get it over with and confess her plight.

Squaring her shoulders, she entered and stood before Mrs. Mitchell.

Maude looked up with a smile. "Laura, sit with us for a while. It seems we're all rushing in six different directions and seldom are together anymore." Her smile faded when she noticed her daughter's face. "What's wrong, dear?"

"It's Mr. Blair," she blurted out. "He's recommending my expulsion from school." She sank into a chair.

"Expulsion!" Sarah said, horrified. "But, why?"

Laura twisted the fringe on her belt. If only she had confided in her mother before and told her about playing hooky. Briefly she described Monday's rally and her part in it. The words were low, and it was difficult to squeeze them past the lump in her throat.

"Now," she finished, "Mr. Blair is trying to expel me." She flung out her hands in a helpless gesture.

"I always knew your suffragist activities would bring you nothing but trouble," Sarah chided.

Laura glanced at her but bit off her angry retort when she noticed the tears sparkling in Sarah's eyes. Besides, she was in no position to be defiant.

Daring to look at her mother, she saw little sympathy in her usually gentle eyes.

Maude cast her knitting to one side and shook her head reprovingly. "Sarah is right. How could you let the suffragists interfere with your schooling?" she admonished.

"I'm going to see Miss Emerson tomorrow," Laura said hopefully. "She'll have some ideas."

They talked for a short time, but what was there to say? There were only more of Sarah's tears and more of her mother's reproaches.

Sadly Laura went up to bed.

When she slid beneath the covers, her lips quivered. How could she have hurt her mother like this? She turned her head into the pillow, heaping blame on herself.

Later Mrs. Mitchell came in and tenderly kissed Laura's forehead. "Things will work out, darling. Don't give up hope. If you need me I'll come to school."

Laura should have felt better when her

mother switched off the light, but the darkness enveloped her as if she were lost, stumbling and falling into a deep abyss. Despite her weariness, she slept very little that night.

The next day, however, after school was out and she was on her way to see Miss Emerson, her problem loomed large once more — almost too large to overcome.

In history class Mr. Blair had been his usual caustic self, giving a brief lecture on how Miss Paul's suffragists were impeding the war effort. Knowing his talk was directed at her, Laura slid down in her seat, trying to close her ears and, for once, not having a comeback. She didn't want him to know that she was rallying her forces.

As she opened Miss Emerson's door she squared her shoulders, determined to tackle this problem. With Miss Emerson's help she'd be able to extricate herself from a messy situation.

"Come in, Laura." Miss Emerson looked up, her gray eyes filled with compassion. She indicated a desk for Laura to sit down in.

Laura's eyes filled with tears again as she slid into the desk, which was bolted to the floor, and gazed at Miss Emerson with trepidation. It was true her English teacher was kind and liked her, but what could Miss Emerson really do? However, as she looked at this energetic woman with her vibrant face surrounded by waves of dark hair, Laura knew that if anyone could help her solve this problem it would be Miss Emerson.

"Now, Laura," Miss Emerson said confidently. "I know why you're here."

Laura shot her a fearful look. Where had she found out? Was it all over school?

"Yesterday," Miss Emerson went on smoothly, "Mr. Blair told me he wants you expelled." Her bright eyes seemed to peer inside Laura's heart. "Ever since class, I sensed something was wrong, even before Mr. Blair bragged about what he intended to do." She grimaced. "What an oaf!" she said with exasperation, briskly unclasping the celluloid cuffs that protected her crepe de chine blouse.

"Listen, Laura, here's what we'll do. You make an appointment to see Mr. Cole the first thing Friday morning. I'll go with you. Mr. Cole is strict, but fair, and," she added dryly, "he also likes good teaching and competent record-keeping. He'll listen to me." She waggled her yellow pencil to and fro. "You need to tell your story exactly as it happened with no embellishments. Don't sell yourself short, Laura, for you're an attractive, articulate student. I'll vouch for that. When we're finished presenting our side to Mr. Cole, I'll wager he'll decide that your case won't be worth the attention of the Board!"

She rose. "By tomorrow it will be all over, and you can go about helping the White House pickets once again." She put a hand on

Laura's shoulder. "Just don't get yourself arrested. That would really give Mr. Blair a case."

Laura looked up and smiled. "I'll try not to. The arrests haven't been as heavy this week as anticipated. Only twenty women were sent to jail."

"How long is Police Chief Bentley going to continue to harass the pickets?"

"You should come to the meetings and find out," Laura teased.

Miss Emerson wrinkled her nose and grinned. "It's term paper time, but I'll be there tomorrow night."

Laura stood, too. "Chief Bentley said no more arrests after this week. We'll have proved our point, and he'll have proved his. I feel better," she said. Inside, she suffered a few doubts. After all, both Mr. Cole and Mr. Blair were not known for their love of suffragists. Hesitating, she went on, "Even if I'm not expelled, how will I ever be able to get through the rest of the year with Mr. Blair?"

"You'll manage," Miss Emerson said crisply. "After all, you're a suffragist. How many times did they have to stand patiently and listen to a senator berate them and their cause? Certainly you should be able to deal with Mr. Blair."

Chapter
Thirteen

ON Friday Laura, accompanied by Miss
Emerson, walked fearfully into Mr. Cole's
office.

How forbidding he looks, she thought,
waiting for him to look up from his paper.
His head was covered with a mane of white
hair, and his steady eyes and square jaw
did litle to reassure her that it was to be a
merciful interview.

Mr. Cole looked up. "Ah, come in, both of
you and have a seat." He studied Laura. "I've
just gone over a number of grievances Mr.
Blair has sent me, Laura. It's a rather im-
posing list." He picked up the paper again.
"You are, according to Mr. Blair, willful,
disobedient, impudent, and a poor student
with a bad attitude."

The blood raced to Laura's cheeks. "I may

disagree with Mr. Blair in class," she said, trying to keep the tremor from her voice, "but I'm not a poor student." Her tone became defensive. "Mr. Blair dislikes me because I'm associated with the suffragists."

"Hmmm." Mr. Cole leaned back in his chair, eyes narrowing and making a pyramid of his fingers. "I must admit," he said dryly, "I don't have much love for them myself."

Laura's heart sank. There would be no justice at the hands of an antisuffragist!

"Nonetheless," he continued, "the suffragists have nothing to do with this."

Miss Emerson spoke up. "Let me tell you about Laura Mitchell, Mr. Cole."

Mr. Cole swiveled his chair around and gave Miss Emerson a piercing look.

Miss Emerson, attractive in a dark dress with a large red bow at the throat, smiled reassuringly at Laura, and then calmly addressed Mr. Cole. "Laura is an excellent English student and does very well in every subject except history. In fact" — she dug into her briefcase — "here's a sample of several of her papers."

Mr. Cole took them and leafed through them, nodding approvingly.

"Laura is also a very caring person," Miss Emerson continued. "She's involved in other activities besides the suffragists, such as a motorcade unit and the Red Cross."

Laura looked down at her hands to hide

the pleasant glow brought on by Miss Emerson's praise.

Mr. Cole cleared his throat. "I respect your opinion, Miss Emerson, and I don't think cutting one day of class warrants an expulsion hearing before the Board."

Laura's head jerked up, and she was unable to hide her broad smile.

"But," Mr. Cole proceeded sternly, "you must serve a week's detention, and any more incidents with Mr. Blair will be severely dealt with." He paused. "Do you understand, young lady?"

"Oh, yes, sir," she said softly, happiness bursting inside her like fireworks. Mr. Cole was actually giving her another chance. How wonderful! She couldn't wait to tell her mother and Sarah.

"Very well, then," Mr. Cole said firmly. "We'll expect exemplary behavior from you, Laura." He gave her a nod. "You're dismissed."

She jumped up, wanting to hug him, but she only backed toward the door and said, "Thank you, sir," and as she turned the knob, she repeated, "Thank you, sir."

When Miss Emerson came out a few minutes later, Laura couldn't contain herself. She hugged Miss Emerson and exclaimed, "I have you to thank for helping me. You don't know what this means to me."

"Nonsense," Miss Emerson said with a

twinkle in her eye. "You could have persuaded Mr. Cole on your own, but one thing I'm not so certain about. . . ."

"And that is?" Laura asked.

"Being an exemplary student." She grinned. "Think you can manage that?"

"Just watch me," Laura promised, and she laughed gleefully.

After school Laura raced toward Cassie's locker, eager to share her news.

Down the hall, Cassie was opening her locker.

"Cassie!" Laura shouted. "Cassie! It's all right! I'm allowed to stay in school!"

Cassie spun around, dropping her books and, even in her hobble skirt, managed to run and hug Laura. "You're not going to be expelled?" she asked. Usually so dignified, she was fairly jumping up and down. "Tell me what happened."

The two girls walked back, picked up Cassie's books, and went out the double doors.

Laura squeezed Cassie's arm. "I still can't believe it. Mr. Cole was very stern, and I thought he would no more listen to me than to a mop. When I saw that he was intent on what I had to say, I relaxed a little."

"Was Mr. Blair at the conference?"

"No, thank heavens, but Mr. Cole read a list of grievances that he'd sent." She grimaced, glancing at Cassie. "You should have heard them. Mr. Blair kept mentioning 'class attitude.' Fortunately Miss Emerson spoke up in my defense, and she refuted every charge Mr. Blair made against me. I wish you could have seen her — she was sincere, vital, and humorous. She even had brought in several of my A essays.

"What a week for you, Laura. I'm glad it's almost over, not only for you, but also for the suffragists!"

"Yes, worrying about leaving school was the worst part. Today, when we read that phrase from James Russell Lowell in English class, I thought how well it fit me. Remember the line, 'The misfortunes hardest to bear are those which never come'?"

Cassie turned to face Laura. "I'm so glad for you." She gazed steadily at Laura, her eyes warm. "You know, I should have been in Mr. Cole's office with you." She slightly moved her elegant, broad shoulders. "But you know Father forced me to attend school on Monday."

"It's okay," Laura said gently. "I'm glad to have you as a friend. We always seem to agree, and no one will ever separate us. I could have been dragged to school, too, that day, if I'd confided in Mother. But that's all behind us. Now we've got to get through history. At least we're facing Mr. Blair together. I don't think I could stand another day of his class if you weren't there also, Cassie." Her eyes softened. "It's a good feeling to know you're in this whole thing with me, and I don't mean just Mr. Blair but the suffragists, too."

"And what would I do without you?" Cassie said, smiling. Then she glanced at her watch. "In fact, I'm supposed to be on duty right now, from four to six o'clock. The pickets will want their coffee right on the dot of four-thirty." She shifted her books, glancing at Laura. "What are your hours?"

"From six to eight." Laura sighed, feeling it was all about to end. "Just think, at midnight it will all be over, and Chief Bentley has promised to leave us alone."

"Why are you headed toward the White House? Aren't you going in the wrong direction?" Cassie asked curiously.

"I promised to meet Shawn for a cup of tea at the corner of Fifteenth Street." She caught her breath. "In fact, there he is now," she said, pointing.

"Hmmm," Cassie said, observing the soldier leaning against a lamppost. "He's handsome." Just then Shawn turned his head and saw them.

"The way he's rushing to meet you, it looks like you two are long-lost lovers." Cassie's laugh lingered in the warm May air. "It looks serious between you two." She gave Laura a sidelong glance beneath long, dark lashes. "What about Joe?"

"Joe's still special." Laura paused. "Both boys are special but in very different ways."

Her pace picked up, and so did her heartbeat, as she returned Shawn's wave.

"Well, the main thing is that you're enjoying them. Just stay out of trouble so you can keep on enjoying them," Cassie warned. "I don't want you taking any more trips to Mr. Cole's office."

"Believe me, that's one place I want to keep away from! In fact, if I'm sent there again for my suffragist activities, Mr. Cole personally threatened to take me before the Board."

When Shawn crossed the street and caught up to the two girls, he was breathless. "Laura, hi!"

"Oh, Shawn. It's good to see you," Laura said, her face beaming. "Everything is all right," she said, almost bubbling over. "I'll be able to stay in school."

"Great!" He gave her that old familiar grin, wrapped his arms around her waist, and pecked her on the cheek. Lifting his head, he peered quizzically at Cassie.

"Shawn, this is my good friend, Cassie Whiting. Cassie, meet Shawn O'Brien."

"Well, hello," Shawn said in a low voice, stepping forward and holding out his hand. "Where has Laura been hiding you?" Folding his arms across his chest, he gazed approvingly at Cassie's tall, lithe figure. "I've heard a lot about you from Laura."

Cassie's eyes twinkled, looking first at Shawn, then back at Laura. Her face with its straight, delicate planes made her seem grown-up. Her dark hair, short and wavy, ruffled a bit in the slight breeze.

Laura managed to return Cassie's smile, but she was none too pleased at Shawn's flirtatious manner. Maybe Joe was right. Maybe Shawn could never be loyal to one girl. The memory of her first meeting came back to her, when Shawn had looked with such admiration at her, too. She chuckled, dismissing the nagging doubt, and said lightly, "I haven't been hiding Cassie at all. She's one of the most popular girls at Jefferson High."

"I can understand that," Shawn said. "So, Cassie, you're a suffragist, too." His tone was unbelieving as he appraised her expensive pink linen suit.

"I am," she said with a pert nod, "and I'm already late for duty at the White House."

"Don't be tardy," he admonished teasingly. "The soldiers will miss you if you're not on time."

His mocking tone, however, didn't upset Cassie, and she held out her hand, shaking Shawn's again. "I've got to run." With a careless wave she hurried off, calling over her shoulder, "I'm glad to have met you, Shawn."

"Same here," he shouted back. Turning to Laura, he said, "What a looker your girl friend is!"

Laura nodded, no longer feeling jealous.

That was just Shawn's way, and what was wrong with appreciating a lovely girl? "Cassie could be a model," she agreed.

He tilted up her chin with his forefinger. "She's too aristocratic-looking for me. I prefer freckles and a dimpled chin."

She giggled. "It's a good thing, Shawn O'Brien, because you're stuck with them." Hand in hand they strolled toward Lee's Tea Room and Gallery.

When the steaming tea arrived, Laura squeezed lemon into hers but Shawn added nothing. He only wrinkled his nose at his first taste. "I'd rather have Irish coffee." Then he reached for her hand. "It's so good to see you." His brown eyes became serious. "You know, Laura, you're playing with fire. Don't you think you've tempted fate once too often? The next time you could get burned."

"What do you mean?" she asked, dabbing her lips with her napkin to hide how flushed she was. Did he think she was flirting with both him and Joe? And although her throat was dry and she could feel a blush sweep across her face, Shawn's next words reassured her. That wasn't what he had meant at all.

"This suffrage business has gone far enough, Laura. It's only a game to you. Don't you see that it could mean prison?" Carefully he set the dainty cup down, awaiting her reply. As he watched her an amused expression spread across his open face. "But you love danger, don't you, Laura? You crave excitement!"

She bridled at his words and stiffly took a sip of tea, cautioning herself to be ladylike and not to shout or carry on. "I'm not playing a game, Shawn," she told him in measured tones. "I know there's a possibility of being arrested, but it's highly unlikely. After all, I'm not a picket." She observed Shawn over the rim of her cup, willing him to understand. If he cared for her he must try to see her viewpoint and to respect her beliefs. "I feel very strongly about the suffragists and what they're trying to accomplish."

For a moment his eyes clouded, then he leaned his head back and laughed. "Don't be so serious, sweetness, or you'll become wrinkled before your time. Your eyes are sending out storm signals, and I could drown in those green depths of fury." His mouth curved downward. "Laura, surely you must realize how men view this nonsense when they see women running around with placards, organizing parades, obstructing traffic, going to jail, and generally making fools of themselves."

She gritted her teeth but said nothing. *Not all men think we're nonsensical*, she thought. Joe understood. Besides, many men had come over to their side, including legislators. Why did Shawn have to cling to the old ways and old ideas? What was it? Did he feel threatened? Why should he? He was handsome and had everything going for him — why should he resent women having the ballot?

His voice softened. "You're not like one of them, Laura. You're lovely and a woman who desires a man's arms around her." His smile didn't reach his sober eyes. "I don't want to have you turn into a spinster like Miss Paul."

"Miss Paul has dedicated her life to our cause." Laura's hands shook, and she felt so angry she could cry, but she wouldn't give Shawn the satisfaction.

"All right, but we've been going out for several months and I'm constantly competing with the suffragist meetings. In fact, I wish you'd take me as seriously as you do Miss Paul." His words were clipped and abrupt. "A little of that treatment goes a long way."

It suddenly occurred to her that Shawn had never had to take no for an answer, certainly not when it came to girls. When he asked, they accepted. She wondered for a brief moment if she were doing the right thing. If he were put off too many times he'd move on elsewhere and not give her a backward glance. She didn't really want to lose him. Shawn was bright; she could enlighten and change him.

"Now," Shawn said, his good humor restored. "I'm as willing as Joe to indulge your whims, but you need to have a little fun, to go dancing," he said with a lopsided grin.

"If you stick around those fanatical old hens in the Women's Party, you'll even start cackling like one."

Flushing angrily, she pushed her teacup aside. He was hopeless. "Really, Shawn. I don't appreciate the comparison."

"Sorry," he said briefly, toying with his spoon.

She took a deep breath. She hated to shy away from an issue that was obviously on both their minds, and she knew it would come up again, but right now she wanted to enjoy Shawn's company. She hadn't seen him all week, and she didn't want him leaving angry. "Let's not discuss the suffragists anymore," she said as pleasantly as she could.

"Suits me." He lightly touched her fingers. "Next month General Long is taking a few of the military brass on a tour of the White House — June twentieth, to be exact — and I've wheedled an invitation for you. Would that please you?"

"Oh, yes," she said. "It's been about" — she squinted at the ceiling fan — "about nine years since I've been there. Mother and Dad took Sarah and me one summer day. The rooms were gorgeous, and even then I was impressed. At the end of the day we had a picnic along the Potomac's banks." She swirled her teacup, studying the residue at the bottom. How long ago that seemed. Her father had been so exuberant, lifting her high on his shoulder and carrying her around, explaining what this painting meant, who donated that vase, and what president had decorated the Red Room. It had been a glorious outing.

"And July twenty-first," Shawn continued, "I want to take you to an army dance. That is, if you can tear yourself away from the suffragists. The dance is especially for the officers, so it should be posh. I want you to wear your best dress. I like your violet gown."

"I'll wear it, because it's the only party dress I own. I wish I could have a new dress, but the war curtails everything, what you can eat, what you wear . . . I'll be so glad to be able to buy some new clothes."

"I don't blame you. See this uniform?" Shawn said distastefully, running his finger beneath the high collar. "I'm getting rid of it as soon as peace comes. I can't wait for my discharge."

She was a little surprised, for Shawn had made a comfortable niche for himself in the military. He was personable, and General Long, waiving protocol, had more than once invited him places where only dignitaries and Washington society mingled. Shawn had been promoted in a matter of the few months that he'd been stationed here, so her puzzlement must have shown on her face.

"Surprised?" Shawn asked with a twitch of his eyebrow.

"I did think you might make the army

your career. Look at you" — she grinned, pointing to the three-stripe chevron on his sleeve — "you're a sergeant already."

"No, I've done my hitch. I'm enrolling in law school right here in the city and be the best damn lawyer east of the Mississippi." He winked. "And earn piles of money defending anyone with the greenbacks to pay. You'll have plenty of new dresses then, Laura."

Did that last statement mean what she thought it did? Did this handsome, carefree soldier sitting across from her really love her? She wanted to ask him what he meant but instead said, "You'll be a good lawyer, Shawn." And he would, too, but somehow she wished he'd not worry so much about fees. He should be more concerned with people that needed his help, regardless of how many greenbacks were offered to him. Her thoughts turned to the suffragists who had been arrested. Doubtless they'd still be in prison if it hadn't been for lawyers who donated their time and energy to free them. Well, she had to be practical and realize that Shawn would no doubt become a prominent, wealthy Washington lawyer and magnanimous only when it suited his purposes.

The sun's slanting rays caused her to ask Shawn the time.

"Holy smoke! It's almost six!" He jumped up, offering her his hand. "We've been here almost two hours, and I'm to report to

General Long, and you're to report to General Paul!" His eyes twinkled, and she smiled back at him. They did have fun together, even if they didn't always agree.

As they parted company she thought of the two events Shawn would take her to — the White House tour and an officers' dance. Silently she vowed to keep those two engagements with him, no matter how many rallies Miss Paul called.

Chapter Fourteen

With a last glance back at Shawn, Laura turned down Pennsylvania Avenue, loving the wide street with the tall trees lining either side. In the distance the pristine whiteness of the White House shone in the sunset. The sidewalks were crowded with people, but there was little doubt that it was wartime. She passed three women in YWCA outfits, a group of sailors who doffed their caps in elaborate exaggeration in her direction, several army officers followed by a navy officer whose uniform was festooned with gold braid. On the street a line of supply trucks rattled by.

A newsboy thrust the *Washington Post* in her face, but she shook her head, walking faster. However, the glimpse at the newspaper's headline — U-BOATS TORPEDO 30 SHIPS

THIS MONTH — made her buoyant spirits sag a little. The killing continued, and the Germans seemed stronger than ever, winning one battle after another throughout France. Despite Michael's assurances that the Germans would never cross the Marne River, she was not so positive.

A contingent of Red Cross nurses jostled her. As they swept by, laughing and chatting, she wondered if their smiles would be quite so wide if she were wearing a yellow sash across her dark blouse.

The tower clock struck six, and she broke into a run. How could time slip by so fast?

As she walked through the corridor of the mansion with its noise and bustle and the constant clacking of typewriters, several secretaries nodded and smiled at her. Laura was pleased, for she was becoming known. Her loyalty, and always doing her job and attending rallies, had paid off.

Dashing past the switchboard operator and the Press Room, she headed to the rear of the house.

Entering the kitchen, she fastened on her Votes-for-Women ribbon and began filling the vacuum bottles with coffee.

"Ah, Laura, I was afraid you might not come tonight," Lucy Burns said as she poured two cups of tea. "I'd heard you might be expelled from school."

"Mr. Cole, my principal, gave me a reprieve," Laura said with a shy smile, for this woman was one of the main leaders in the Women's Party, second only to Alice Paul, and though she'd heard Lucy Burns speak, she'd never had a conversation with her.

"I'm glad you can stay in school. We need more women in the professions," Lucy said firmly, looking down at Laura. She was a tall woman, and her rolled-up shirtsleeves, held in place by an elastic garter around her upper arm, showed she was quite muscular and physically fit. "When we were in prison, we demanded to be examined by women doctors, not that they sent us any."

Placing the two cups on a tray, Lucy reached for a large jar. "Alice and I need a molasses cookie before we go out on the line." She glanced at Laura. "You do plan to go to college, don't you?"

"Yes," she responded without a second thought. It was as natural as if Lucy had asked if she had planned to go on breathing. She hadn't really thought about college, not since that day when she had burned the blueprints. It was as if from that day on she wasn't concerned about her future. Now, talking to Lucy Burns, this staunch ally of Alice Paul, she wanted to be a professional, maybe a doctor like Joe.

"Are there many women doctors?" she asked curiously.

"Very few." Lucy's lips tightened.

Nibbling a cookie, Lucy leaned against the counter, shaking her head. "Alice is tired and run-down. I'm anxious for her. She's worried about the arrests."

Laura knew that Lucy had the reputation of the eternal optimist while Alice was the pessimist. Lucy's good spirits were known throughout the Party, even when she had served her sentence at Occoquan Workhouse. "How many arrests have there been?"

"We've had thirty this week, but they're a token," Lucy said grimly. "Chief Bentley knows it and we know it."

"Then why does he do it?"

"He's a vindictive little man. After our seven months in prison we were released by a court order. Since then we've filed sixteen suits against the government for arresting us and we've won." Abruptly she laughed, slapping the kitchen countertop with the flat of her hand. "Those court sessions were worth all the money we've collected. It gave us an open forum for our views, and believe me, we expressed them loud and clear."

Laura was puzzled. "Doesn't Chief Bentley know he can't hold us?"

"Oh," Lucie said, chortling, "he knows all right, but he's determined to harass us and push us as far as he can. I think our eternal vigils at the White House have infuriated him, and he means to show us that we can't upset his city. After what we've been through, does he think we'll stop now?"

"I admire you for your time in prison," Laura said hesitantly. "I know it was awful

167

because I've been reading Ada Kendall's journal."

"It wasn't pleasant, but we gave each other strength. See this?" Lucy pointed to a silver pin, a tiny replica of cell doors, on her collar. "When we were set free, a mass rally was held at the Belasco Theater, and we were each presented with a pin like this." She tapped it proudly with her forefinger. "Just over eighty-six thousand dollars was raised in our behalf, and they dubbed us 'prisoners of freedom.'" She chuckled. "We had other names, too. The other inmates called us the 'Strange Ladies.'"

Laura marveled that this raw-boned leader had spent so much time talking with her. What she said made sense. Indeed, she wouldn't give up. Maybe, just maybe, she could do something with her life that would help women like Lucy Burns and Alice Paul. If she could serve such great women her life might be worth something. She smiled. There would be years to figure out her life. Who knows, she thought bitterly, maybe she'd *still* be on the picket line in years to come. Surely not. But she'd never leave here until the nineteenth amendment had been passed, that was certain! Never. She grasped the vacuum bottle and with firm steps hurried out to the pickets.

The week was almost over, and even if the pickets were arrested, the courts would order an immediate release. Everything was fine. She wanted to change her determined stride to a skip and a jump as she neared the brave women who patiently held their placards.

Dusk, mingling with the fog that had rolled in from the Tidal Basin, gave the scene before her an ethereal appearance. The women in white, with their large-brimmed hats, standing very still and straight, and the purple, gold, and white tricolor billowing out from the White House fence, was a breathtaking sight.

As Laura poured a cup of coffee for Rowena Green, one of the youngest and prettiest suffragists, there was a loud clatter of horse hooves. Suddenly, from behind the shrubbery, policemen jumped forward, dashing to arrest the pickets. One on horseback shouted, "Women, surrender. You're surrounded."

The scattering women, however, paid no heed and rushed in every direction to escape the policemen. A patrol wagon chugged into the square, and Laura ducked out from under the grasp of a burly officer. Her heart in her dry mouth, she raced toward the statue of Andrew Jackson but realized almost at once that the bronze horseman would be scant protection.

Frantically she veered to the left and dived into the bushes. The fog might enshroud her in a misty gray cover. She heard heavy footsteps and scrambled deeper into the brush. Bunching up, she clasped her knees tight against her chest. Not daring to breathe, she waited fearfully as the thrashing came closer. Laura squeezed her eyes shut and murmured in a low voice, "Please don't let them find me." She mustn't be arrested. But even as this thought flickered through her mind, a harsh, panting voice said, "Over here, Clancy. Here's the little weasel!"

Through the branches she could see the blue uniform and tried to make herself smaller, but it was no use.

"Come out of there," a voice snarled. "Burrowing in like a rat in a hole!"

She tried to scurry away from his reaching hands, but his nightstick came crashing down on her shoulder, sending an agonizing flame of pain down her arm. Then all at once she was lifted out of the shrubs. She yelped. Her arms, she thought, were being pulled from their sockets as the policeman jerked her to her feet. Dragging her toward the patrol wagon, she tried to hang back, but his fingers were like iron talons.

She bit her lip to keep it from trembling. She must be brave and show the mettle of which suffragists were made. Her shoulder was a ball of fire, but she mustn't think about it. Suddenly she bent her head, sinking her teeth into the policeman's hairy wrist and squirmed free, but she didn't get far. Without a moment's hesitation the officer lunged after her, entangling his fingers in her long, thick hair.

"You vixen!" he roared, pulling her back.

Surely the man was pulling her hair from the scalp. Wincing, all she could do was follow meekly along with her head twisted to one side.

When they reached the rear of the wagon, he lifted her up. "Get in there," he growled. "You witch!"

As she was roughly shoved into the patrol wagon, all she could see was a row of women staring down at her as she lay sprawled before them. Suddenly the faces blurred and became hideous, disapproving masks that resembled Shawn, Mr. Cole, Mr. Blair, Sarah, and her mother.

Chapter Fifteen

COMPELLED to relinquish her skirt and blouse at the district jail's front desk, Laura was given a straight-cut cotton dress. Donning the coarse gown that reached to her ankles, she already felt like a criminal.

As Laura was thrown into the dim cell she was frightened, aching, and angry. The room was barely lit by a single bulb dangling from the ceiling, but it was enough to illuminate a cot crisscrossed by wooden slats, with the bedding roll at the foot.

Fetid air assailed her nostrils, and the cramped space caused her to cringe. She had a horror of small enclosures ever since the time, as a child, she had played hide-and-seek in the backyard with Sarah. She had run around the house, ducked through the front door, and hidden in the hall closet.

When Sarah didn't come inside to search for her, she had decided to come out and show herself, but when she had tried the door, the knob only slipped around and around in her hand. She couldn't get out, and her muffled cries couldn't be heard. She had beat on the door until her fists ached. It wasn't until Sarah came in, over an hour later, and could hear her wails that she was liberated. Her sobs and ragged breathing alarmed Sarah, but after a few minutes, she had recovered. However, she'd never forgotten her fright, and since that time she had refused to venture into any tiny space.

She gazed around and shivered. Now she was in a little room with a cold concrete floor, damp heavy air, and iron bars that would keep her locked in for God knew how long.

As her eyes grew accustomed to the gloom she could see how dirty the washbasin and corner toilet were. She glanced across the corridor, and in the opposite cell saw Rowena Green, sitting dejectedly on the bed, and her roommate, Mrs. Lawrence Lewis, grasping the bars and staring gloomily at her.

Mrs. Lewis was one of the dauntless suffragists who had been arrested in 1917 and who had kept a diary of what had happened to her. Because of her vivid descriptions of what had been done to the women prisoners, they had gained the public's sympathy. The outcry that followed forced the government to release the suffragists sooner than they had wanted to.

Rowena, white-faced, stretched out on the bed, her arm flung across her eyes.

Mrs. Lewis, square-jawed but with large, gentle eyes, said soothingly, "Don't worry, Laura. We should be out of here in a few days."

"A few days?" Laura echoed dumbly. "I thought the authorities couldn't hold us."

Mrs. Lewis smiled. "Oh, they can detain us as long as they please. Remember, this is Friday night, and over a weekend it will be difficult to expedite a court order for our release."

The words caused Laura's heart to lurch. How could she stand being cooped up in this suffocating cell? What if she missed class on Monday? Then she would not only have a prison record, but she'd be expelled from school as well. Tears stung her eyes. What could she do?

"How can we notify Miss Paul?" she asked fearfully, looking wide-eyed at Mrs. Lewis. "Or our families?"

Mrs. Lewis chuckled, showing even, white teeth. "Miss Paul already knows. And your family? She'll take care of that, too. If you need —"

"Shut up in there!" a prison matron shouted, all at once materializing in the corridor. "No talking! Absolutely none!" Banging her nightstick smartly across the bars for emphasis, she paced back and forth in front of them. A large, beefy woman with a scowl on her long face, she wore a dark uniform. "If there's any more noise out of either cell," she boomed, "I'll toss you into solitary!" Enjoying her authority, she thrust her big face between the bars. Her narrow eyes glinted maliciously at Laura.

Laura shrank back, her legs bumping against the cot. Solitary! She must never be thrown into solitary. She would go crazy in a dark hole!

Turning her back on the matron, she silently unrolled the thin mattress. Trembling, she lay down and pulled the worn blanket up to her chin. When she dared to peek out, the threatening guard had left.

She stared into the darkness, hearing the drip, drip from the faucet and a scurrying, scratching noise. What was it? Her blood ran cold. Rats! It had to be rats! She turned on her side and curled up in a ball, shuddering. Her shoulder sent sharp shooting pains down her arm. She tried her best not to cry again. How could the suffragists stand a seven-month jail sentence? She closed her eyes against the scratching noises and tried to sleep, praying for freedom. She must have more confidence in Miss Paul. She would have them out in the morning.

However, the morning light, streaming through the barred window, brought no news. Only a breakfast of watery cereal which, when she lifted the spoon to her mouth, she was sure held a maggot. She threw down the spoon, retching. Perhaps she was just imagining worms, thinking of the many journal entries she'd read of the suffragists in the Virginia Workhouse. The inmates had been given moldy, wormy food, day in and day out. She glanced in the direction of Rowena and Mrs. Lewis. Rowena tasted the thick mush that passed for porridge, while Mrs. Lewis had disdainfully pushed her bowl aside.

Laura remembered Mrs. Lewis's diary and recalled the force-feeding scene. Would they force-feed them in this prison if they didn't eat? She stared at the bowl's contents, but there was no way she could pick up the spoon and try to swallow the awful lumps.

Gingerly she sat on the cot's edge with her stomach churning. She thought of Mrs. Lewis's ordeal when she had been in prison last winter. Five people had held her down, forcing a tube between her lips and shoving it down her throat, letting the fluid gush into her stomach. Laura observed this quiet woman who had been so stalwart that she had tried to stop moaning, for fear it might upset her friends in the next room. What courage and concern she had! Just looking at her serene face gave Laura renewed strength.

She clenched her teeth. She'd never let a tube pass her lips. Then she groaned audibly. They had ways of force-feeding other than through the mouth. In Lucy Burns' journal she had written that five people forcibly held her, and when she wouldn't open her mouth, they had shoved the tube up her left nostril. Laura pressed her clenched fist against her mouth. She had to get out of here. Where was her mother? Where was Miss Paul?

The matron, with a contemptuous flourish, removed the bowl. "You can starve if you want to, Missy. You ain't got much meat on those bones the way it is, so if you want to get sick, go right ahead!" She sneered, shrugging her massive shoulders.

"The food is buggy," Laura retorted, coldly staring into the matron's eyes.

"Hmmpf! Miss High and Mighty. We'll see if you're still so uppity after you've gone without eating for a few days!"

Laura almost jumped, but she wouldn't give this witch the satisfaction of seeing how her words panicked her. *A few days!* Who knew how long they'd be shut in this terrible place?

Suddenly the iron door at the end of the corridor clanked open, and Alice Paul and Lucy Burns walked down the aisle. They spoke encouraging words to each cell's occupants.

When Lucy Burns stopped at Laura's cell, she said, "We've made a special plea in your case, Laura. After all, you're only sixteen, and we want you back in school on Monday."

Nodding quickly, Laura swallowed and tried to smile. "Oh, yes," she said, almost pleading. "I need to be back by Monday morning or Mr. Cole will see that I'm expelled."

"The court order is in Judge Murphy's hands right now," Lucy said confidently. "We'll keep checking on your release." The small silver pin glinted in the early-morning light, and Laura thought, *I hope I won't earn a bar emblem for a seven-month imprisonment like she did.* Maybe, Laura thought, in the next hour she'd be free.

But the next hour brought no news. Alice and Lucy had left with promises of a quick release, and Laura knew they were sincere, but she also had misgivings. The courts moved slowly, and there was no guarantee she would be out by a specified date. She hit her fist on the bars. Time was so important! Even if she were released Monday afternoon it would be too late. She would be expelled! If that happened she might as well run away from home. What could she do all day? Her mother and Sarah would be humiliated and wouldn't want her underfoot.

She squinted up at the tiny window, wishing she could open it and let in some fresh air, but it was bolted shut. She should do what Miss Paul had done months ago when told the cell window mustn't be opened. She had thrown a book by Elizabeth Barrett Browning through the window. The smashed pane allowed a breeze to blow throughout the cell block, and several prisoners had commented that it was the first time in years they'd had fresh air. Alice must have been an obstinate prisoner for the wardens to deal with. Despite her petite frame, she was ninety-five pounds of pure stubbornness.

Laura smiled grimly as she braided her hair. She'd seen several roaches, and braids were better than thick hair flowing over her shoulders. She quivered at the thought of bugs in her food and bugs in her hair.

"Laura Mitchell!" the matron yelled. "You have visitors in the waiting room." Her heavy footsteps resounded down the hall, and when she appeared, fitting a large key in the lock, even her unpleasant face was a welcome sight. To escape confinement if only for a few minutes would be sweet, Laura thought.

Entering the large room with a table and three chairs, her heart leaped at the sight of her mother, Sarah, and Joe. Joe grinned when he saw her and gave the thumbs-up sign.

Tremulously she smiled back, suddenly conscious of her drab prison dress with the rounded neckline and too-large sleeves. Her hair pulled back and pale face must shock her mother.

Mrs. Mitchell and Sarah both rushed to her side, hugging and kissing her. They offered what sympathy they could. She was only glad they didn't say "I told you so."

"Oh, poor Laura," Sarah exclaimed. "If only we could get you out." She clucked her tongue in dismay, looking around the room distastefully. "It's horrible in this place."

"I — I know," Laura said, fighting back tears and wishing she were going back home with them for a lovely lunch. She was hungry, and her stomach rolled. She glanced over Sarah's shoulder at Joe. How wonderful he looked.

He stood with his arms folded across his red-checked shirt, watching every move she made. When his eyes met hers, a grin spread across his dark face, reassuring her.

Disentangling herself from Sarah and her mother, Laura moved into his arms. "Joe, Joe. I hate it here, and they don't know when we'll be released!" She wiped her eyes, determined not to cry.

He patted her back and said, "Be patient, little one. Miss Paul has Opal Zacks working on the case. She's one of the top women lawyers in the city."

"Yes, but can she get me out by Monday?" she inquired, sniffling. "If I'm not in school Monday I'll be out for good."

For a long moment they said nothing. With his arms around her she felt safe and secure. Never mind that she didn't know when she'd be free. "Do you think I'm stupid for getting involved in the Women's Movement?" she asked in a whisper.

"Of course not. You know I approve of what you're doing." He cupped her face in his hands. "When you come home, I'll show you how much I care, little one."

Their eyes locked. What a sweet feeling to be with Joe. He was her strength, and he *did* care for her!

"You know, the time you spend in here will scarcely be remembered." He stroked her hair.

Disagreeing silently, already she was beginning to tremble at the thought of returning to her dismal, cramped cell. "I — I wish I were going home now," she said in a light voice, trying to be cheerful, but she could scarcely get the words past her closed throat.

"Soon, soon." Solemnly he leaned down and kissed her cheek. "Be brave, little one."

"Time's up!" snapped the matron. "Back to your cell, Laura Mitchell!"

"She's only sixteen. You've no right to hold her," Mrs. Mitchell said indignantly.

"I know nothing about age or sentences. My job is guarding prisoners. The judge makes decisions about whether this miss should go free or not."

Maude, eyes worried but filled with love, slipped her arm around Laura's waist and pulled her close. "She shouldn't be thrown in with hardened criminals."

The matron snorted. "She's in with her own kind — those infernal suffragists. If you call them hardened criminals, then she's in with the worst!" She grasped Laura's upper arm. "Come on, missy."

Sarah ran up and kissed her. "We'll keep working to get you out. Our next stop is Miss Zacks's law office." Then she leaned close and whispered, "Shawn will be here tomorrow."

Laura smiled. "I'm glad," she said in a low voice, giving Joe a sidelong glance. She didn't know why she was being secretive. Joe knew about Shawn, and it didn't seem to bother him. In fact, she wished he would show a twinge of jealousy, just a twinge once in a while, but he didn't.

The matron's fingers dug into her arm and, with a rough tug, pulled her along. Laura winced, for a tongue of flame burst across her shoulder blade.

As she allowed herself to be led away, she turned and blew first Joe a kiss, then her mother and Sarah.

The clanging of the corridor's iron door sounded so final, and she drew back in front of her cell and halted.

"Hey, missy!" the matron rasped. "None of that!" With a yank she moved her forward. "Don't give me any trouble!"

Anger exploded within Laura against this bully, and she wheeled about, confronting her. "Leave me alone," she said between clenched teeth. "My shoulder is black and blue, and you're hurting me."

Immediately the matron released her arm. "All right, but don't try any funny stuff!"

Amazed, Laura stared at her. It was as if the matron was afraid to touch her. Then Laura smiled. Now she knew the reason. There had been too much national attention focused on the suffragists' treatment in jail. A little spunk, rubbing her arm, and standing up for her rights, thought Laura, caused this woman to let go of her arm.

Opening the cell door, the matron glowered at her but didn't touch her again. "In with you," she snarled.

Once the cell doors shut, Laura sank down on the cot. The day stretched interminably ahead.

The long hours dragged by, and she still couldn't bring herself to touch her food. She glanced at Mrs. Lewis and Rowena, who were eating their bread. The corridor was very quiet. How frustrating not to be able to speak to one another! The silent corridor with its long shadows appeared ominous and eerie.

Later, when the lights were turned off, she stood on tiptoe on the cot's edge to peer through the bars. The Capitol dome shone in the streetlights. Bitterness flooded through her. The dome was the symbol of freedom, democracy, justice! Words, words, and more words. They meant nothing.

Saturday night was almost gone, and there had been no messages all day.

Throwing herself on the cot, she lay awake, staring at the ceiling. Was it all a hideous nightmare? Would she wake up tomorrow in her own bed? But as she stared at a roach skittering across the wall, the bars throwing black stripes along the moonlit wall, she knew this was real.

Chapter Sixteen

SUNDAY'S subdued morning light filtered through the rain-streaked windowpane, but the steady patter didn't diminish her spirits. Today, please God, she would be released.

Although she was starving, she hadn't touched her breakfast gruel. She couldn't. If Alice and Lucy could go on a three-week hunger strike, she could manage without food for two days! Her bruised collarbone was a constant, dull throb. Nonetheless, she knew it wasn't broken. Her spirits lifted even more when she thought of this afternoon and Shawn's arrival. She was eager to see him and tried to look as clean as she could under the circumstances. She splashed water on her face, combed her thick hair, then rebraided it. Her gray gown was wrinkled, and the coarseness was scratchy against her skin.

She wriggled, feeling like such a clod in it. What she wouldn't give to scrub every inch of herself in a sudsy bath and then wash her hair. Still and all, she was able to smile at Rowena and Mrs. Lewis across the way.

When lunch came, she ate a few bits of the stale bread, then began her constant watch toward the corridor door. Surely the matron would come any minute and tell her Shawn was here. Visiting hours were over at three, so he had to come soon.

Two o'clock and still no Shawn. She lay down, her spirits plummeting. Had he forgotten her?

Just as she'd almost given up hope, the frowning matron, without a word, unlocked her cell door and jerked her head toward the waiting room, saying gruffly, "You've got someone waiting."

Her heart soared. As she hurried to the visitor's room she looked around and there he was, leaning nonchalantly against a chair. The khaki uniform he wore fit him as if a tailor had measured him first, and the match-leggings were neatly wrapped around his muscular legs. His brown hair was in perfect waves, and his blue eyes danced as he stood with his hands on his hips, surveying her. "I don't know," he said, teasing. "Is this my Laura of the cascading hair?" He moved closer, pretending to inspect her, lifting a braid and letting it fall across her breast.

She smiled feebly. She knew she looked

awful, but she had worked hard to make herself presentable.

"Oh, Shawn," she murmured, moving into his comfortable arms.

He stroked her head, holding her tighter.

"Ouch," she whispered.

"What's wrong?"

She smiled ruefully. "When I was arrested, the policeman hit me with his nightstick, and my shoulder is still sore."

He shook his head, holding her more tenderly. "Laura, my poor Laura."

She muttered against his rough-grained wool jacket, "I thought I'd be home by today."

"Isn't this home?" he said dryly. "The suffragists seem to inhabit this district jail more than anyone else!"

She stepped back, her blood rising, but she was too weary to fight with him. "We'll be here as long as it takes," she responded quietly as she moved out of his arms and sat in a straight-backed chair.

"And what about school?" His eyebrows lifted, and he drew up a chair, straddling the seat with his arms resting on the chair back.

Crossing her ankles, she sat with her eyes cast down. "I don't know just what I'll do if I'm thrown out of school, but I've been weighing my options." She looked up and met his eyes unflinchingly. "I may work full-time at National Headquarters."

Abruptly Shawn pushed his chair forward

and walked around the room, hands in his pockets. "I don't know how you could get yourself into this mess. The suffragists are no good for you, Laura. Get out of their organization before they ruin you!" He stopped and watched her reaction, but she kept her face immobile. Shawn continued. "You've been beaten with a nightstick; you've landed in jail; you've been near expulsion; and in all likelihood you'll be kicked out of school; and you still talk of helping these crazy women!"

Stricken, she could only stare at him.

Shawn stopped pacing and confronted her, his dark blue eyes probing and intent. "When you're let out of here, and you will be soon, I promise you, I want you to relax for a while. Stop going to your motorcade drills, too. You can't win the war or win the ballot single-handed!" His voice softened, and he cradled her cheeks with his palms, bringing her face near his. "I love you, Laura. I want to take care of you. Don't you want that?"

She gazed into his searching eyes as if mesmerized, and a smile spread across her face. His words sounded wonderful — he was wonderful, like a safe haven, and if she ever needed taking care of, it was now!

He smiled, bent his head, and kissed her.

His lips were sweet and lingering. How pleasant it was to lean against him and let him handle her problems. She needed him, she thought, as her arm slid around his neck, pressing her hand against the nape of his neck.

When he released her, her knees wavered, and she felt dizzy. She smiled wryly. Was it love or hunger pangs?

As if reading her thoughts, he brought out a napkin with four dried apricots and handed them to her. "You're so pale," he said sympathetically. "Your mother told me you couldn't eat the food in here, so I thought you might appreciate some nourishment."

She ate one of the wrinkled apricots, savoring each mouthful while surreptitiously watching the matron who was seated by the door, reading. One after the other she ate the apricots, hiding her mouth with her hand, for it was forbidden for food to be smuggled into the prison.

Shawn nodded approvingly.

Eating the last of the fruit, she didn't know what she needed more, this food or Shawn's arms around her. "You know, Shawn," she said slowly, "perhaps you're right. Maybe I *do* need taking care of. I only get myself into trouble." She noticed his pleased reaction and hastened to add, "But one thing I can't give up until women have the vote is following Miss Paul."

His mouth set in a straight line. "You can't or you won't?" He reached for her hand and coaxed gently, "Not even if I ask you to?"

Her gaze was steady, despite feeling as if

his eyes would melt her into submission. "Not even if you ask me, Shawn," she said softly. "Please try to understand."

He shrugged, reaching for his hat, twirling it. He looked so jaunty and self-possessed. "I've got to go, Laura."

Her hands became cold and clammy. "You're not angry with me, are you, Shawn?" she asked in panic.

"Of course I'm angry!" he said hotly. "I'm tired of coming in a poor second to the suffragists." He tipped his hat farther over his brows and eyed her levelly.

Her lower lip trembled slightly at the thought of his leaving so angry. She wasn't as brave as she thought. She reached out to him, but he ignored her hand.

"I'll stop at the front desk and see if there are any new developments on the court order," he said matter-of-factly. "When I came in, that woman lawyer was arguing with the police captain, and she had a sheaf of papers she was waving beneath his nose."

Her pulse picked up a beat. "Perhaps Opal Zacks is negotiating my release, even while we talk. If only I could get out of here today."

"I'll do what I can," he said cryptically. "But you can't force them to hurry things along. You ought to know that!"

She closed her eyes and said, "To eat a wonderful dinner, to go dancing with you, to weed the garden, to be free. I can't wait!"

He eyed her dress. "I can't wait, either. To see you with your hair done up and wearing your lavender dress." He glanced around. "If I could have brought you a saw file, I would have done that, too." He grinned ruefully. "There must be more than one way to break you out of jail!" Impishly he pinched her cheek. "I'd like to see those cheeks rosy and a smile on those pretty lips."

She smiled tremulously, relieved at his mood change.

"Time's up!" the matron ordered. "Back to your cell." She paused and sneered. "Suffragist!"

With a heavy heart at the thought of the confining cell, she blew Shawn a kiss and accompanied her guard.

As Laura paced back and forth in her small room, she expected Opal Zacks to appear with discharge papers, but no one came, and when the lights were turned off and all the prisoners were ready for bed check, Laura blinked back her tears until the matron had peered into her cell. After her heavy footsteps had receded down the hall she buried her face in the thin pillow and let the torrent gush forth. She cried until she had no more tears. Then, exhausted, she finally dozed fitfully.

When she awoke, it was dark, and she sat bolt upright. Her dream had been so terrifyingly real. With fear she looked about her cell, but it was the same stench-ridden room with the same dirty window. The same cot and sink.

She recalled vividly what she had dreamed. She had been chased by a dozen uniformed officers, all brandishing clubs. Up one corridor and down another she had dashed, frantically trying to find a way to elude them. But every time she reached a cell, the barred doors clanged shut against her. Breathlessly, she had run until she came to the end of a long, narrow passage. Then suddenly the floor had opened out from under her, and she had fallen, fallen into a deep pit. The taunting jeers of the police were followed by a large sheet of iron pulled over the opening. The space was no larger than the closet she had locked herself into years ago, except this area had a dirt floor and dirt walls. It was a terrible nightmare. No wonder she had awakened with such a start. She dared not go back to sleep.

She lay awake until the first streakings of dawn.

Monday morning and she was still in prison. School started at eight-thirty. It was too late. Too late!

"Laura Mitchell!" the matron called gruffly. "You're wanted at the front desk!"

Stunned, Laura stared at the raw-boned woman who opened the door and pointed to the end of the corridor. Was she to be set free?

When she reported to the desk, the police captain handed her her clothes, indicated a small room where she was to dress, and told her she was discharged.

"Am I free to go?" she asked incredulously, hugging her clothes next to her.

"What do you think I said?" The captain waved her away. "Get dressed and get ready to leave."

"Wh-what time is it?" she stammered.

"Eight o'clock. Miss Zacks will be here at eight-thirty. You're to wait here for her," he said shortly.

"School starts at eight-thirty," she whispered.

Uncaring, the captain had returned to his paperwork.

She wheeled around and rushed into the dressing room, banging the door shut behind her. She was going to school. Jerking off her prison dress and flinging it in a heap, she grabbed her blouse and plunged her arms into the sleeves, nimbly buttoning up the front. Then she fairly jumped into her skirt. Eight o'clock! How could she ever make it to her first-period class when Jefferson High was clear across town? Did her mother know she was to be released? Why wasn't she here? For once, though, she didn't care. She needed someone with a car, and General Long's limousine came to mind. If only Shawn were here to drive her!

The captain, his nose still buried in his

books, looked up when she cleared her throat impatiently.

"Well?" he growled.

"Sir," she blurted out, "I can't wait for Miss Zacks. I need to get to school!"

Raising his bushy gray brows, he eyed her in surprise. "You're going to school like that? Your hair's undone and you've buttoned your blouse the wrong way!"

"I don't care, I've got to leave here at once!" Her words tripped over one another.

The captain hunched up his shoulders, and then let them drop. "It's okay with me. If you're gone when Miss Zacks gets here, then it's too bad for Miss Zacks!" He handed her a pen. "Here, sign these release papers."

With trembling fingers she scrawled her name across the bottom line. "There!" she exclaimed, flinging the pen down. "What time is it?"

"Eight-fifteen," he retorted, guffawing. "I've never seen anyone quite so wild to get to school."

"Is there a trolley line near here?" she asked desperately, tucking several loosened strands from the braid behind her ear.

He indicated with his thumb. "Over on Calvert Street, one block south of here." His eyes sparkled, but his mouth was sober. "You'll make it if you run."

"Thanks," she called, turning on her heels and racing for the door. "Tell Miss Zacks I'll see her later at Headquarters."

Out the door she flew, taking the steps two at a time.

A car chugged to a shuddering halt, brakes squealing. "Hey, lady. Want a lift?"

Joe! There he sat, bouncing in the cab of the Menottis' delivery truck. She had never been so glad to see anyone in her life.

"Joe," she said between breaths as she clambered up beside him. "I've got to get to school by eight-thirty. You don't know how happy I am to see you!"

"I think I do," he shouted above the revving engine. Then, shifting gears, they sped down the street.

"Will we make it?" she questioned desperately, still not believing her good fortune that she had been set free and that Joe had come to meet her.

"If old Betsy doesn't conk out on us, we'll make it. Hang onto the side strap, for you're in for a ride." He glanced at her. "Do you think Mr. Blair will let you into his class?"

"He'd better! If I'm not late there's nothing he can do about my arrest. After all, what happens over the weekend is no concern of his." She shivered a little, thinking of her three-night ordeal. "How did you know I was to be released this morning?"

"Miss Zacks called your mother just as she was leaving for work. Maude, in turn, called the store." He winked at her. "When Papa heard you were released, he commanded me to get you to school this morning and not to worry about the deliveries until later." He honked at a dog that ran alongside, barking at the wheels. "Papa, of course, considers you part of the family, and you couldn't ask for a more fierce protector."

Smiling and holding a hairpin between her teeth, she tidied her hair. "I needed a fierce protector with the matron we had. She was a terror, and I'm not so sure I'd like to see Aldo tangle with her."

"He could handle her, believe me." Joe swore under his breath as he pulled on the steering wheel, veering the car to the left to avoid hitting a young boy who almost darted into the street. He pressed the rubber bulb, and when the boy heard the honking and saw the truck with its side canvas panels flapping, he stepped back quickly.

Along the sidewalk wide-eyed pedestrians watched the careening truck with disbelief.

"Faster, Joe, faster," she urged, clinging to the strap, swaying and bouncing first one way and then another as they hurtled down the avenue.

"Old Betsy can't go much faster," Joe answered, but nonetheless he pressed his tennis shoe firmly down on the accelerator.

A second dog yapped from the safety of the sidewalk as Joe continued to honk the horn and skillfully maneuver his truck around a horse-drawn milk truck.

"It's eight twenty-four," Joe said, pointing to the school's towers. "We made it!"

Jolting to a screeching stop, Laura scrambled out of the front seat. "Joe, you're a love!" She barely touched the running board as she broke into a race against the clock. She fleetingly wondered if Shawn would have made this same stupendous effort in her behalf.

She pounded up the walk, gulping in mouthfuls of air for her bursting lungs.

Hair flying, she ran down the hall and stopped at Mr. Blair's classroom. Scarcely able to catch her breath, she threw back her shoulders and entered, just as the late bell rang.

Chapter Seventeen

LAURA'S adventure in jail the week before was over, and even Mr. Blair seemed reconciled to having her in class. Although he did his best to ignore her, she nonetheless had become quite a celebrity. Students, boys and girls alike, came up to her and congratulated her on her bravery, and even Olaf Jorgenson had wanted to know more about the suffragists. She was pleased by the renewed interest in the Movement. But what she was pleased most about was the fact that she was still in school. Thanks to Opal Zacks, her lawyer.

Ever since last Monday, when she'd come dashing down the hall into school, she had been on her best behavior. She didn't want to jeopardize her last three weeks in school. Then, being rid of Mr. Blair and beginning her senior year next September, would be a joy. Now she had the summer to look forward to with time to really work for the Movement and to sort out her feelings for Joe and Shawn.

After school on Monday she and Cassie walked to the Women's Headquarters. Cassie was still on her four o'clock duty, and Laura had kept her usual six o'clock duty. Even though the arrests had stopped, the White House picketing continued. At first going out with her vacuum bottle of coffee had unnerved Laura. She had been apprehensive that the police would come charging down upon her again and drag her to jail, but she needn't have worried, for all was calm. Chief Bentley had issued a statement that the White House pickets would not face arrest, but if hoodlums harassed them, it would be at their own risk.

"Isn't it wonderful, Cassie? Woodrow Wilson is for the passage of the Susan B. Anthony Amendment, and more and more senators are, too. How can we lose?"

Cassie, moving beside her in long, fluid strides, looked doubtful. "He's coming on our side awfully late. Most of the senators have already decided on how they're going to vote."

"It will pass the Senate, you'll see. Women aren't pouring into Washington for nothing. They'll have influence on their own state senators."

While Cassie went on duty, Laura quietly drank a cup of tea in the mansion. As she squeezed the lemon slice into the steaming brew she smelled the daisies on her table and felt a buoyant radiance. The room was alive with women from every state in the union. They had massed here for the big vote on the Women's Amendment on June twenty-seventh. And to think she was part of it! Could anything be more exciting, more exhilarating? Their amendment had already passed the House of Representatives and needed only eleven votes to pass the Senate. President Wilson had recently taken to writing letters on behalf of the bill's passage, but there would be some legislators he wouldn't be able to persuade. Take Senator Shields from Tennessee, for example. He would be a hard man to crack. John K. Shields was known for his antisuffrage stance and hated being "nagged," as he called it, by the women's group from Tennessee. But with or without his vote the amendment would pass the Senate; then ratification by three-quarters of the states would be easy.

Laura gazed around with a sense of nostalgia. In a few weeks the amendment she and others had worked for so hard would pass, and their work would be finished. She would miss this yellow room, bedecked with flowers, humming with good conversation and good fellowship. Would this national headquarters mansion still be retained, or would everything be dismantled? She hoped the women would stay together and implement their gains. Laura enjoyed this company of women and the closeness that had developed within these walls.

"Hello, Laura," said Opal Zacks, standing by a chair. "May I join you?"

"Oh, please sit down," Laura said enthusiastically, smiling at her lawyer-benefactor, who had obtained her release from prison sooner than any of the other suffragists.

The pleasant woman, her large hazel eyes bright with intelligence, studied Laura. "Well, your stint in prison didn't hurt your appearance, that's for sure. You look positively ravishing this afternoon," she said with a broad smile.

Laura said, "I can't tell you how much I appreciated your help in getting me discharged. It means a lot to be able to finish my junior year."

"Glad to do it! You've been a good worker for the organization." Opal ran her fingers through her curly hair. "Now we have another big job ahead of us."

"I know," Laura answered. "The Senate vote, right?" She grimly pressed her lips together.

"The Senate vote," echoed Opal. "But we'll win, Laura — without a doubt, we'll win!" She laughed, showing prominent white teeth, all the whiter against her brown suit, the same color as her chestnut-brown hair.

Her positive attitude was reassuring. "I hope you're right," Laura said, then suddenly asked, "Is it difficult being a lawyer?"

"You should qualify that question, Laura. Is it difficult being a *woman* lawyer?" She pondered her answer, moving her shoulders in her lightweight summer suit. "At times it's not easy, and I've had to prove myself more than once in the courtroom, but when male attorneys see that I'm competent, efficient, and quite sane, they relax and treat me as one of them." She paused. "What do you intend to study in college, Laura?"

"I'm not certain, but I think I'd like to do something that would help women."

"That's a girl! Why not become a lawyer?" she asked half-teasing, half-serious.

Laura shook her head. "I don't know. I just don't know. This experience with Miss Paul and then being thrown in jail have made me grow up, but I still haven't hit upon a career. How long have you been a lawyer for the suffragists?"

"Ever since 1913, the day before Wilson's inauguration, when Alice Paul organized almost ten thousand women to march down Pennnsylvania Avenue without any police protection." Opal chuckled low in her throat. "That was an experience and took all the nerve I could muster. We had to fight our way through unruly mobs and hecklers all along the way. It was hard to keep our dignity and keep in military formation, but we did," she said proudly. "The mobs were so unruly that the Secretary of War was forced to call out the troops from Fort Meyer." Her eyes had sparks of fire in them.

"I wish I could have been there," Laura said.

"Oh, it was a sight to see! Bands playing and yellow banners everywhere. Huge contingents of women had come from all over the country and held their state flags high." She sobered. "From that day forward Wilson realized we were a force to reckon with!"

Laura's eyes shone. "You must be so proud of your accomplishments!"

"Oh, I am. I worked hard for my law degree, and so far I've put it to good use. Let's hope I can continue to be successful in helping women, because there's a long struggle ahead of us, even if the amendment passes. You can rely on that!"

Laura watched Opal as she left, wondering how her father would feel about her becoming a lawyer.

As Laura brought a replacement for a torn banner to one of the pickets, she paused, for coming through the White House gates was the President's large black limousine.

Inside she glimpsed the President and his wife. As the sober-faced leader passed by he lifted his top hat in her direction. Stunned, Laura held up her hand, not knowing whether to wave or salute. The president replaced his hat atop his thinning gray hair.

His glasses caught the glint of the late-afternoon sun, and a brief smile flitted across his long face. His wife, partially hidden by a black ostrich-plumed hat, lifted her head, but all Laura could see was a vivid splash of crimson across her lips.

Suddenly the president tapped the driver's shoulder, and the car ground to a halt. He rolled down the window and shouted, "Don't give up hope!"

Laura stood with her mouth agape. "Thank you, Mr. President," she at last was able to gasp as his car picked up speed and circled out of sight.

"Don't give up hope," she whispered. The President of the United States had actually stopped to speak to her!

She was still thinking of the President when she arrived home and entered the front door. The quietness after the hustle and bustle of the mansion was quite a contrast. Where was everyone? Surely her mother and Sarah were home by now.

"Laura?"

Startled to hear her name called from the darkened parlor, she hastened to switch on the lights.

Mrs. Mitchell hastily blew her nose, then stuck her hanky in her pocket.

Small fingers of alarm danced across her spine. Laura asked, "What's wrong?"

"It's Sarah . . ." Maude paused to compose herself. "Frank has been killed in action."

She drew forth the handkerchief once again.

"Frank?" she repeated dully. "Frank is dead?"

"We just received the letter from the State Department." A tear ran down Maude's cheek. "Nothing I say comforts Sarah. I wish I could do something to help her."

"Oh, Mother." Laura ran to her, falling to her knees and hugging her. "Not Frank. What happened?"

"The letter was brief. They said his plane had been shot down over German soil."

Laura, crying softly, lay her head in her mother's lap. Good, decent Frank, she thought. Good, decent Sarah. Life was so harsh!

Maude smoothed Laura's hair and said in a choked voice, "Go up and see what you can do to console her."

"I'll do what I can." She wiped her eyes and, with leaden feet, ascended the steps. How could she say words to help Sarah when there weren't any? Frank was dead. There were no words that would change that.

Slowly swinging Sarah's door open, Laura stood quietly, observing her sister's prostrate form across the bed. In her hand she clutched a letter edged in black.

"Sarah, Mother just told me."

Sarah sat up, and when she saw Laura, she jumped up and the two sisters embraced. "I can't believe it, Laura. I just received a letter from him yesterday. He talked about our wedding. . . ." She began weeping, and unable to continue, she turned and stared out the window.

"I know, I'm so sorry," Laura said softly. She put her hand on Sarah's shoulder. "It's hard to understand why these things happen. But Frank was fighting for a safer world." She knew her words had a hollow ring to them, but she didn't know what else to say. "You know there's hope for a better tomorrow." She hesitated and patted Sarah's back. "I just saw the President tonight, and his very words were 'Don't give up hope!' "

Sarah wheeled on Laura. "Don't give up hope!" she lashed out angrily. "What did Wilson say that for? Did you have your stupid Votes-For-Women sash on? Hope for the suffragists? How does that relate to Frank? The suffragists! I'm sick to death of them. I hate the suffragists! They've done nothing to help the war, and now," she said, sobbing, "my poor Frank is gone forever."

Stunned, Laura moved back, stumbling against a chair and sinking down into it. Did her sister despise her and the suffragists that much? She couldn't breathe but could only stare at Sarah's furious face.

Chapter
Eighteen

LAURA, astonished at her sister's outburst, was too paralyzed to move. Surely Sarah didn't mean she hated *her*. She was too distraught over Frank's death to realize what she was saying.

Sarah stood in the middle of the room twisting her handkerchief and staring disconsolately at Laura.

Carefully standing up, Laura approached her. "I know you didn't mean what you said about the suffragists, Sarah. You couldn't. You're too kind." She enfolded Sarah in her arms.

"I don't want to discuss it," Sarah said, tight-lipped. "Please go away. I need to be alone."

"Sarah," she said gently. "I love you. I can't leave when you feel this way."

Tears glistened in Sarah's violet-blue eyes, and her plump figure sagged in her dark, wrinkled dress as she reached out to grasp the bedpost. "Frank is gone," she said in a disbelieving voice. "Shot down for what? Why? It was three weeks ago today that he was killed, and it was only yesterday that I received his letter. Only yesterday everything was perfect — his writing was filled with our wedding plans." She gave a shuddering breath. "I answered him last night, and now Frank will never read it." She rested her head against the bedpost. "I — I don't know what I'll do now. The future is so meaningless."

"That's nonsense and you know it, Sarah Mitchell," she said evenly. "You'll continue your work at the factory; you'll attend your Red Cross meetings; you'll go on with your life." She reached out and put a hand on Sarah's shoulder. "Frank would want you to do that."

For a long moment no word passed between the two sisters, then Sarah lifted her head. "I suppose you're right," she said mechanically, and with trembling fingers she swept back her disheveled blonde hair, usually so perfectly waved, and faced Laura. "I'm all right, really, I just need to be alone." But her appearance said otherwise. Her eyes were red-rimmed, and her pale cheeks were tear-streaked.

"Very well," Laura agreed doubtfully,

hating to leave her, especially after she had said she hated suffragists. Laura was a suffragist. Did Sarah actually mean that she hated her, too?

As if reading her thoughts, Sarah managed a wan smile. "I love you, Laura. Forget what I said."

"Oh, Sarah." She hugged her sister tightly, but the close affection between them had disappeared some time ago. Although she held Sarah, things had changed. Sadly Laura turned and left, wondering how long it had been since she and Sarah had sat down and really talked. She remembered when she was fourteen and had confided in Sarah about her feelings for Joe and how his indifference bothered her. Sarah had laughed and told her to have patience . . . that she was growing up too fast as it was. Now confidences were no longer shared. Their conversations were limited to housework, lectures, and the war effort.

In the next few weeks school was let out for the summer, and things returned to normal. All except Sarah, who was quieter than usual. Nothing seemed to restore her good nature, nothing that is, until a letter arrived from a Lieutenant Bill Crowley.

As they were seated around the table, Sarah held Lieutenant Crowley's letter. "It's my turn to read a letter aloud," she said softly.

Laura gave her a sharp look. This was

something Sarah had never done before, but perhaps Lieutenant Crowley's letter would help ease her pain. "Good," she said, "then I'll pour the tea." She knew this wouldn't be an easy letter to listen to, for she could see by the address that Lieutenant Crowley had been in Frank's 94th Aero unit.

Sarah nodded her appreciation as Laura poured the tea; she took a sip and began to read in a composed manner, although the words were scarcely audible:

Chamery, France

Dear Sarah,

Frank has talked of you so often that I feel I almost know you. This is a hard letter to write, but while I'm in the rest tent, I'll attempt to describe how Frank died.

Captain Eddie Rickenbacker, our commander, ordered a special service with military honors for Frank, who was shot down behind German lines on May eleventh. He was attacking enemy observation balloons, which is a particularly dangerous target, because there are German Fokker planes above them and machine-gun protection underneath. His French Sqad plane was no match against those kinds of odds. So you see, Sarah, Frank died a heroic death, and we're all immensely proud of him here. He will be remembered by the men in the 94th squadron.

I guess I was as close to Frank as anyone. He was a shy fellow but one you could always depend upon. When he gave his word, it meant something. As you know, you are Frank's only family, so I'm gathering his personal effects, including his posthumous Medal of Honor, and if it is all right with you, I'll bring them to you after the war is over. I'm a Virginia boy myself, so Washington is close to Richmond, my home.

We'll both keep fond memories of Frank, and I know you must be a special girl to have been engaged to him. I know you are very pretty. I have not packed your picture with Frank's things and will keep it by my bed. I hope you don't mind, but it brings a little cheer to my dreary barracks.

Would you please answer this letter so I know you got it?

With my sympathy,
Bill Crowley

With a catch in her throat Sarah folded the letter, stuffing it in her apron pocket. "I'll save this letter. Bill Crowley sounds like a good man, and I'm glad Frank had him for a friend."

"I am, too," Laura replied. "Sarah," she

asked, brightening, "would you like to go with me to the motorcade unit this morning? The corps is planning to fill trucks with food and medicine for the drive to New York. Even though I'm not eligible to drive, I'll help load the trucks. It seems the trains are overloaded."

"Sorry, but I can't," Sarah said. "Mother and I are going to a pot luck this noon at the Red Cross." A small smile made her seem more like the old Sarah. "But thanks for asking."

Lieutenant Crowley's letter had helped, thought Laura. "Maybe next time," she said, feeling good about asking Sarah. She began to clear the table. "I'll see you later."

As she washed the dishes she felt so free. It was great not having school and the daily confrontations with Mr. Blair. Even the C he had given her was worth it to be rid of him. Now she had time for her suffragists and more time for Shawn and Joe. She was glad, too, that Sarah had renewed her interest in the Red Cross. For a week she hadn't gone out of the house, but she had started to do her routine jobs, although the deep hurt she had suffered left a sadness in her eyes that hadn't been there before.

As Laura went down the walk toward the motorcade drill grounds, she thought of how her mother and Sarah always seemed to be together. Their relationship had been like that even before her father died, except that she and her father had been inseparable then. How she missed him! Sometimes she felt like an outsider in her own home.

When she arrived at the drill grounds, the Packard trucks were lined up, hoods shining, and ready to be loaded. The five women drivers were dressed in long duster coats, the shaded cap and goggles and the hat with the closely tied veil ready for their two-day drive. Laura examined the packages of hospital supplies and foodstuffs, not wanting to look too closely at the drivers, for she was filled with envy. The trucks would be driving from Washington to New York, where the supplies would be shipped overseas. She wished she could be part of this "Express Run."

After the loading she watched as the five women climbed aboard their vehicles. The engines were cranked into action by fellow drivers, and with the American flags waving smartly in the wind atop the radiator ornament, they started off.

Wearily, Laura turned homeward. She was tired, but she had promised Shawn she would accompany him on the White House tour. What she really would like to do was to spend the time at Headquarters waiting for the results of the Senate vote. Today, June 27, 1918, it would be decided if the amendment would pass or fail, and she longed for the companionship of women she had worked with these past months. The tearoom would be jammed.

As she hurried along, the five trucks led by a motorcycle policeman drove by, with the women honking and waving at her. Huge signs on the trucks' sides proclaimed their destination: "The Washington–New York Express."

After she bathed and changed into a blue summer dress and her lisle stockings and pumps, with an azure satin bow atop her hair, she was ready for Shawn to call for her.

Later, with Shawn on the White House steps, waiting for the guide to begin, she felt every bit as attractive as the two officers' wives on the tour. A breeze came up from the Potomac, blowing loose several curls and tumbling them down onto her forehead. As she shaded her eyes to gaze down the mall at the Capitol she wondered what was happening on the Senate floor. Were Alice Paul and Lucy Burns sitting in the gallery?

Shawn took her arm. "We're ready to start the tour." He looked at her and winked. "You look prettier every time I take you out! I'd like to think I was the one who brought such a sparkle to those emerald eyes. Wherever did you find that beautiful dress?"

"It's just a summer dress, which will be new to you, but I can assure you, it is old for me."

As they proceeded into the great hall, passing the former presidents' portraits, Laura was pleased with Shawn's compliments. Sometimes she felt like a drudge, doing housework, driving, serving coffee, but Shawn made her feel as pretty as a glamorous movie star.

Going into the State Dining Room, the largest room in the White House besides the East Room, she stared in wonder at the heavy oak paneling and big game trophies that Theodore Roosevelt had collected and that Mrs. Wilson was planning to dismantle. Following the group, she marveled at the ornate centerpiece with its sixteen carved figures, each holding up a giant candlestick. The gilt grouping was set on a mirrored base. Laura glanced at Shawn, lifting her eyebrows. "How would you like to live like this?"

"I think I could handle it," he said with a chuckle.

And he could, too, she thought. Shawn was meant for a luxurious life. She turned back to view the high-backed chairs and velvet drapes, imagining President and Mrs. Wilson entertaining one hundred guests from all over the world with the women in jeweled tiaras and men in black tuxedos. The waiters would bring in gleaming silver platters of food, which, with a wide flourish, they would uncover before the guests.

Shawn leaned over and whispered, "General Long is invited here next week for a state dinner for an Arab prince."

"Will you be . . ." she left the question hanging in the air.

Grinning, Shawn shook his head. "I'm afraid I'll be waiting for the general in the car."

The sergeant-at-arms motioned Shawn to his side and the two conversed quietly.

It wasn't until the tour had moved into the East Room and she was admiring the famous Stuart portrait of George Washington that Shawn rejoined her. "Laura?" His blue eyes were troubled.

"What is it?" she questioned, puzzled at his expression.

"It's . . ." He cut the air with his hand. "It's nothing. I'll tell you later."

Uneasy, she again turned her attention to the white-and-gold room with its three crystal chandeliers. It was here that State functions were held.

She gave Shawn a sidelong glance, wondering what he had heard, but she kept her voice light as she said, "Wouldn't it be fun to see the second and third floors where the President has his private living quarters?"

Shawn nodded. "Of the one-hundred-thirty-two rooms, we've barely scratched the surface."

As they went out to the South Portico, one of the four entrances, the beauty of the

White House grounds was striking in the sunlight. The president's rose garden shimmered with pinks and reds, and the birds flitted here and there through the flowers and trees. The magnificent magnolia trees had been planted by Andrew Jackson in memory of his wife, Rachel, who died before she ever stepped inside the White House.

The tour members continued out the gate and dispersed, but as soon as they were alone, Laura confronted Shawn. "Now, what were you going to tell me?"

He laughed, a bit too loudly. "It's nothing. I just didn't know how you'd take it, and I didn't want to ruin the tour for us."

"Take what, for heaven's sake," she said with exasperated impatience.

"The Senate voted down the Women's Amendment by two votes."

"Two votes?" she repeated slowly, feeling as if her heart were being twisted in half. The years the suffragists had worked! Only two votes! Turning her back on Shawn, she put her face in her hands and wept bitterly.

"For heaven's sake, Laura, don't take this thing so seriously!" He touched her shoulder.

Wheeling around, she angrily brushed away his hand. "Don't you see? This *is* serious! Getting the vote means everything to me!" She could feel a flush creep across her cheeks, warming her face.

Shawn held up both hands, smiling. "All right, all right, sweetness. I won't fight about it, but the way you're caught up in this fanatical movement could do you more harm than good."

She gave him a long look, then walked away, too disheartened to argue further. She had thought she could change Shawn's views, but she was beginning to have doubts.

Chapter Nineteen

LAURA had been at Headquarters every day, and the new strategy would be no longer to condone President Wilson's speeches. Too long he had "said" he favored the amendment, but when it came down to the wire, he didn't push through the legislation. It was well known how Wilson would go over a senator's head to the people if he really wanted a measure passed. Alice Paul had promised to unveil a new plan that was certain to renew Wilson's interest in their cause, but she wouldn't reveal her strategy just yet.

As Laura sat at her dressing table, she thought of the Joan of Arc role she was to play in the upcoming parade scheduled for July twenty-first. Of course, it had to be on the very day of the Officers' Ball that Shawn had invited her to. She smiled ruefully as she brushed her hair, remembering how she had vowed that nothing would interfere with the two events he had planned. The White House tour on the day of the losing vote for the Susan B. Anthony Amendment had ruined what was left of a delightful day, and now, July twenty-first. At first Shawn had laughed uproariously at her playing Joan of Arc in a parade, then he'd been furious when she told him that she wouldn't be able to go to the ball, because of the rally later. But he got over it. Shawn never held a grudge or his anger very long.

As she tilted her head to one side, brushing until her hair shone with golden highlights, she was pleased with the plans she had with Joe for today. Her thoughts drifted back to the festive Fourth of July they had had last week. The Menottis, Otto Detler, Sarah, and her mother had all gone to the band concert in the park. She had sat next to Joe in her white dress with the green sash and her new sailor straw hat. She had stabbed several hat pins through the green hat, but it had perched precariously atop her hair like a bird's nest out on a limb.

She smiled at the closeness she felt to the Menottis and her family. Holidays were special occasions and meant for families. Even Sarah had responded to the fun and been more like her old self.

After the patriotic speeches following the concert were finished, they had taken the trolley to Glen Echo Park. There, Aldo and Joe had spread blankets on the grass, and Maude and Bertina brought out two large wicker hampers brimming with food. A patriotic fever rose in Laura as she thought of the warm scene. There was Otto, a German, the Menottis from Italy, and the Mitchells, who had emigrated to this country from Ireland during the Great Potato Famine of 1846. Only in America would there be such a melting pot at one table, she marveled.

She slipped into a pink dress, as pink as cotten-spun candy, and twirled before the full-length mirror, loving the new shorter length. Why, there were at least eight inches of her slim legs that showed! Naughty! She giggled. The sun-splashed day was gorgeous, and she hoped she and Joe would have as good a time today as they had had on the Fourth! It had been such fun, she reminisced, playing ball with Aldo and Joe, then eating a delicious lunch of fried chicken, potato salad, and apple pie.

Later she and Joe had walked hand in hand along the riverbank to the Little Falls of the Potomac. What was it Aldo had called them — the two *Uccello D'Amore?* Lovebirds. She liked that, but she felt a twinge of guilt, too. Was she a tease going with two fellows at the same time? Sarah thought so. Her sister, never one to mince words as far as Laura was concerned, warned her about finding a fine boy and going *only* with him. Playing the field wasn't what nice girls did. A smile played around Laura's lips as she remembered the night of Fourth of July with its bursts of fireworks against the night sky and Joe's arm carelessly around her shoulder. When she was with Joe, she felt warm, relaxed, and happy. Her feelings must have been reflected in her face, for she had caught Aldo's eyes on them, and he had winked and nodded his approval. What a glorious Independence Day that had been!

Today, she thought as she perked up the puffed sleeves on her dress and caught her hair with a ribbon, they would have just as much fun as on the Fourth. She examined her face and was pleased when she saw that her cheekbones were more prominent and that the planes of her face were taking on a leaner look. She peered more closely at her freckles, and although the summer sun always brought out more, especially on her nose, still there didn't seem to be as many as last summer.

"Admiring yourself?" her mother asked dryly.

Embarrassed, Laura wheeled around and flushed. Mrs. Mitchell was leaning against the doorjamb and smiling.

"I like to admire my pretty daughter, too."

Laura blushed even more.

"There's no harm in an admiring inspection once in a while."

Laura smiled in return. "Do you think I'm pretty?" she asked shyly.

"I think you're a rare beauty, dear."

"I hope Joe likes my dress." She put forth her left foot and held her full skirt at arm's length.

"Ha! Now you're preening!"

"Do you think Joe will like the dress?" Laura persisted.

"He should!" Her mother raised an inquiring brow. "And what about Shawn? What is he doing on this lovely Sunday?"

"Attending a garden party with General Long at Blair House."

"Oh, and you weren't invited?"

"Not this time," she answered, thinking of the many fancy parties and balls that she had been able to attend because of Shawn.

"He's a nice lad," Maude said, coming farther into Laura's yellow-and-white bedroom. There was a brief hesitation, then she asked casually, "How much do you like him?"

"A lot," Laura said. "He's fun and has a wonderful personality." How could she tell her mother that with Shawn she sprouted wings and could fly over rooftops?

"He's a charming lad, but I think you're dazzled by his magnetism and the exciting places he takes you. Perhaps you should tell Joe about Shawn."

"But, Mother," she protested. "He already

knows about Shawn. He doesn't care. Joe is only a good friend, has been since I was a little girl."

"But you're grown now, and I saw the way Joe looked at you at the picnic." She moved closer, straightened the hem of Laura's skirt, and affectionately patted her arm. "I just don't want to hurt Joe, but most of all, I don't want *you* hurt!"

She yearned to hug her mother, but something held her back. Her throat tightened, but she had to say what was on her mind. "Look at Sarah, Mother. She dated Frank all through high school. He was her one and only boyfriend. Now look at her. She just had her twentieth birthday, and she doesn't have a beau in sight."

"Is that what's worrying you!" Her mother chuckled. "You'll never lack for boys, Laura. Don't rush yourself and don't lead Joe on —"

"What about Shawn?" Laura interrupted.

"Oh, you're not leading *him* on." There was a small smile on Maude's usually sober face as she looked knowingly at Laura. "That boy can take care of himself, and besides, I've seen the color rise on your cheeks when he calls for you. The two of you go well together." She took Laura's hand in a show of fondness, which had been lacking between them for so long. "But you go even better with Joe."

Laura placed her hand in her mother's.

"Mom, trust me. I'm enjoying myself now. For the first time in my life I have two boyfriends, and I don't know what harm there is in that. Who knows what will happen, but one thing I know is that I won't hurt Joe. He's been my big brother too long."

The doorbell rang, and Laura squeezed her mother's hand. "Speaking of big brothers, there's Joe now."

"Have a good time," Maude Mitchell said, "and tell Joe about Shawn."

She didn't look back as she hurried downstairs. She knew what her mother meant. Joe knew about Shawn, but he didn't know how her heart raced when she was with him. Why did she have to tell Joe? She was comfortable the way things were. She wanted their easy relationship to continue without the complication of Shawn O'Brien's image hovering between them. If there was an opening in the conversation, she promised herself, she'd tell Joe. Otherwise she'd wait.

Relaxing because of her decision, she greeted Joe with unusual warmth. Joe, responding to her effusiveness, kissed her. It was a brotherly kiss, she assured herself.

Later, as they sat under three oaks on a grassy knoll overlooking the Potomac, which wound below them like a green water snake, she nibbled on a chicken leg. As she licked her fingers she frowned. Should she tell Joe now? She looked up to see Joe watching her.

He grinned, white teeth flashing against olive skin. His thick black brows arched as he flipped a shiny penny. "I'll give you this for what you're thinking."

"Hmmm, just something Mother and I were discussing." She gazed out at the field of primroses and bluebells. "Mother and Sarah are good at giving advice." She felt mean talking about them this way . . . they both wanted only her happiness, and she was belittling their conversation.

"Their advice wasn't about your love life, was it?" Joe asked teasingly, pouring out two glasses of cold lemonade.

"You'll never know, Joe Menotti," she answered smartly. Too late she realized that this was the opportunity she needed to confess how much she was seeing Shawn and to give Joe warning that he shouldn't take her for granted.

Although she knew Joe's feelings were no longer like those of a big brother, taking his little sister for an excursion, still and all she didn't want their outings to end. She enjoyed his company too much.

"You look very summery in your pink dress," he said.

"Thank you," she murmured, seeing herself reflected in his dancing liquid eyes.

"You're a remarkable girl. What new adventure have you been up to?"

"Well, next week the suffragists are parading down Pennsylvania Avenue and having a rally afterward." She hesitated. "I'm leading the parade on a white charger, dressed in armor."

"You're wearing a suit of armor?" Joe asked incredulously.

"Yes," she said in a low voice. "I represent Joan of Arc." She hadn't mentioned her role before, for fear Joe would laugh at her, but she should have known better than that by now. Joe took her too seriously to poke fun at anything she decided to do.

"Joan of Arc! You'll be the champion of women's rights. I can see you now on your white horse with your hair flying and banner waving. That's what I call dedication." He gave her a warm, admiring look. "What a sight. I wouldn't miss it for the world!"

She smiled then. Joe always supported her. She loved Joe. She loved Shawn. Which was the right one for her? She cast a probing glance at Joe and felt her heart stir. Then she remembered what Shawn did to her heart, causing it to pound with excitement. She had to admit that Shawn left her breathless with his persuasive love.

He reached over and took her hand. "I have something to tell you."

She looked down at his long, slender fingers, which were gently tracing a circle on her wrist. A delightful tremor tingled through her. Joe had the delicate, sensitive touch of a surgeon's fingers. She kept her eyes fastened on his tanned hand, hoping he wouldn't tell her he loved her. Yet when she looked up into his dark eyes, she didn't know why she was afraid. Hadn't she loved Joe Menotti since she'd been nine years old? She'd always love him but not like Shawn.

"What is it?" she asked. "If you're going to give me bad news, save it until later. Why spoil such a perfect day?"

"It's not such bad news." He sat up and draped one arm over his bent knee, reaching for a blade of grass, and ran it through his fingers. "It's just that I'm to be inducted into the Army Medical Corps." He glanced at her to see her reaction. Then his eyes shadowed. "Laura, please don't look so stricken."

She sat up straight. "When?" was all she could utter in a choked, dry voice.

"September first."

"That's less than six weeks. Oh, Joe. I'll miss you."

"I won't be far away," he said wryly. "I'll be trained right here at Fort Myer. I thought you'd be pleased."

She bent her head. "I'm not. What will I do without you?" And she meant it, too. How she would miss him! Joe's love was dependable and sure, and it felt wonderful to be in the warm protection of his strong arms. If only the war would end and he could stay here.

"Look," he said matter-of-factly, "I got tired of seeing the poster all over town. 'On Which Side of the Window Are You?' Remember?"

She nodded. The poster was everywhere and showed a young man in a suit gazing out his living room window at a regiment of marching soldiers.

"I want to do my part. Besides" — he laughed — "I know you like uniforms. Now, maybe I'll be able to give Shawn O'Brien a little competition."

Her eyes widened. She didn't need to tell Joe about Shawn. He knew.

Chapter Twenty

On July twenty-first, walking to headquarters, Laura thought all week about Joe's enlistment. He would be a superb army medic, but it was a shame he couldn't finish his schooling. How many of the men she loved was this war going to destroy? Frank was already dead, Michael was at the front, Shawn might be sent overseas, and so might Joe. What would happen to them? The morning newspaper reported that the Germans were pushing into the Allied lines at Amiens, Château-Thierry, and Saint-Mihiel. Never had she studied a map of France so closely. Marshal Foch admitted that the Allies' position was desperate, and he was depending on American troops to hold the line. Where was Michael in these vast troop movements? Was he still in a trench near Cantigny? Was he on the march? She prayed he would come home safe.

Well, she thought as she strode purposefully through the double doors, she had her own battle to fight today. This parade was drawing the battle lines between the suffragists and the President of the United States.

"Laura," Lucy Burns called out to her, "are you ready to be our lady in shining armor?"

"I'm ready," she called back cheerfully. "I've polished the armor until it will dazzle old Senator Shields."

"Three cheers!" Lucy exclaimed, holding up a clenched fist. "We'll show them that we won't give up!"

Laura hurried to the dressing room, for the parade would begin in an hour. Groups of women were holding banners, tuning band instruments, arranging flowers in each other's hair, and lining up their placards.

Catching the excitement, Laura strapped on her leg armor, but before she could pick up the breastplate, Cassie hurried to her side.

"Let me help you, Laura." As Cassie moved toward her she adjusted the yellow sash across the chest of her white voile dress, looking slender and elegant as usual.

"I can use some help. This is heavy!" Together they lifted the armor over her head, and Cassie fastened the side straps.

"I hope I won't embarrass anyone by falling off my horse," Laura said nervously.

She straightened the armor. The metal would be hot on such a sunny July day, and she had to hold the purple, gold, and white banner high, plus sit on her horse straight and tall. "I haven't been on a horse for two years, Cassie. I don't know how I'll handle the charger."

"You haven't ridden since your father died, right?" Cassie asked softly, handing her the mail gauntlets.

Laura nodded, finding it difficult to speak. Her weekend horseback rides with her father were among her fondest memories. "Dad used to take me to the stables every Sunday." Then she stopped, not being able to speak of the painful memory of their Sunday canters through the park. She remembered that glorious September morning, she on her chestnut mare, and her dad on his bay gelding. It was after that last ride when her father dismounted at the stables that he had complained of chest pains. Later that night he suffered his fatal heart attack.

"I'd better go out and try mounting the horse," she said in a tight voice. She didn't look at Cassie, only grasped her rolled banner and headed outside.

"Good luck," Cassie called after her.

"Thanks, Cassie, I'll need it."

Her great white stallion, although beautiful and pawing the ground, was fortunately gentle. She mounted and unfurled her banner, which, unlike Joan of Arc's standard with the dauphin's royal emblem, bore only three words: EQUALITY FOR WOMEN.

Starting at the Capitol with trumpets blaring, the dazzling parade began. A contingent of women dressed in white with yellow sashes each carried a purple banner. A long line of yellow taxicabs, the suffragist color, had signs on the doors proclaiming: VOTES FOR WOMEN. A band played "America, America" with Laura leading the procession. Her heart was beating faster than the drum's tempo. The great white horse pranced and bobbed his head in a stately gait, and she found that her old riding skills were not forgotten.

Past the District Building, the Willard Hotel, and the Treasury Building they marched. Crowds lined both sides of Pennsylvania Avenue, cheering wildly as she rode past. Flowers were everywhere — strewn in their path, in the marchers' hair, on her horse's bridle, and small bouquets on the taxi hoods. How different this parade was from the parade of five years ago that she had read about, she thought, as she kept her head high and her eyes steadily ahead on the Capitol dome. Today they had flowers thrown at them instead of tomatoes, and they no longer had to fight their way through mobs of unruly hecklers. Today the leafy branches of the trees seemed to welcome them forward.

She wore a silver helmet, but it couldn't hide her lovely hair, which fell loosely around her shoulders. Even though the sun glinted off her armor, she didn't feel uncomfortable — only proud to be bearing the standard of the suffragists. When the trumpets sounded and her banner snapped smartly in the wind, she felt as if her heart would burst.

Reaching Lafayette Square in front of the White House, the women congregated to listen to Alice Paul. Laura's armor was beginning to chafe, and her horse had to be led through the huge clusters of women. She was thirsty and wished she were dressed in her own clothes. She craned her neck. Where was Miss Paul? She was supposed to speak now. All of a sudden her eyes focused on another figure — Shawn! He was threading his way through the crowd toward her. She wasn't hard to spot, she thought ruefully, in her cumbersome armor, a plume waving above her helmet.

"Hi, sweetness!"

"Shawn! What a surprise!" She couldn't hide the fact that she was pleased at his unexpected appearance.

"I caught a glimpse of you in the parade, my warrior maiden. You looked very regal." He winked broadly. "Too bad there wasn't a battle for you to fight."

"Miss Paul is about to speak. Please," she coaxed, "stay and hear her."

"No thanks. I have better things to do with my time." He smiled warmly into her eyes and took her hand; however, he soon pulled it back. "Do me a favor," he said, "and take those metal gloves off."

She chuckled, removing the gauntlets.

He took her hand again. "That's better. Look," he said earnestly, "it's not too late to go to the dance. It's near here, only over at Blair House, and it's the social event of the summer. Please," he wheedled, his hand squeezing hers.

Gazing into his expectant face, she patted her horse's nose and shook her head. "You just don't give up, do you, Shawn?" She hesitated, then abruptly said, "All right. I'll make a bargain with you."

He cocked an eyebrow upward and grinned. "Anything for thee, fair maiden."

"If you'll stay and listen to Miss Paul I'll go to the dance with you." At the sight of his frown she hastened to add, "Her talks are always short." She wanted to add "and inspiring" but thought better of it.

Shawn's eyes sparkled. "You've got yourself a deal, but don't expect me to become a convert."

"Oh, I won't." She laughed, but she secretly gave him a sidelong glance, for that's exactly what she hoped would happen. Miss Paul could sway anyone to her way of thinking.

There was a drumroll, and Miss Paul jumped up on a flower-decorated cart that had been in the parade.

As Laura predicted Miss Paul's speech was

short. The applause was loud and long. Then the band struck up the "Star Spangled Banner."

Miss Paul lightly leaped to the ground.

Lucy Burns next hoisted herself up on the cart. "Ladies, we'll go back to Headquarters, where Mrs. John Melmon has sent in a catered dinner."

"Too bad you'll miss the dinner," Shawn said.

"Yes, I would have liked to have gone." She looked at Shawn's crestfallen face. "But I'll have to go with you to the dance and have a good time instead. Besides, I can't wait to get out of this armor!"

He chuckled. "You do look pretty ridiculous."

She frowned with annoyance.

"Hey! No frowns tonight." He leaned over and put his arm around her waist. "I just meant you'd look much more attractive in your lavender dress"—he gave her a lazy look—"and much easier to touch." He gave the back of her armor a sharp reverberating knock.

"Oh, Shawn," she said, laughing, "you're impossible."

"I know," he said, winking again. "It's the devil in me." He sobered. "Listen, I need to drive General Long to Blair House in twenty minutes. I'll pick you up around eight-thirty. How does that sound?"

"Fine. I'll be dressed and waiting in my lavender dress."

But as she returned the horse to the stable and hurried home, she suddenly felt she wasn't doing the right thing. The suffragist dinner, the culmination of the whole exciting day, was important, and she had planned to attend. How could Shawn always coax her into veering off in an opposite direction than the one she had planned? She shook her head, feeling that she had been manipulated again, yet the decision had been hers, so why did she have this niggling doubt in the back of her mind?

Later, as she and Shawn climbed the steps leading to Blair House, she thought how much fun she was going to have attending a dance in this wonderful old mansion. How its rosy bricks and white trim shone in the pale carriage lights! It was fitting that this was the State Department's guest house for foreign dignitaries. And this week, in honor of an Arab emir, the green shutters were thrown wide and she could see through the lace curtains that the dancers were circling and swaying to the music that drifted out over the oleander bushes and magnolia trees.

As she glided across the polished dance floor, inlaid with dark and light woods, and had Shawn's arms around her, she felt lighthearted, but not lighthearted enough to forget where she should have been.

At the end of the gavotte, Shawn swirled her downward until her back arched and her hair touched the floor.

"I wish I had a picture of you dancing," Shawn said softly. "You're as graceful and lithe as a wood nymph."

"Shawn, are you sure it isn't more of the Irish blarney that has sneaked past that sweet-talking mouth again?"

He chuckled, sweeping her back onto the floor when the small orchestra struck up a fox-trot. His dress uniform was set off by immaculate white gloves and puttees. The glittering couples and the hundreds of tapers that lit the hall made her feel like a princess.

It wasn't until the end of the evening that her guilt resurfaced. She should have gone to the dinner to hear Miss Paul's plan for the amendment's passage.

Shawn snapped his fingers before her eyes. "You're far away."

"No, I'm here, Shawn." She mustered a smile, but even Shawn couldn't restore her happy mood.

At eleven Shawn took her home in General Long's auto, so that he could return by twelve-thirty to pick up the general.

When they turned down Cherry Alley and stopped before her house, she touched the door handle.

Reaching over, Shawn grasped her hand. "Sit here for a few minutes."

Glancing at his handsome, smiling face, so close to hers, she felt her heart hammer and her knees weaken. If he planned to kiss her she was more than willing.

Gently he bent his head and fulfilled her wish. Responding to his kiss, she felt as if she could melt in his arms.

"I love you, Laura," he whispered in her ear, his fingers entwined in her hair. "You're my girl — no one else's," he murmured in a low voice. Then he sat back, his blue eyes gazing into hers and repeated firmly, "No one else's."

"Shawn," she said shakily, "I — I am your girl," but her tone couldn't mask her uncertainty. Even as she said the words a stab of guilt went through her. What about Joe? she thought bleakly.

He faced the windshield, putting both hands on the steering wheel. "I doubt that!" His tone was harsh.

"Shawn," she said, placing her hand on his sleeve, "what's wrong?" Her voice seemed to echo back at her in the roomy limousine.

He turned then and looked at her.

Did she see a flicker of pain in those darkened eyes? She smiled and restarted her question. "Is everything all right?"

"You've said you're my girl, Laura." He cupped her face in his hands. "Now prove it."

Her pulse stopped, and in the stillness surely her heartbeat could be heard. "How can I prove it?" she asked huskily.

"I don't want you to see anyone else — not even Joe Menotti." The name came out with bitterness.

"Joe's my friend," she protested. "He lives above us. I can't avoid seeing him."

"That's not exactly what I mean. I don't want you going on picnics alone with him along the Potomac."

Astonished, she said nothing.

Shawn went on, "I called the other day, and Sarah told me where you'd gone. I was crazy. I almost went after you to pull you away by your hair." He took a deep breath, faced her, and grinned. "But I knew you wouldn't appreciate a caveman approach." He kissed her lightly on the nose. "Will you stop seeing Joe?"

"I'll — I'll think about it," she said, too stunned to say no. Why did Shawn always demand her wholehearted attention? She was so torn. Was it only a few short months ago that her only yearning was for Joe to recognize that she was a young woman and to put his arms around her? Now, suddenly Shawn wanted her to see only him. Was she ready for that?

Chapter
Twenty-one

LAURA, taking a respite from weeding the garden, swung lazily to and fro in the hammock. As she glanced through the green leaves, the golden sun rays filtered across her face and on the green grass. She thought of the past few weeks and of how little she'd seen of Joe. They hadn't gone out since their picnic, and not because of Shawn's request, either, but because of her work and Joe's studies. She had told Shawn that she didn't intend to stop seeing Joe, for he was her friend, but in spite of herself there had been a pulling away. Shawn was keeping her busy, and if she had a suffragist meeting one night, then he would ask to see her the next.

These days, however, the news took precedence even over Shawn. She, along with everyone else, eagerly devoured the papers.

The German offensive was coming up against strong resistance, and over one million American troops along the western front had given a renewed fighting spirit to the Allies. The news today had been encouraging. Last week, on a misty morning with over four hundred tanks, the British had surprised the Germans and pushed them back east of Amiens. The Germans' previous gains had placed them in a vulnerable position, for they no longer had the heavy fortifications of the von Hindenburg line to protect them. At Amiens the Allies had captured over thirty thousand prisoners and taken some five hundred guns. General Ludendorff had called this the "Black Day of the German army," but according to the *Post*, there was plenty of hard fighting left.

Despite the German offensive's being broken, Laura was concerned about Michael. She worried constantly about his whereabouts. The casualty lists were mounting, as hundreds of names were printed daily. Surely the Mitchells wouldn't lose *two* men in the war. Every day she watched for Clara, along with Sarah and Mom, and every day the postmistress shook her head. No letter from Michael. Clara knew what the black-edged flag in their window meant and knew the fear of adding a second one.

Leisurely Laura swung back and forth in the hammock, and her thoughts strayed to Opal Zacks and the talk they had had. Maybe she should think about becoming a lawyer, too. At least she needed an idea or two about her future. She was no longer a child, she thought with a sigh. In just a few months so many things had happened that made her grow up. The transformation of her body, two beaux awakening her love, becoming a suffragist, being jailed, helping train recruits at the motorcade, and Frank's death. Yes, it was time she had some direction in her life. Miss Zacks had convinced her that more women needed to go into the professions, and although a lawyer could help, wouldn't a compassionate teacher like Miss Emerson prove to be just as important?

A warm breeze drifted across her face, and the scent of the yellow roses was pleasant. She watched a pair of bluebirds flit from tree to tree. They were sure of their place in the world. Why couldn't she be?

It was two weeks later when the whole world exploded for Laura. The suffragist arrests had started all over again — including Alice Paul's. As Laura washed her hair she rubbed the soap into her scalp so hard that it tingled. When was the President going to do something for them? When was he going to see how many wrongs had been done against women? Her eyes burned, not from the soap, however, but when she thought of the forty-seven women who had been arrested. To think she had been out with Shawn. She hadn't attended the rally and

243

thus missed the fiery speeches at the foot of the Lafayette monument.

"Laura! Laura!" Sarah said excitedly, rushing into the bathroom. "I've put the teakettle on!"

Rinsing her hair, Laura almost banged her head against the faucet. "Sarah," she said, her voice sounding muffled as she bent over the sink, "does this mean there's a letter from Michael?"

"Yes, it just arrived. Hurry. Mother's cutting the cake."

"Pour the vinegar solution over my hair, please, Sarah?"

Carefully Sarah poured a stream of the solution over Laura's rich hair, cutting the soap. The pungent, acrid odor hung in the air.

"I'll be right there," Laura said, wrapping a towel turban-fashion around her head.

Coming into the kitchen, she squeezed her mother around the waist. "At last, eh, Mom?"

The letter was propped against her cup, ready to be read. Laura slit open the envelope, took out the contents, and began to read in a clear voice:

> July 30, 1918
> Charlons-sur-Marne

Dear Mom, Sarah, and Laura,

The Rainbow Division has left the British sector and joined the French army under General Gouraud. The German offensive we expected didn't materialize, so the general ordered us to work on our main line of defense. It's a good thing, because the Germans charged us the other day. You can't believe how the Germans are still trying to cross the Marne and capture Paris. The prisoners we've taken are mainly either old men or fourteen-year-old kids. Today, though, Foch has ordered a massive counteroffensive and we move forward in three hours. There's something in the air that spells victory for us! I can feel it! The Americans have given a good account of themselves at Cantigny, Belleau Wood, and Château-Thierry. Even our Chief of Staff, Douglas MacArthur, has won the Distinguished Service Medal. I predict he's going to go far in the army! Today was a sad one; the poet of our division, Joyce Kilmer, was killed by a sniper's bullet — you remember, he wrote "Trees." I'm sorry about Frank, Sarah. Those airmen put their lives on the line every time they take up their planes. You don't know how much they've done, though, and how much the infantry depends upon them when we go into battle.

I have the photo of the three of you that Shawn snapped propped up on my knapsack. Every time I think this war will never end, I look at your smiling faces and know that nothing can keep me from coming home to you. When we go through a French town, we're offered crusty bread, cheese, and wine. The villagers almost kiss the ground we march on. There hasn't been time to really meet anyone, so I'm eager to get back to Washington — to see you, to sleep in a soft bed, and to eat a meal without the sound of exploding shells.

I enjoyed your letter, Laura. I see you're going out with Shawn. He's my good buddy, but in all honesty, he can be a heartbreaker, too. No, I don't think you're silly for being a suffragist. That takes a lot of grit, something you've always had!

Tell everyone hello. I won't be able to write too often as new marching orders come almost every day.

With all my love,
Mike

P.S. Send me socks. Dry socks are as scarce as German beer. I'll bet I could sell a pair for five dollars!

"Today's August eighteenth," Laura mused. "I wonder how far they've gone and where they're fighting since he wrote this."

Maude Mitchell looked up, eyes bright with tears. "He'll be in the thick of it, that's for certain. He's like you, Laura — Michael never was one to hang back."

"He's right about the pilots," Sarah interjected. "Bill Crowley wrote yesterday and said their planes fly low and go in ahead of the infantry. The American Expeditionary Force really depends on them."

Laura's eyes grew round. "So Bill Crowley said the AEF really depends on the pilots, eh? How many letters have you received?"

Smiling, Sarah said, "Only two."

"And you didn't say anything?" Laura said. "Sarah, you're a sly dog. You are such a private person, isn't she, Mom?"

"Yes, she is," Maude answered, raising her brows. "Did this Bill Crowley write anything about the war in his last letter?"

"Very little." Sarah threw out her hands and with an apologetic smile said, "He told me a little of his upbringing, that's all. He'll be discharged September first and will bring me Frank's things soon after."

"September first," Laura said in a low voice. "That's Joe's induction day." She must stop by the Menottis' store and see them. It had been weeks, but she'd had other things on her mind, although that hardly excused her from spending a few minutes with old friends.

Laura's mother pushed her glasses up onto the bridge of her nose. "It's almost time to go to the Canteen Center, girls." She glanced at Laura with a worried frown. "You're going with us, aren't you, Laura?"

"Of course. I promised, didn't I?" She flushed.

"Promises don't mean much if Alice Paul beckons," her mother said dryly.

"Mother, you know the past two weeks have been turmoil at Headquarters."

"Oh, yes, who hasn't heard of the arrests?" Maude drained her cup, remaining calm.

"I thought the arrests were to be over after you had been released from jail, Laura," Sarah said, puzzled.

"So did we," said Laura bitterly.

"You'll have to admit," Mrs. Mitchell said, "that the parades and speeches these last few weeks at the Lafayette monument have been inflammatory." She rose, standing with her hands on the back of the chair. "How many were arrested last week?"

"Forty-seven" — Laura's tone was grim — "including Alice Paul, and she wasn't even in the parade. Lucy Burns, Rowena Green, and Mrs. Lawrence were all arrested, too." She made a fist. "I wish I had been there." Her face felt warm when she thought of how she and Shawn were having a good time canoeing along the river that day.

"I was in court the next day, though, and you should have heard the trumped-up charges."

"Trumped-up charges?" Sarah's pink-and-white face wrinkled into a questioning look. Her voice was quiet, as if trying to soothe Laura.

"The women were charged with climbing the Lafayette statue! Can you imagine?"

Laura asked indignantly. "You can't go there without seeing someone climbing all over the monument or eating their lunch at its base." She banged her fist into her hand. "It's infuriating!"

"I'm just glad you weren't there to be arrested again," Sarah said.

Laura shuddered. "So am I!" She didn't think she could take a cell again, not even for Alice Paul. There was a moment's silence, then Laura's mouth twitched with a smile. "It was funny when the women were arrested last Thursday, though. There were nine of them making speeches at the statues, and when the police pulled one down, another would clamber onto it and begin to speak. The officers were going crazy trying to catch them. It was like trying to catch fireflies!"

"They don't give up do they?" her mother murmured in a low voice.

"No, we can't give up!" Laura emphasized the *we*. "Not after all these years! There will be another protest today," Laura dared to say, "and I intend to be there." She looked defiantly, first at her mother and then at Sarah.

Laura's mother sighed. "Do what you have to, Laura. But don't forget the boys overseas. I think you'd do more good knitting a pair of socks for Michael!" Her wry look and crooked smile softened her words.

"I am helping the war effort, Mother," Laura countered. "Doesn't my motorcade

249

unit, Red Cross, or canteen work count for anything?"

Mrs. Mitchell reached out and touched her hand. "Yes, my darling Laura. Come," she urged gently. "The troop train will be in at eleven o'clock. We'd better go."

Laura looked at them. No tongue lashings? Were both of them becoming reconciled to the suffragists? Maybe Michael's approval helped. Perhaps now they had a glimmer of belief in the suffragists' ideals!

Sarah smiled at her and grabbed her elbow as they left. "Time to feed those marines some coffee and doughnuts."

For the first time in months the two sisters went out arm in arm.

Chapter
Twenty-two

AFTER working at the canteen Laura hurried to meet Cassie at Headquarters. Cassie, looking cool and sophisticated in her pale apricot dress, was sitting in the tearoom having an iced tea.

"Cassie" — Laura waved, dashing to her table — "how is everything here?"

Cassie's small mouth turned down at the corners. "Not good. They brought in the women from the workhouse this morning. They're being nursed upstairs."

"That workhouse hasn't been used for years," Laura said, appalled that the suffragists would be kept there. "Not since the days of Teddy Roosevelt."

"Melinda and Josephine came back with rheumatism because those underground cells are so cold and damp that you need blankets even in this ninety-five-degree heat."

"I'd like to round up Chief Bentley and all the antisuffragists in the city and throw them in the very same workhouse for a year," Laura said vehemently, her chin jutting forward.

"They'd never last," Cassie said, her eyes liquid fire. "Our women were only there for two weeks, and look how they came out. I've been upstairs rubbing arms and legs until I think I've got rheumatism in my own hands." She held out her slender fingers, and to Laura they looked perfectly manicured without a mark on them. Cassie continued, "Many of the women got lead poisoning because the water pipes hadn't been used for years."

"I could cry for them," Laura said. She glanced around. The tearoom didn't have its usual exuberant noise. Women were subdued, talking quietly in small groups. "Is our duty schedule the same?"

"No, we're to help the nurses upstairs."

Laura nodded grimly.

After the two girls parted Laura went upstairs to see how she could help.

Lucy Burns was in the front bedroom, and when she saw Laura, she called, "Laura, come in. Am I glad to see you! We've been up to our elbows in work." She meant that literally, too, for her sleeves were rolled to her upper arm.

"Whatever you want me to do I will." She

glanced at the four beds occupied by four women.

"Bless you, child. Will you fill the water pitchers and fetch some clean towels from the supply room?" Her square face was red with perspiration, and she patted Laura on the back. "If you have time, of course."

"I always have time," Laura said, but silently she wondered if Lucy was taking a barb at her because she hadn't been anywhere near the protest meeting when Lucy and the others had been imprisoned.

"Oh, one other thing," Lucy said. "Would you read to Mrs. Lawrence?"

Taken aback, she asked, "Is Mrs. Lawrence all right?"

"A headache and chills." Lucy rubbed her forehead. "I think it took a lot out of her this time. She demonstrated in the rain, then was thrown into a damp cell. No wonder she came in chilled to the bone."

Laura looked over at Mrs. Lawrence, who had been with her in prison, and remembered how brave she had been. Now Mrs. Lawrence huddled beneath the blanket.

"There are six bedrooms on this floor," Lucy explained. "Each room contains four very sick women. Anything you can do to cheer them will be a big help."

"You — you don't suppose any of them have the flu, do you?" She felt like a coward asking, but there was a little flutter in her heart when she thought of the disease sweeping Europe.

"No," Lucy said matter-of-factly. "I haven't heard of any cases in Washington yet. There have been a few reported in New York and Boston. Don't worry, Laura. These women don't have anything contagious. What most of them have are aches in their backs, arms, and legs." She had an iron glint in her eye. "I'm afraid they'll have those pains for the rest of their lives." She wrung out a cloth and placed it on Mrs. Lawrence's forehead.

For a moment Laura couldn't move, only stand and stare. Why this constant persecution? Why? With leaden feet she moved to refill the pitchers with fresh water. When she finished, she noticed that Mrs. Lawrence's eyes were open and following her.

"Hello, Laura," the woman said in a weak voice. "This time the workhouse got the best of me."

Laura smiled down at her.

"Oh, Mrs. Lawrence," Laura said, impulsively grasping her hand and holding it. "You'll feel better in a few days. You need rest and quiet and then you'll be back on the line."

"As long as it isn't back in prison," she whispered.

"Lucy said you might like to be read to, is that right?"

Her eyes brightened, and she struggled to

sit up, a determined expression on her square face.

Laura chuckled. "I see you like that idea." She picked-up the leather-bound book, checked the spine, reading the title aloud, "*A Tale of Two Cities* by Charles Dickens." She settled herself comfortably in a chair and ordered Mrs. Lawrence to lie back and listen.

Laura began this novel about the French Revolution. " 'It was the best of times, it was the worst of times. . . .' "

She paused, thinking that this 1859 sentiment was just as relevant in 1918. There were so many good things in her life, such as love and the suffragists, yet so many bad things, such as the war.

"Is that as far as you're going to read?" Mrs. Lawrence asked wryly, smoothing the covers.

"Sorry," she muttered with a small smile, and continued.

After Mrs. Lawrence had drifted off to sleep Laura quietly made her way downstairs.

By September the women had recovered from their imprisonment and Laura was back in school. Her senior year promised to be a good one, for she liked all her courses and her teachers. Miss Emerson was her adviser and the only time she saw Mr. Blair was in the halls or the main office, which suited her just fine.

On Friday, walking home from school, the sky was as azure blue as Shawn's eyes. The only clouds in the distance were fleecy white, but there were gray clouds on her horizon, and they made her fearful. There were cases of the flu being reported in D.C. now.

However, her heart lifted along with the breeze that blew through her hair when she thought of tomorrow, for Joe would be back from Fort Myer on a weekend pass. She smiled. Dear Joe. She longed to talk to him about her teachers, the suffragist meetings, and just . . . everything. How she had missed him! Even if she hadn't seen him as frequently in the past few months, still knowing that he was there gave her a good, safe feeling. Her muddled feelings were so frustrating. Perhaps when Joe came home she'd be better able to sort out her emotions.

Tomorrow she planned to visit the Menottis' store and hoped he would ask her out. Just for old times' sake. She was disappointed that he hadn't called to ask her to the movies or for a picnic by the river, but perhaps it wasn't too late. She had deliberately not made a date with Shawn so she could be with Joe. She breathed in the honeysuckle and thought how much Joe would like going to the zoo and a picnic.

Right now, however, she was on her way

to a protest meeting at the Lafayette monument.

When Laura reached Lafayette Square, she stopped short, for there at the base of the statue was Alice Paul and Lucy Burns. She also recognized Julia Emory holding a flaming torch. What was happening? she wondered. There was an expectant edginess to the forty or so women assembled.

Alice had climbed up and stood directly beneath the statue of the Marquis de Lafayette. "Ladies! We've heard many speeches about how we need the same freedom that Lafayette helped to bring to this country, but as yet this freedom has been denied to women!" She looked around calmly, but beneath her serenity was an indomitable spirit that fairly radiated from her small face. "And so it is time to do something that President Wilson will listen to!" Her tone was firm and her eyes like steel.

The women, never taking their eyes from her face, stood silently waiting for their leader to proceed.

"We have just learned from Senator Overman that the Senate has no intention of presenting our bill this session. . . ."

There were grumblings and the shuffling of restless feet.

"Here, ladies, are the words that President Wilson spoke to our delegation this morning!" She turned slightly to a tall woman next to Julia Emory, who immediately held up a sheaf of papers.

Without a moment's hesitation she took the torch from Julia Emory and touched it to Wilson's speech, sending the papers up in smoke.

Laura gasped. The President's words were being burned. If nothing else, this would make the people and the President open their eyes in astonishment.

Alice Paul ground beneath her heel a piece of the charred paper. "We want action, not words! From now on," Alice continued smoothly, "the President's speeches will be burned in front of the White House. We will guard an urn with a perpetual flame!"

Laura then broke into a cheer along with everyone present. How dramatic! She just hoped that more arrests wouldn't be forthcoming as a result of this action.

But there were no arrests. Indeed, the very next day Senator Jones introduced the suffrage amendment in the Senate, and the discussion began. It remained to be seen when the vote would be taken. Laura, however, was more concerned with seeing the Menottis and Joe, for today Joe was home. Her excitement was evident as she tried to capture her thick masses of hair with a large pink bow at the nape of her neck. Twice she had tried it and twice it was crooked, but the third time it stood out crisply. She gave herself a final look in the mirror and approved of what she saw. Her pastel pink blouse and her hobbled skirt gave her a grown-up air. Her nose, straight and well formed; her wide, big green eyes; and the loose hair falling gently around her face gave her a more sophisticated look than Joe had seen before. She looked closer into the mirror, and her smile was slightly impish. As she stepped back she staggered. Drat these narrow hobble skirts. They might be extremely fashionable, but she didn't much like her stride being hampered. Taking small, mincing steps was not her style.

Nonetheless, she felt like quite the coquette as she hobbled into the store. Aldo, on a stepladder, stacked tins of tuna on the shelf as Bertina handed them to him.

When the bell jangled above the door, they both saw Laura at the same time, and Bertina rushed over, holding out her arms.

Aldo, for all his bulk, stepped down quickly.

"Tressora!" Aldo boomed.

Bertina hugged her, then kissed both cheeks. She stepped back, surveying Laura, and nodding her approval. "You look beautiful, *ma bambina*. Beautiful!" She rolled her eyes. "You wear latest style, eh?" She examined the long skirt with a slit up the front, then blew her a kiss.

Beaming, Aldo swaggered forward, smoothing his thick mustache. "Still too skinny! You eat something?"

"No, thanks." She chuckled. "I just finished breakfast." Casually she glanced around. "Is Joe here?"

"We tell him to sleep late," Aldo said. "The bugler get him up too early. No bugler here."

"He come to shop soon. You sit." Bertina indicated a barrel. "Sit and wait, yes?"

"Can't I help you?" Laura asked.

"In that skirt?" Aldo's laugh reverberated throughout the store. "Too tight for working."

"Ah. *Sardino!* What you know, eh? We go back to work." Bertina turned and smiled. "Sit, Laura."

Just then the bell tinkled again, and Laura wheeled around, almost upsetting herself.

"Careful," Joe cautioned, running to catch her. He held her in his arms, and they both burst out laughing.

"If it isn't Laura — my little girl all dressed up in the latest fashion," he teased.

"Joe Menotti! If it isn't the grocery boy in a U.S. Army uniform!" Her face was as pink as her blouse. "It's — it's good to see you," she said, all at once very flustered.

He grinned, still holding her hand. His straight black hair had been cut so that it stood up like barbed wire. He was tanner; his black eyes sparkled.

She hoped the sparkle was brought about by the sight of her. She knew the glow she felt was brought about by his presence. Was she in love with Joe?

"Hey, Papa, want some help?" Joe called, looking beyond her to his parents.

"No, no. You talk to our long-lost girl."

He turned back and sat across from her. "How's school?"

"Fine. My history teacher is super." She laughed and nervously touched her hair ribbon. "Not at all like Mr. Blair."

"And the suffragists?" His grin widened.

She drummed her feet against the barrel. "That's a long story. I'll tell you about it when you've got an hour." She smiled mischievously. There, she thought, that should give him the opening to ask her out. How handsome he looked in his smart uniform, which fit his tall, slender figure to perfection.

When he didn't ask her out, however, she decided other tactics were needed.

"Well, I'd better get back. I just came by to say hello. I hope I'll get to see more of you Joe," she said, her smiling eyes twinkling at him.

"I wish I could see you tonight," Joe said.

"And what's keeping you?" she questioned a bit too cheerily.

"We're having my Uncle Vito and Salvatore and their families for dinner. Maybe I'll see you Sunday."

"I hope so," she said, her heart sinking. She'd better leave before her chin started to tremble. Already tears were near the surface. She was surprised at how disappointed she was, but she had so planned to be with Joe tonight!

That night, as she lay in bed, she could hear the Italian music and the laughter above. She knew all of Joe's relatives. How many meals had she eaten there? Why didn't he invite her? She turned over and thumped her pillow.

If she didn't see Joe tomorrow she'd die! She needed his love! She was becoming more and more sure of that. The problem was that he didn't seem to care about seeing her!

Chapter
Twenty-three

THE next afternoon, a lazy Sunday, Laura wasn't idle. Sitting in the backyard, she kept her eyes studiously on her knitting, hoping that Joe would glance out the window and see that she was alone. Where was he? He had seemed distant yesterday when she had expected hugs and kisses. Her fingers flew angrily. If he didn't come down soon she'd take a plate of cookies up to the Menottis. That was rather a feeble pretext to see him, but what other excuse was there?

Putting down the bulky sweater she was knitting, she gazed out on the orange-and-yellow marigolds interspersed with asters lining the fence. She missed the bachelor buttons that used to be there, but since they were the national flower of Germany, they had been weeded out. It was such a pleasant fall day. Oh, where was Joe?

Then, as if in answer to her prayers, she heard his rich, deep voice behind her.

"I see you're doing your war bit," Joe said, a trifle amused.

She picked up the brown yarn and began to knit furiously.

Joe came around and faced her, dressed in his khaki uniform. "I've never seen you quite so domestic," he said, a smile tugging at the corners of his large mouth.

She bent her head over her work, paying particular attention to a cable stitch she had dropped. "Hello, Joe," she said as nonchalantly as she could. "I'm not being particularly 'domestic,' as you call it. This sweater is meant for the Red Cross shipment." She stopped knitting and looked up. "How is your Uncle Vito and your Aunt Gemma?"

"Brimming with life. Vito's leather shop is doing very well, and Aunt Gemma works there, too. She has built up quite a fashionable clientele."

How marvelous he looked, she thought, admiring his lean good looks. He had always been tall and slender, but somehow today he seemed taller. His Roman nose, straight and regal, dominated his face along with his dark, gentle eyes. She smiled when she remembered how he used to scoop back his thick hair off his forehead — he'd no longer be able to do that — not with such a bristly haircut! She refocused her attention on his conversation.

She seemed to be seeing Joe with new eyes since she'd been going with Shawn. Joe had some qualities that she wished Shawn had more of, such things as steadfastness, caring about her activities, warmth, and understanding.

Oh, she wished he'd stop talking about his relatives. She didn't really care about Uncle Vito's family. She wished he would talk about the two of them.

Joe went on, heedless of her exasperated look. "Uncle Salvatore's bakery on Wisconsin Avenue is thriving, and Aunt Ida is doing —"

"Joe!" she cut in impatiently. "When do you need to report back to your base?"

He lifted his brows in mild surprise at the interruption, then grinned. "Are you anxious to get rid of me?"

"Oh, no. It's just that I thought we could spend some time together and maybe . . ." She left her statement unfinished.

"I leave at four o'clock," he stated, watching her thoughtfully.

"Oh, no." She glanced at her watch. "It's two o'clock already." She almost groaned aloud. "I thought with Fort Myer so near you might not have to leave until morning. After all, the base is just across the river in Arlington."

He chuckled. "Oh, then you *do* want me to stay?"

"Yes," she breathed. "Oh, yes. I've missed

you, Joe." She didn't care if it did sound as if she yearned for him to remain. It was true, and she'd never been one to hide her emotions. "There are so many things I want to tell you. About my schoolwork and the drama reading I'm doing in English, the suffragists' arrests, and the burning of Wilson's speeches." Her words tumbled out.

"Hey, little one, slow down." He laughed and threw back his head, showing even, white teeth. He sank down in a lawn chair with his long legs stretched comfortably out before him. "When you were small, you used to get so excited that I couldn't understand your rapid babbling!"

She smiled. "I guess I was talking too fast, but it's so good to have you here and to tell you what's been happening. You're the only one that I can talk to about the suffragists," she ended lamely.

"I read about the arrests in the *Post,*" he said. "What spunk! No wonder you're a suffragist. I'm only surprised you didn't join them when you were twelve!" He shook his head and his face sobered. "But burning the President's speeches! That's serious. Some folks look on that as treason, and they'll be alienated from your cause."

"That's too bad," she retorted sharply. "We've waited too long as it is for Wilson's promises to be fulfilled, but he never delivers."

Joe stood up and walked to her chair. "Laura, let's walk over to the gazebo in the park." He offered her his hand.

"That would be fun," she said, happy at last for his attention.

Sitting in the gazebo with the lindens and weeping willows all around them, she longed for Joe to take her hand, but he was too engrossed in asking her questions.

". . . and what is this drama reading you're doing?"

"I'm preparing excerpts from the Pankhurst journals."

"The Pankhursts were early suffragists, weren't they?"

She nodded. "They're called suffragettes in England. Alice Paul demonstrated with Mrs. Pankhurst and learned many techniques from her."

"Just be careful you don't upset your teacher right at the beginning of the year. Remember Mr. Blair!"

She shuddered. "How could I forget him? No, this assignment on journals and diaries is for English class. Miss Foster is very understanding." She stopped and observed him. "Now it's your turn to talk. How is boot training?"

"It's not too bad," he said, slinging his arm atop the balustrade behind her. "We've learned how to take a rifle apart, put it back together, how to clean it, how to stand formation, how to march step, how to make a bed, and how to pack a knapsack. Nothing very exciting, like your suffragist meetings!"

Ignoring his friendly barb, she asked, "What's Fort Myer like?"

"Fort Myer? Bustling. It used to be only for ceremonial troops, escorts, and firing squads for military funerals. Now there are ten thousand of us there."

"Do you like your officers? I hope you don't have anyone like Mr. Blair."

"Worse. My commanding officer is Colonel King, who's a real tyrant. In the two weeks I've been there, the only orders he's given are with a shout or a growl." He gave a low chuckle. "It will almost be a relief to be sent overseas, just to get away from him."

Her heart stopped. "Overseas?" she said weakly. Why hadn't she thought of that? "When will you be leaving?"

"Our sailing date is November fifteenth."

"I'll write to you," she said shakily, not able to think of a response. If only he could be stationed in Washington like Shawn!

"By the way," he casually asked, "how's Shawn?"

Startled, she hesitated. Should she tell him how much she was seeing him? "He's fine," she said brightly. "I haven't seen him for a while." Not since last week, she thought, but Joe didn't need to know that. She wouldn't tell him that Shawn was coming later this afternoon, either. She didn't know why she was trying to hide these facts from Joe; she only knew she wanted his undivided attention with no complications about Shawn. Briefly she wondered if Joe would care how often she had been seeing Shawn. She sighed. Probably not. The turmoil she felt was the same old story. Shawn was such a delight, but so was Joe. It must have been nice to have things so clear-cut as when Sarah had Frank.

He rose abruptly. "Time to go. The sun is moving westward, and I need to pack."

"Will you be coming home soon?" she asked hopefully.

"Once in October and once before I sail."

She nodded dumbly, not saying anything. She couldn't. Her heart was too full.

He reached for her hand, and it felt so good to have him enclose her hand in his.

As they turned down Cherry Alley her pulse beat faster, for there on the front doorstep stood Shawn. He was early.

"Well, well," Shawn said, stepping down to meet them. "I got off duty early. I didn't expect to get here this soon." He cast a glance in Laura's direction. "Obviously," he said drily, "neither did you."

"Shawn," she said, a trifle nervously. "Joe was home from camp this weekend and I wanted to talk to him . . . to ask his advice about a few things." *Another lie,* she thought.

Why did she do it? How could she juggle the two of them and try to keep them in separate compartments? She glanced uneasily at Joe, who was looking at her with a faintly amused expression. He knew now she had been seeing Shawn and frequently. He knew, too, that she hadn't asked his advice, about anything.

Shawn stood with his arms folded, looking Joe up and down. "I see you finally joined the army," he said. He paused. "Or were you drafted?" His wide-brimmed hat was cocked jauntily to one side.

Joe said nothing but his black eyes flashed.

Shawn smiled, but his blue eyes were chips of ice. "Listen, Joe. Laura doesn't need a guide anymore. I know all about how you helped watch over her growing up years and it's a very touching story, but Laura's a big girl now." He jabbed a finger against Joe's shoulder. "I'll thank you to keep away from her!"

"Do you have a claim on Laura?" Joe asked softly.

"Look," Shawn said, "Laura and I have plans for this afternoon, so why don't you take off?"

"I'll repeat my question," Joe said levelly. "Do you have a claim on Laura?"

Shawn looked boldly at Laura and puffed out his chest. "She's my girl," he said proudly. "Take my word for it, Joe. She doesn't need or want you anymore."

"Is that true, Laura?" Joe's eyes were flinty.

Stricken, she started to reply, but the words choked in her throat.

"Why don't you beat it," Shawn said, jerking his thumb beyond his shoulder. "You're not wanted here!"

Joe looked bitterly first at Shawn and then at Laura. "I can see that."

"And when you come back again," Shawn said, bunching his fists, "don't see Laura!"

"We'll settle this later," Joe muttered, attempting to brush past, but Shawn, with both hands on Joe's chest, gave him a short shove backward.

When Shawn repeated the shove, Joe flushed angrily, holding up his fists.

Immediately Shawn jabbed at Joe's face and Joe's head snapped back. With another quick stab Shawn bloodied Joe's nose.

Joe pushed Shawn, causing him to fall backward and his hat to fly off. Scrambling to his feet, Shawn furiously attacked Joe, hitting his chest and face.

"Stop it!" Laura yelled. "Both of you. You're behaving like ten-year-olds!" She thrust herself between them, and with hands defiantly on her hips, she dared either one to push her aside.

Pulling a handkerchief from his back pocket, Joe wiped his nose. The white square soon had bright red splotches on it.

Laura ran to Joe. "Oh, Joe, are you hurt?"

"Only a bloody nose," he answered rue-fully. "Your friend Shawn is a bit too feisty." He cast a baleful look at Shawn.

"I'm so sorry," she whispered, brushing off his jacket.

"Forget it," he said abruptly, scooping up his hat. "I've got to go, Laura."

"I know," she responded in a low voice. "I'll miss you."

Joe's eyes had a mocking twinkle. "It seems you won't be too lonesome."

She put a deterring hand on his sleeve. "Good-bye, Joe. Hurry home." She looked into his eyes, but the corresponding warmth she wanted to see wasn't there. "I hope to see you next month."

He quickly patted her hand, still holding a hanky to his nose. "Good-bye, Laura."

"Maybe you'd like a black eye to go with that bloody nose," Shawn said, pulling Laura near him.

"Next time we'll see who gets the bloody nose," Joe said between clenched teeth. Wheeling around, he strode around the corner of the house.

Furious, Laura spun around. "What's wrong with you, Shawn O'Brien? Can't you get it through that thick skull of yours that Joe's my friend?"

Shawn picked up his hat, slapping the dust off his trouser leg. His reddened face was gradually returning to normal.

"Now, Laura, me girl, me sweet colleen," he said in an Irish brogue. "Sure an' you can't blame a fellow for lovin' the likes of you." His eyes were as appealing as a spaniel's, and a smile played about his mouth. "You can't blame me, can you now?" he wheedled, approaching her.

She held up her hands. "Stay away from me, Shawn."

Heedless of her warning, his fingers walked up her arm. "I'm sorry, sweetness. I really am. But how do you think I felt when I came to take out my best girl and saw her walking toward me, holding hands with some other fellow?"

Her heart sank. Shawn was right, of course. He must have been upset. She attempted a small smile. "I'm sorry, too, Shawn, but after what happened I don't much feel like going out and having a good time."

Shawn's blue eyes shadowed, but he said lightly, "Let's just walk over to the zoo like we planned and watch the monkeys. They'll make us laugh and we'll forget this whole thing."

She shook her head reproachfully. "I don't feel much like laughing, Shawn."

He shifted his feet, eyeing her. "If that's what you want. I guess I'll just have to go with Melinda, General Long's daughter, instead," he said with a grin, but she wondered if the statement wasn't too far from the

273

truth. He pulled on his ear and smiled at her. "Can we start over again next Saturday night?"

She nodded silently and started up the steps. Shawn reached for her hand, but she sprinted out of reach, up the stairs.

"I'll call you," he said, his usual bravado returning.

She didn't answer, just ran into the house and closed the door.

As she sat at her dressing table she untied her neck scarf and stared dully at her image in the mirror. Wrinkling her nose, she whispered, "What a mess you've made of things! You sat home last night, hoping Joe would call, and tonight you'll sit home alone because you sent Shawn away." Maybe Sarah was right. It was time for a decision. Who was it to be? Shawn or Joe?

The next few days she threw herself into her studies and her suffragist meetings. Time went quickly, and it wasn't long before she and Shawn were back on their usual footing. He had called her every night, and he was so sweet that it wasn't hard to forgive him.

Saturday they went on a canal-boat ride pulled by mules all the way to Lock Five. She had packed a lunch, and the afternoon was most pleasant. Still, at times, the encounter between Joe and Shawn haunted her, and she wished Shawn weren't so possessive and that Joe was more so.

Joe would be home in October — then perhaps she would make a decision. She certainly couldn't have Joe and Shawn embroiled in another fight over her. Maybe she shouldn't see Joe anymore. She probably shouldn't see Shawn, either, at least not for a while, but he was irresistible, always attentive, clever, funny, and yes, even lovable.

Sarah was right — she shouldn't play the field and pit her two beaux against one another. She must straighten out this situation — and soon. This, she promised she would do, for it was only fair to Shawn and Joe.

Chapter Twenty-four

THE influenza epidemic had hit Boston, with over five-hundred deaths reported. By law Bostonians could only venture outside if they were wearing a face mask. But New York was one of the hardest hit cities in the country, with almost twenty-five thousand registered deaths.

By the first part of October there were over seven hundred flu cases reported in Washington. No one, however, least of all President Wilson, seemed too alarmed. In fact, the president had a little limerick he recited about the flu:

I had a little bird
Its name was Enza,
I opened the window
And in-flu-enza.

Laura wasn't too concerned about the flu, either, as she sat in English class, ready to give her recitation on Emmeline Pankhurst. She was well prepared and spoke clearly and firmly.

When Laura finished and gathered up her notes, she was greeted with a round of applause. Even Olaf Jorgensen beat his large hands together in approval.

"That was terrific, Laura," he whispered after she was seated. His ruddy, large face was beaming.

Laura was pleased also. After class she was delighted to learn that Miss Foster had given her an A+.

Walking home, she felt the brisk air enlivening her step. The pin oak, red oak, and silver maples were beginning to change to new autumn colors, and she spied a yellow finch darting from one tree to another.

Fall was her favorite time of year. She loved the tangy air, the red and yellow fall leaves, and the brisk breeze from the north. She smiled when she thought of Washington's nickname — "the green-and-white city" — because of all the trees with white buildings nestled in between. In the autumn, however, the city didn't live up to the name, for the trees took on too many vibrant hues.

She was happy about life, too. Shawn was beginning to listen to her and recently had said nothing derogatory about the suffragists. Perhaps she was making a difference in his attitude after all. She did long for the old casual footing she had with Joe, but that seemed to have disintegrated even before his confrontation with Shawn. Maybe when he came home on October twenty-second, things would be different. But even as the thought flickered through her mind, she was afraid it was only wishful thinking. She'd been doing too much wishful thinking lately. Joe seemed bent on stepping aside for Shawn, and perhaps he was right. Her mother had tried to steer her to Joe, but now she was the one that needed to make a choice. The old frustrated feelings welled up inside, closing her throat. What should she do?

She patted her knapsack bulging with note cards. Because of her neat handwriting, Lucy Burns asked her to recopy fifty cards for the index. She had agreed but would much rather have been the one to be calling the senators or what the newspaper called "tele-suffing." Although all the suffragists had received a "Don't List" on how to talk to a senator, it didn't do her any good. She was too young. She remembered some of the "Don'ts" on the list that each new interviewer was given, though, such as:

Don't nag.
Don't boast.
Don't threaten.
Don't lose your temper.
Don't stay too long.

She sighed. It was always her age that stood in the way. A person-to-person interview with a senator she could understand, but why couldn't she call? She could crank the phone, give the operator the number, and talk pleasantly to a senator just as well as the older women.

Dashing up the steps, she took the mail from the box and unlocked the door. As she sifted through the mail — the *Ladies Home Journal,* an advertisement for a shampoo — she noticed that her mother and Sarah were gone. Her heart lurched when she saw a letter from Michael; at least his name was on the return address. But it wasn't his handwriting. She shed her long, loose vest and tore open the envelope. Something must be wrong!

Hastily she scanned the contents:

> Field Hospital
> Near Paris
> September 15, 1918

Dear Mom, Laura, and Sarah,

Here I am in a field hospital about fifteen miles northwest of Paris. There's nothing to be alarmed about. I landed here because my shoulder caught a piece of German shrapnel — it's a souvenir from our offensive attack on Saint-Mihiel. As you can see, this isn't my handwriting. I dictated this letter to one of the prettiest French nurses you've ever seen. Her name is Françoise Giraud and she reminds me of you, Laura, except she has raven-black hair.

Before we began the attack, the German line was bombarded for four hours and the U.S. Gas Regiment gave our troops a smoke screen. The 42nd Division had only a few casualties. Wouldn't you know I had to be one of them!

We easily took Saint-Mihiel. Next we're to open an offensive in the Meuse-Argonne, a sector sixty miles west of here, but I'm stuck here with a beautiful nurse instead! War is hell!

We did ourselves proud at Saint-Mihiel. Even Premier Clemenceau and the president of France, Poincaré, came to the front to offer their congratulations.

Well, Françoise needs to make her rounds, so I'd better quit for now.

Don't worry. I'm getting lots of tender loving care. I don't know when I'll be sent home, but it shouldn't be too long before my medical discharge comes through.

As the song says, "Keep the Home Fires Burning."

All my love,
Mike

Dropping the letter in her lap, Laura stared at the grandfather clock with its gilt

Roman numerals, but even when the chimes rang, the time didn't register. She was thinking of Michael, who had helped shape her ideas and taught her, as her father had done, to stand firm in her beliefs as long as they didn't hurt people. How much fun she had growing up with Michael! The memory of their fishing expeditions on the Potomac, where they fished for brook trout, came flooding back. Smiling wistfully, she remembered how Mike had allowed her to wear his old knickers and vest and how she had tucked her mass of hair beneath one of his large caps. With a pole balanced on her shoulder she marched proudly by his side.

Her eyes brimmed with tears when she thought of how things had changed. Mike was lying wounded in France, and she was involved in other interests. Becoming an adult was often filled with loss and pain. She sighed. There was little chance they would ever recapture those carefree fishing days.

She propped the letter on the hall table where her mother and Sarah would be certain to see it. With a sad weariness she went up to her room to work on the note cards.

In the next few weeks Laura was involved in the Banner Campaign, which consisted of picketing the Senate and especially the thirty-four senators who had voted against the amendment.

On Saturday she, along with Cassie and other suffragists, marched to the Capitol.

She glanced at Cassie, feeling a deep commitment to her country and the women with whom she marched. The impressive white dome with its many columns representing states of the union and the Goodness of Freedom crowning the cupola all made her tingle with pride.

They mounted the steps with the banner held between, each girl holding a wooden support. The columns surrounding them and the marble entrance were splendors Laura had forgotten. Perhaps she should return to her dream of becoming an architect.

Quietly she and Cassie stood atop the steps as men and women passed, some stopping to read their banner and others pointedly ignoring them. Dressed in her wine-colored suit, Cassie was the epitome of grace, while Laura, in the bulky navy sweater and skirt, made quite a contrast. Still, their yellow sashes indicated they were of one mind!

All at once the heavy brass doors were flung wide, and a number of office boys came whooping and hollering as they descended on Cassie and Laura like yapping prairie dogs. Their banner was torn from their hands and ripped to pieces.

"Cassie!" she shouted. "Run!"

But Cassie had plastered herself against a white column and looked like a martyr to the cause. In the meantime Laura picked up a wooden support, brandishing it back and forth like a baseball bat. Just let them attack, she thought. She'd give them such a lump on the head that they'd not soon forget the Women's Party!

As quickly as the boys had dashed among the suffragists, wrested signs, and shredded them, they disappeared. The boys no sooner were gone, however, when the police came and herded the women inside.

Through the rotunda, the huge, circular hall, the eight women were taken, then ordered into the guard room.

They were detained about fifteen minutes and then released.

When they emerged into the sunlight, more banners and more suffragists had already taken their place.

"Oh, Cassie," Laura said fervently. "I wish we could stand on top of the dome with our banners for all Washington to see!"

Cassie laughed. "The Senate would have to pay attention then!"

Suddenly Laura grasped Cassie's arm. "I have an idea. Let's smuggle a banner into the Senate. We'll unfurl it from the visitors' balcony!"

Cassie shot her an astonished look. "Laura! We wouldn't dare!" But there was an impish gleam in her dancing eyes.

"Well," Laura said excitedly, "are you game?"

For a second Cassie said nothing. Then she brought her hands together in a sharp clap. "Let's do it!" she answered firmly.

Chapter
Twenty-five

ON the way to Cassie's house Laura stopped at the Menotti's store.

When the bell jangled, Aldo glanced up and nodded in her direction, but his big smile was missing as he went back to slicing mozzarella cheese for an older woman. His broad face drooped, including his mustache. Laura looked around but didn't see Bertina. Any minute she'd probably come from the back room with a tray of cookies.

After the customer had left Laura said, "It's quiet this morning. Aren't you lucky, no Joe or Bertina around to argue with," she teased.

Aldo didn't respond with his usual bellow. He didn't even smile. In a helpless gesture he threw out his hands. "Bertina sick. Last night. This morning." He rubbed his forehead. "I tell her stay in bed. The doctor he come this afternoon."

Her pulse jerked. Immediately she thought of the flu. "It's not serious, is it?"

"No. No." He placed his hands over his large stomach. "She sick here, that's all." But before he turned to lift a glass canister from the shelf, she noticed a worried frown on his face.

He held out the peppermint sticks to her. "Take, take," he urged.

"Thank you," she said, tucking the peppermint candy in her pocket. "I'm sure Bertina will be fine. I'll stop in to see her this afternoon." She paused. "Is Joe coming home tomorrow?" She knew that October twenty-second was the date but hoped he didn't have a change of plans.

"Tomorrow," Aldo reiterated. "I miss Joe." Then, lest she think he was too soft-hearted, he grinned. "I need my son to sack onions and potatoes. Sweep floor."

"Of course," she said, a twinkle in her eye.

Aldo eyed her black suit and black stockings. "All dressed fancy?" His thick eyebrows lifted in a question.

"Yes," she responded brightly, pleased that he had noticed her short jacket and matching skirt, for she had taken special pains in dressing. In her black and white polka-dot blouse with the saucy tie, she felt pert and glowing. "Cassie and I are going to the Senate this morning."

"More picketing, eh?" His eyes took on a mischievous glint.

Nodding, she said quickly, "I've got to hurry and meet her. We mustn't be late for the opening session." Hiding her secret behind a smile, she wheeled about and, with a wave, was gone. Never would she tell Aldo her plot. He would be horrified. No one should do anything bad against this great country, he would say. Well, what she and Cassie planned wasn't bad, she told herself, swinging up Fishing Lane, but it was electrifying! The rolled banner was heavy, and they carried it between them into the Rotunda. The magnificent paintings and the many bronze and marble statues thrilled Laura. In her eyes the most overpowering statue was the marble likeness of a standing, pensive Abraham Lincoln sculpted by Vinnie Ream, an eighteen-year-old woman. She paused before Lincoln, giving the sixteenth president a snappy salute. "Government of the people, by the people, and for the people," she murmured. "We're getting there, Abe."

"Laura! Hush!" Cassie hissed. "Do you want to be thrown out before we even get inside the chamber?"

Laura grinned. "All right. I'll behave." As they walked down the corridor, painted with vivid blues, reds, and greens, they passed on either wall frescoes of animals, birds, and flowers, but Laura could only see the line forming behind the silken cords. "Hurry, Cassie."

The two guards, stern and forbidding, waited for the bell before they lifted the cord and swung wide the heavy doors to the Visitor's Gallery.

Shifting their heavy burden, easy to smuggle in because it was wrapped in an American flag, they rushed along the star-studded pattern on the blue carpet and down the stairs to obtain a front-row seat.

Spectators dashed in after them, but Laura and Cassie threw themselves into a seat. Carefully they placed the banner under the seats until they were ready.

With their arms resting on the railing they watched the senators come in and sit at their desks. One hundred desks were on the floor, the Democrats on one side and the Republicans on the other. Pages scurried back and forth with messages or to place pads and pencils on each desk.

Finally, Vice-President Marshall came in, rapping his gavel on the podium. Once there was silence, he called on the chaplain to open the session with a prayer. Senators stood and bowed their heads, but once the prayer was finished, the chamber went back to noisy confusion.

After watching the proceedings for ten minutes, Laura clutched Cassie's wrist. "There he is! Senator Shields! The old buzzard!" she whispered close to Cassie's ear. "Let's get the banner ready!"

They bent over, loosened the cord around the middle, then tied the end cords to the bolted-down chair legs. Laura glanced around, but the people were giving their rapt attention to the senator from Iowa.

"Go fast!" Laura muttered, hefting the banner up onto the balustrade. From the corner of her eye she saw a guard sprinting down the aisle.

"Now!" she shouted, and with a flourish, the girls unleashed the huge white, purple, and gold banner. The large black letters emblazoned across read: VOTES FOR WOMEN!

All at once a whole battery of guards bore down upon them, but not before they yelled in unison, "Senators! Don't delay the Women's Amendment!"

The startled senators, goggle-eyed, stared up at them. They were pointing, gesticulating, and sputtering when they noticed the banner swaying above their heads. A number of men applauded but others shook their fists.

"You vixens!" a burly guard shouted. Two guards, each one grabbing Laura's arm, dragged her up the aisle.

The guards pulled so hard on her arms that she kept back her tears with difficulty. With blazing eyes and a rage boiling up inside, she viciously kicked one sharply in the shin, causing a sharp yelp of pain.

Cassie, too, fought her captors, but it

wasn't any use. They were dragged and shoved into the Senate's Guard Room. Laura's guard pushed her into a high-backed chair where she sat, glaring at him.

Not knowing what would happen next, she wasn't too surprised when the door was flung open and in strode Colonel Ridley.

The short, dapper man was furious, his face a contorted red blotch. "You dare to interrupt Senate proceedings!" he thundered. "I'll send you to prison on treason charges!"

Laura glimpsed Cassie's calm face and wondered if underneath she were as frightened as she was. Treason! Her blood chilled at the thought. That was an offense punishable by death!

Colonel Ridley paced back and forth, every once in a while stopping to confront them, ranting and raving at them for what seemed like hours.

A guard opened the door. "Excuse me, sir. The vice-president."

Colonel Ridley replaced his glower with a sober, calm expression and straightened his shoulders.

William Marshall brushed hurriedly past the guard.

Laura sat stunned. The vice-president of the United States!

The vice-president, however, scarcely glanced at them as he conferred in low tones with the colonel.

The colonel's face reddened, but he nodded

his head and said, "Yes, sir, right away, sir."

Mr. Marshall departed, leaving Colonel Ridley staring at them for a moment. Then he spat out the words, "You're free to go."

"Free to . . ." Laura gasped.

"You heard me!" the colonel snarled.

"But, why?" Cassie asked, as puzzled as Laura.

The colonel's face flushed angrily. "The vice-president says they don't want any more publicity than necessary about your incident." He glowered at them. "If I had my way I'd throw you in the nearest cell for twenty years!" In disgust he turned his back on them and shouted, "Guards!"

Two soldiers immediately appeared.

"Escort these two radicals out of here."

"Yes, sir." They smartly saluted and walked the girls into the hall, through the Rotunda, and out onto the marble steps.

As they walked down the mall, Cassie and Laura couldn't believe their fantastic luck.

Laura giggled. "I wonder if our banner is still waving in the Senate Chamber."

"I imagine it was ripped down about two seconds after we were forced out," Cassie said dryly. "Laura," she said thoughtfully, "do you think Miss Paul will be angry with us?"

"I'm afraid she might, but if we had waited for her permission we'd never have done it!"

But Miss Paul was not angry. In fact, she was pleased at their bold move. However, she did admonish them not to do it again, for they would need all their energy for the upcoming October thirty-first demonstration in front of the Senate.

The next day Joe came home, and she dreaded to face him, for his mother was very sick with the flu. Poor Bertina! Yesterday when she went up to visit her, Aldo had barred the door, shaking his head helplessly.

"Bertina has flu," he said gruffly. "You go home."

She had looked into Aldo's large sad eyes, and her heart ached for him.

This morning, before eating her breakfast, she had to find out how Bertina was. Joe was staying downstairs in Otto Detler's apartment, for the flu was too contagious. Aldo would allow Joe in the house only for a few minutes at a time. He was needed to tend the store.

Laura gazed out the kitchen window at the bright fall leaves and wished things were as bright in the Menotti household. How quickly things could change!

"Ah, Laura," her mother said, hurrying in, dressed in her coat and hat. "I need to go to work. They're short of conductors. Please take the soup that's on the stove to the Menottis." Her eyes softened. "You mustn't go in, Laura. Leave it on the doorstep."

"But if it's so contagious, won't Aldo get it?"

Mrs. Mitchell smiled, stirring the soup. "He says he's 'strong like lion.' Sometimes people in the same household of an influenza patient are immune."

"Mother," Laura said thoughtfully, "this epidemic is serious, isn't it?"

Maude's eyes clouded. "I'm afraid so. Over five hundred cases have been reported so far in Washington."

Just then Sarah entered and poured her coffee. "Good morning, Mother, Laura."

"Hi, Sarah." Laura looked back at her mother. "I just hope our family stays healthy."

"We're strong like lions, too," her mother said with a short laugh.

And Laura could almost believe her. They would remain untouched, she thought. Just look at her mother's ruddy, strong face and Sarah's rosy glow. Yes, she felt better. The Mitchells would be fine. But Bertina was another question. "I hope Bertina will be all right," she said. "I'm worried about her."

"We all are." Laura's mother hugged her around the waist. "Don't forget to deliver the soup. I know it will make Bertina stronger."

"What are my Saturday chores?" asked Laura, hugging her mother back.

"Rake leaves. Otto will be busy cleaning the eaves and drainspouts."

"And Sarah?"

"I work at the factory today," Sarah interjected. "They're stepping up rifle production."

"You've been putting in long hours," Laura said.

"Yes," Sarah replied. "And I'll be home late again tonight."

After her mother and Sarah had left for work, Laura cleaned the kitchen, put a lid on the steaming soup kettle, and hauled it upstairs. Setting it on the doorstep, she rang the bell and waited for Aldo to answer.

The door opened slowly, and Laura backed away when she saw his drawn, haggard face. "How is Bertina?" she questioned anxiously.

Aldo moved his massive head back and forth. "Not good, not good."

"The soup will help," she said in a low voice, indicating the container.

"*Grazie*," he murmured.

"*Prego*," she answered his Italian with the Italian "You're welcome." Her eyes filled with tears as she ran downstairs.

Joe was just coming up from Otto's apartment. "Have you got an extra cup of coffee?"

"Oh, Joe," she said, hastily wiping away a tear. "Come in." She felt so sorry for him. What a gloomy homecoming.

After she had poured two cups of coffee she reached over and touched Joe's hand. "I hope your mom will be better soon. The soup should help."

"Mama is too healthy. It's sad to see her like this. The only time Papa will let me see her is when I wear a mask and stay for only a few minutes at a time." He drank his coffee, but his gentle eyes were no longer filled with dancing lights. "At least I can help out at the store, and since we prepare army provisions, I'll be given an extended leave. I'd like to take you out tonight," he said, "but I need to be close to Mama." He looked at her, and a crooked grin lit his face. "Maybe we can just sit and talk. I need that right now."

Her hand tightened on his fingers, and her face reddened. She felt wretched not to be with Joe when he needed her. "I'd like that," she said lamely, "but I won't be home until late tonight."

"Shawn?" He gave her a rueful smile.

"We're going to a dance at the Officers' Club tonight." He must think she was an awful playgirl. "It's the first time we've been together for a long time," she finished dispiritedly. Sadness overwhelmed her, and she wished she could sit with Joe.

"Sure." He finished his coffee and rose. "Time to open the store."

"If there's anything I can do let me know, won't you?"

"Of course, little one. I'll call you." He wheeled about and was gone.

But somehow his voice wasn't as convincing as it might have been. She missed the old warmth and ease between them.

Later, while dancing with Shawn at the Wardman-Park Hotel, she was quiet, thinking of not being able to talk to Joe tonight when he needed her.

Shawn held her out at arm's length, looking into her eyes. "Why so pensive tonight, sweetheart?"

She smiled at his concern. "Just thinking of the flu and Bertina Menotti. . . ." her voice trailed off.

"And Joe Menotti, too, I'll bet," Shawn said, mocking lights in his blue eyes.

"And why not?" she flared. "He needs me now."

"You still care for him, don't you?" Shawn said, arching his brows, his eyes riveted on hers.

"I-I don't know, Shawn." She remembered her resolve to no longer see Joe. That had changed with Bertina's illness. She could never turn her back on him. Oh, why did she always make the wrong decision? Here she was dancing in a new dress of white chiffon and Joe was home, worried to death.

"Pretty dress," Shawn complimented.

"Thanks," she said briefly. If Shawn only knew she had made the dress for the suffragist rally at the end of the month, he wouldn't think it was so pretty. Alice Paul had a new demonstration in mind. No longer would they carry signs but they would wear white dresses with black arm bands to indicate the death of justice in the Senate.

"A pretty dress," Shawn murmured, "for a pretty girl." He pulled her close. "But you're a little wild, too. That latest stunt you and Cassie pulled in the Senate was crazy!"

She stiffened. Would Shawn ever understand?

"All right, all right." He laughed. "We won't even mention the suffragists."

The waltz music swirled around her, and Shawn, with big, sweeping steps, moved her out in the middle of the dance floor.

His eyes were shining and his broad smile dazzling. "That music makes the blood race, doesn't it?" He held her lightly. "Are you happy with me, Laura?"

She laughed then. He could make her so angry and so happy at the same time. It was like being on a roller coaster. "Yes, Shawn," she responded warmly. "I'm happy."

But Shawn's smile disappeared when he glanced over her shoulder. All at once he pulled Laura close and kissed her.

"Shawn!" she said indignantly. "What on earth — ?"

But she didn't have time to finish, for there stood Joe beside her with his hand on her arm.

Bewildered, she asked, "Joe, what is it? Why are . . ."

"What the hell are you doing here?" Shawn growled, hands on his hips.

Ignoring Shawn, Joe faced Laura.

"Just a damn minute!" Shawn said belligerently, standing in front of Laura. "Laura happens to be with me!"

Black flames erupted in Joe's eyes, and he clenched his jaw. "Get out of my way," he ordered, spacing his words far apart.

Shawn snorted. "Make me!" He grabbed Joe's arm.

All at once Joe shoved Shawn so hard that he went sprawling across the shiny floor. Couples stopped dancing to stare.

Shawn scrambled to his feet, face flushed with anger, but Joe contemptuously turned his back on him.

"Joe," Laura gasped, "why?"

"I'm here to take you home, Laura." His eyes softened, and he grasped her hand, saying gently, "Sarah was brought home by ambulance. She has the flu."

Chapter Twenty-six

RACING home in Joe's delivery truck, Laura's heart beat wildly. Joe was grimly tight-lipped. Was he thinking of Shawn's kiss? His mother? Sarah? Everything was descending on her at once.

When they came to a screeching stop, she bolted from the car, leaving Joe and tearing upstairs. Despite the closed door, she barged in.

Maude, sitting by Sarah's bedside, glanced up and placed a finger to her lips. "The doctor just left," she said in a low voice. "Sarah is asleep."

"What happened?" She gazed at Sarah, bathed in perspiration, her rosy glow transformed to a pale ivory.

Motioning to Laura to accompany her out of the room, Maude explained, "Sarah complained of a severe headache during lunch, fainted on the assembly line, and was rushed home. The doctor has ordered complete rest and no excitement." Mrs. Mitchell took a shaky breath. "Her temperature is a hundred and four." She turned away, her face contorted with pain, but she didn't cry.

"Mother, please. You get some rest. I'll sit up with Sarah tonight."

"I don't want you in the same room with her unless you wear a mask."

"Mother! I intend to sit with her." Laura's voice was firm, and she resolved to at least help that much.

"Oh, Laura. I don't know what I'd do if you got sick, too."

"I'm healthy and strong," Laura said confidently. "Sarah is my sister, and I must help her."

Maude lifted Laura's hand, patting it. "I know how you feel, but trust me in this. I'm taking the next few days off from work, but I want you in school. Your senior year is too important. You must finish school."

Laura nodded, too weary to argue.

Mrs. Mitchell continued. "All of Sarah's dishes, sheets, utensils, everything she uses will be kept separate from ours. The next few days will be critical."

"I understand." Laura turned to leave. There was no reasoning with her mother when she set her mouth in that stubborn line.

She sighed. The newspapers advised that you shouldn't go on the trolley, you shouldn't visit people, you shouldn't have visitors, you should always wear a mask. If you feel ill, take a strong drink. Others advised that you dare not touch alcohol. One treatment was hot baths; another was cold, wet sheets. No one knew what to do for this dread disease! Laura stumbled to bed, wondering if they could weather this. Her concern was to be able to get medicine and food. Would they become outcasts in the neighborhood and have people shun them because Sarah had the flu? Thank God for Joe and Aldo. Otto, too, she was certain, would help if called on. Her brain was whirling, thinking of Sarah and her mother, but soon she fell into a deep sleep.

The next few days were a nightmare. Bertina had worsened and slipped into a coma, and Sarah, although awake, was still weak and nauseous.

On Wednesday Laura stayed home as all schools in Washington had closed indefinitely because of the Spanish influenza. Now she could do her share in nursing Sarah. Her mother, exhausted and pale, for once didn't argue with Laura's suggestion to get some rest. Maude, without a murmur, went to bed.

As Laura sat observing Sarah, she thought of the sign in their apartment window: the white sign with a big black *I* for Influenza. She held a cool cloth to Sarah's forehead, and suddenly her sister's eyelids fluttered open. "Laura," she mumbled, "I'm hungry." Her eyes closed again, but Laura was elated. Sarah's color was returning, and she wanted something to eat. For the past few days she wouldn't touch her food, no matter what Laura gave her. Did she dare hope Sarah was getting well?

The doorbell rang. Who would dare call? It was probably Joe, for he had been ever faithful and completely fearless of the flu.

Pushing back her loose tendrils of hair, she ran downstairs.

There stood Joe, slouched against the door frame. "Mama died an hour ago," he said, gazing at her with black, sorrowful eyes. "She never regained consciousness."

"Bertina? Oh, Joe, I'm — I'm . . ." Her eyes shimmered with tears, and for a few seconds they looked at one another, eyes wet.

"Come in," she said, opening the door wider.

"No, no. I need to be with Papa. There's a lot to do, for the funeral is tomorrow." His grief-filled voice wrung her heart.

"I understand." Funerals were immediate these days. She'd seen the stacks of coffins outside the mortuary ready for delivery.

The next morning, getting dressed in a black gown for the funeral, Laura heard a thud from Sarah's room.

Rushing into the bedroom, she saw that

her mother had collapsed beside the night-stand.

"Mother! Mother!" she called frantically but couldn't rouse her.

Panic-stricken, she raced to the phone, cranking the handle for the operator and shouting Joe's number.

In less than two minutes Joe was there helping carry Mrs. Mitchell to her own bed.

"Joe," she said, working feverishly to make her mother comfortable. "First Sarah, now Mother." She looked fearfully into Joe's eyes, then spun around. "I'll bring a basin of water to bathe Mother's face."

Joe glanced at Maude. "Her color is not too bad . . . it may be exhaustion."

"I hope so," she breathed. She knew it was almost impossible to get a doctor. The flu centers helped, however. You could go and purchase medicine and call for free advice. Over two thousand cases had been reported in the city, and the hospitals were jammed to overflowing.

Returning, she pressed the damp cloth on her mother's flaming cheeks and forehead and gazed wordlessly at Joe.

His black eyes swam with compassion. "I think it's the flu, Laura. I checked her tongue, and the tip is bright red."

A definite symptom, she thought in despair, then pressed her lips together. This horrible disease wasn't going to lick them!

"You shouldn't be here alone with two flu patients," Joe said.

"And who will help me? No, I'm able to do this, and besides, we Mitchells are 'strong like lions.'" She tried to smile, but look what had happened to Bertina! Sadly she looked at Joe. "You must leave. The mass is at ten o'clock." She looked down at her black dress. "I'm sorry I won't be able to go to the church. I meant to."

He grasped her arms. "Don't worry about the funeral," he said gently. "Mama will know your heart is with her . . . that's all that matters."

Quietly she moved into his arms and they held one another. Then Joe stepped back, turned, and was gone.

A moan caused her to wheel around.

"My head," Mrs. Mitchell gasped. "It's splitting apart! I ache so. My throat . . . my joints."

"Here, drink this." Laura handed her a glass of water mixed with medicine, which they fortunately had.

Dutifully Maude drank the cloudy liquid.

"You'll feel better now," Laura said, reaching for her wrist and feeling the unstable pulse. She was alarmed but tried to smile reassuringly. "Lie back, try to sleep, and when you awake, you'll be as good as new."

"Sarah?" her mother whispered, her fingers plucking restlessly at the quilt.

"Sarah was awake a few minutes ago and asking for food. Don't worry about Sarah, Mother. I'm the best nurse you can find." And the only one, she thought ruefully.

As her mother dozed fitfully, breathing rapidly, Laura thought of the epidemic. It had started overseas and traveled to New York, Boston, San Francisco. Already over three hundred and fifty thousand had died in the United States alone, the cities being the hardest hit. Why had she thought Washington would be spared? Some people said it was the Kaiser's secret weapon, but if so, it had turned on the German people, too, killing around one hundred and fifty thousand. In India close to five million people had perished. Even the names of this pestilence were peculiar. In Hungary it was called "The Black Whip"; in Switzerland, "The Coquette," giving her favors to everyone; and "The Bolshevik Disease" in Poland. No matter what it was called, to her it was the most horrible illness imaginable! How she yearned for things to be normal again. From a bustling household, their rooms had become dark with drawn shades, and silent, except for soft retchings and dry coughs. Laura put her weary head in her hands and wept.

A moan, more like a whimper, made her straighten up. "Mother?" she said quietly. "Are you awake?"

"Yes." She gazed at Laura with bright, feverish eyes.

Laura reached for an orange wedge, and dribbling the juice on her mother's parched, cracked lips, she thought she saw a sign of improvement.

That night Laura was more relaxed than she had been for days. Every day she talked by phone to Shawn, and everyday Joe brought her fresh fruit or vegetables, but she didn't dare have either of the men in the house. Once in a while, however, Joe insisted and, wearing his face mask, would slip in long enough to say hello to Mrs. Mitchell and Sarah.

It shouldn't be too long, Laura thought, until life would return to normal. Sarah, although still weak, managed to eat solid food, to dress herself, and even to sit for short periods of time with Maude.

These short respites gave Laura time to take a short walk or to sit by the river.

On Sunday, as she sat on the banks of the Potomac, she felt as if every bone in her body would melt — she was that tired. How she needed her father now! What strength he would have given her! The suffragists had been pushed out of her mind this past week, but tomorrow she intended to take part in the demonstration before the Senate wing. She had sewn her black arm band and her white dress was pressed, ready to wear.

Laura took a deep breath. Tomorrow she would take on the most recalcitrant senator, just like Joan of Arc! She smiled as she pulled her cape around her shoulders and sank down on the grass with her back against an oak. It was so peaceful here as she watched the lazy waters ripple and lap against the shore. The sun made the blue river dance with silver and diamonds.

If only the Mitchells and Menottis could be together like they had been on the Fourth of July! How much fun they had had. Now all that was changed. Bertina was gone, and although Joe and Aldo were back in the store, next week Joe was to report back to Fort Myer.

She plucked a red leaf from the ground, twirling it in her fingers.

Next fall at this time she'd be in college. While she had been nursing Sarah she had had many hours to contemplate her future. More and more she was thinking of becoming a lawyer. The Women's Movement needed doctors and lawyers. Her recent nursing experience, however, had shown her that being a physician wasn't for her. She wanted to be around live, healthy people — not taking pulses, doling out medicine, changing bedding, and emptying bedpans. A law career was much more appealing. She could use her head in arguing for or against individuals. She wasn't afraid of a challenge, and she knew she could help women in trouble, just like Opal Zacks. Who knows, she thought, one day she might even run for the Senate! Montana had already given women the vote as early as 1914! Wasn't Jeanette Rankin from Montana elected to the House of Representatives?

Chuckling, she stood up. What an imagination she had!

As she walked briskly along the shore she shivered a bit in her cape against the chilly October wind. She had a slight headache and felt more like sitting down, but it was time for her mother's medicine.

How strange that she should be caring for her mother when, for all her growing-up years, her mother had taken care of her. Fortunately Maude Mitchell was beginning to perk up and had even sat up for an hour yesterday.

Arriving home, Laura first checked the mail and was pleased to find a letter from Michael.

Eagerly she opened the envelope and scanned the contents:

October 1, 1918

Dear Mother, Sarah, and Laura,

The rumors are flying hot and heavy all over the hospital that Prince von Baden of Germany is sending out peace feelers to President Wilson. Seems they want the peace treaty based on his Fourteen Points. I doubt if Old Clemenceau or the English Prime Minister, Lloyd-George, will go along with it. They're too intent on revenge and reparations. Either way, it will be a relief to have the war over with!

Some of the worst fighting the Yanks have come up against has been in the Meuse-Argonne sector. Our offensive started September 26, and the battle is still being waged. The Argonne Woods are so thick, the mists so heavy, and the Germans so entrenched that the 77th Division only made five miles in six days! The Germans aren't retreating an inch, and this could be one of the toughest fights of the war. Don't worry, though. The way the Americans are fighting, the Germans will soon have to surrender.

I've saved my good news till last. I'm to be sent by the boat-train to Le Havre in two weeks. From there a troop transport will bring me home. I can't wait to see each one of you! I should be home by the middle of November, if not sooner.

I hope you are well and in good spirits!

With all my love,
Mike

"I hope you are well and in good spirits,"

she repeated softly. How ironic! Little did Michael know what Sarah and his mother had been through. Carefully she folded his letter and mounted the stairs. This would cheer her mother immeasurably.

As she walked down the hall she suddenly reeled, feeling dizzy. When she touched her forehead, it was burning. The narrow walls converged upon her, and the swirls in the wallpaper pattern spun and wheeled in her head. Then a black wave washed over her, and she could feel herself falling, falling into darkness.

Chapter
Twenty-seven

WHEN Laura awakened, the dresser and mirror blurred, came into focus, and blurred again. "Mom?" she said, and wondered if that tiny squeak were her voice.

"Shhh, lie still, dear. You need rest."

Her mother was right, for her whole body ached with tiredness. Suddenly a spasm shook her. With stomach heaving and bitter gall rising in her mouth, she looked frantically at her mother, who hastened to place a basin on her chest.

The vomiting left Laura spent, and she only wanted to sleep. Despite the perspiration that drenched her sheets, she was chilled to the bone.

She glanced again at her mother. "Mother, are you all right?" she asked shakily, not believing her eyes. Was it only yesterday she was nursing both her mother and Sarah?

"Both Sarah and I have recovered and are doing fine." She measured out a teaspoon of the medicine. "Take this. Now we need to concentrate on getting you on your feet again."

Laura took the evil-tasting medicine and closed her eyes.

After a short nap she opened her eyes to see Sarah looking down at her.

"How — how long have I been in bed?" she whispered.

There was pity in Sarah's eyes as she smoothed the covers. "Two days. We found you crumpled in a heap in the hall, and between Mother and me, we managed to get you into your own bed."

"Two days," she repeated dully. Somewhere in the dim recesses of Laura's brain she remembered that the crisis period for flu patients was three days. She had another day to suffer. Would she live or die? The way she felt now she wanted only to die. Her head was clenched in gripping pain, and each time she moved, her aching joints protested.

Although she tried to lie still and sleep, waves of nausea swept over her, and her watery eyes hurt when she coughed. Was this what it was like to face death? Everything she wanted to do, everything she wanted to be, was over. She had lived sixteen years and accomplished nothing. Her thoughts came in jumbled, hazy spurts. And the suffragists?

She had missed the demonstration. She thought of the black arm band she had prepared for the rally. A wild giggle erupted into the room. Was that maniacal laugh from her? Now that arm band could be worn by her mother at her own funeral.

Laura's fevered wet brow was wiped; she didn't know by whom, but it did no good. Her teeth still chattered.

More images came to haunt her. Shawn's teasing grin . . . Joe's dancing black eyes . . . Sarah's pitying look . . . Mother's sad countenance. All her loved ones were enveloped in a gray, damp mist, and their faces faded in and out. Her heart constricted violently. Here came Bertina with her jovial, laughing face. Now came Father with his black beard and twinkling eyes. Weakly she held out her hand. "Father," she whispered. A raging sea surged and pounded within her, submerging her once more in blackness.

Grimacing images floated before her in a nightmarish delirium — the leering guards . . . the sneering prison matron . . . the dark, clammy cell. It was frigid, and all at once ice water spilled down her spine. She sobbed. What were the guards doing to her? Suddenly she realized they were wrapping her weak, protesting body in a shroud.

In the stillness she heard a whimpering moan and knew it came from herself. Conscious again, she opened her eyes to find Sarah dabbing her cheeks with a cool, wet cloth. Sarah held out an orange slice, but Laura's stomach revolted at the sight of food.

"No," she groaned, and it seemed her strength ebbed from her arms and legs.

"You must eat something," Sarah said matter-of-factly. "This will make you feel better."

Tightly gripping the blanket, she forced herself to allow the squeezed drops to trickle down her sore, parched throat.

"No more," she managed to say. "No more." She turned her head sideways on the pillow. "Oh, God, help me," she murmured. "If I'm dying, take me quick."

Suddenly a masked face loomed before her. She shrank against her pillow.

"Hello, little one," Joe said softly, taking her hand in his. "It's good to see you awake."

"Joe." The name came out more like a croak. Relaxing, she recognized the dark, gentle eyes above the white gauze mask. "You shouldn't be here," but even as she mouthed the words, she was glad he was.

"Nonsense. I'll always be near you — whenever you need me!"

She smiled gratefully. Despite the pain, she would get better. She must — for Joe's sake — and Shawn's. Where was Shawn? she wondered.

Tenderly Joe smoothed back her hair. "You must fight!"

She nodded. What was it she had said?

That the Mitchells were strong like lions? Well, she felt more like a newborn kitten. Her last look, before she drifted off to sleep, was of Joe's sweet face.

On the fourth morning of her death struggle Laura sat up in bed, still weak, but her midsection no longer contracted in spasms. She was even hungry! For the first time she put her legs over the side of the bed and rose shakily, holding onto the nightstand and a chair on the way to the bathroom.

How good it felt to bathe her face in cool water.

Looking into the mirror, she could scarcely believe what she saw. She stepped back in astonishment. Her face had a purplish tinge, and there were black circles under her hollow eyes. Her sunken cheekbones were etched sharply against her thin face.

"Laura?" her mother called. "Are you all right?"

"Much better, Mother. I'm still a little shaky, but I don't have that achy sickness." She came out of the bathroom. Her nightgown was still clean after her mother had changed it last night.

Mrs. Mitchell had brought in a tray of hot broth and tea. There was a bowl of fresh fruit by her bed. Later she would eat a banana, she thought, remembering the doctor's advice. Nothing was better for a flu patient than fresh fruit.

As she crawled back into bed she smiled

faintly. "It's so good to be part of the world once more."

"Believe me, it's good to have you back. Welcome," her mother said, smoothing her covers. Holding the bowl, Maude began spooning the hot broth into Laura's mouth. She returned the bowl to the tray and poured a cup of tea, holding out the cup. "A few days' rest and you'll be as good as new."

Sarah came in and sat at the foot of the bed in her orange Oriental wrapper. "Hello, Laura, dear. You'll have enough to digest with the broth and tea. Later you can eat some fruit." She beamed. "I'm glad you're feeling better."

Laura laughed. "So am I." She gazed at Sarah's healthy good looks. "You look like your old self! How you and Mom kept me hopping!" She gazed fondly, first at one, then the other, and chuckled. "It was only fair that you should both have to take care of me."

Her mother gestured to a few envelopes on the table. "Shawn has been calling and sending cards every day." She touched a red blossom in a vase of roses. "These are from Shawn, too."

Laura reached for the top card.

"No, no." Her mother shook a finger. "Not yet. After your nap you may open them."

Laura didn't argue. She was too fatigued, but when she fell back on the pillow, even though she was tired, she felt oh, so good.

After Laura had rested for two days she dressed and went downstairs. It was a Thursday, but school wouldn't open until December first, which meant she would be attending school through June, but she didn't care — she knew her mother was right. Nothing must stand in the way of her schooling. More and more she was aware of the law and how she could help women.

As she drank her coffee she thought how wonderful it was to be well again. Was it only last month she had wondered if things would ever return to normal?

Her mother kissed the top of her head. "I'm leaving for the day. The trolleys must run on time!" She smiled down at Laura.

"Is it safe?" Laura asked, fearing the closeness of people crowded on the train.

"It is now," Mrs. Mitchell reassured her. "The trolleys are sprayed with disinfectant each morning." She shook her head sadly. "The death rate rose to thirty-two hundred last month, but it's beginning to taper off."

"I hope you can't catch the flu twice," Laura said.

"No." Maude chuckled. "We should be immune."

She watched her mom leave, glad that their love seemed to have been strengthened by what they had gone through.

Sarah drained her coffee and rose. "What's on your schedule today, Laura?"

She shrugged as if she had no plans, but as

she did, she thought better of it. She decided to tell Sarah and risk her displeasure. "I know you disapprove, Sarah, but I'm going to Headquarters." Her tone was defiant, and she braced herself for a lecture.

Sarah dropped her hand on Laura's shoulder. "I don't disapprove anymore. Who am I to censure your activities? Life is too short not to follow your conscience and do what you have to do."

Round-eyed, Laura stared at her sister. Was this the same Sarah who had told her not to be a "playgirl," to forget the suffragists, and to literally tend to her knitting?

In spite of herself she grinned at Sarah's new attitude. "You believe the suffragists are right?" she asked incredulously.

Sarah laughed lightly. "I didn't quite say that, but I do think they've done some good things. I wouldn't even mind voting, although I must say it would feel peculiar." Her smile faded. "When you hovered between life and death, Laura, I was ashamed of how I tried to run your life. You were always very lively — so different from me. I frowned on everything you did." She sighed deeply as if with remorse. "Seeing you lie in bed so still and quiet was terrible. I couldn't bear it. I wanted you back, Laura — back like your old self, a member of the suffragists, having two boyfriends. No matter what you did, I didn't care."

Laura leaped up, hugging her sister. "Oh,

Sarah, we've both been pigheaded. I'll never criticize you again."

Holding Laura at arm's length, Sarah smiled. "Don't make such rash promises. Now," she said in a spritely tone, "run along to Headquarters and don't forget to wear your yellow sash."

An hour later Laura was seated opposite Cassie. It was marvelous to be back in the bright tearoom with fall bouquets on each table.

She watched her friend as she folded letters, creasing them perfectly with her long, slender fingers. "Cassie," she said warmly, "I can't tell you how good it is to see you again!"

Cassie glanced up, smiling. "I missed you, too." Then she sobered. "To think you nearly died and I couldn't even visit you!"

"I was lonesome for you, Cassie — and for everyone here." She remembered how caring Cassie's father had been, calling every day. "Your dad must be almost crazy with patients."

"He is," Cassie responded with a worried frown. "Dad hardly comes home, except to sleep. He even eats on the run. This past week, though, he's been averaging more than his usual four hours of sleep. The patients have either died or are getting well, and very few new cases have been reported. I was so concerned for him." She looked at Laura with compassion. "And you, too, Laura. Was it terrible?"

"Terrible! Awful! Horrible! I'm just glad to be alive." Laura shuddered. "But I don't want to talk about it." She looked around at the almost empty room. "By the way, where is everyone today?"

"Influenza has decimated the ranks here, too, but Alice and Lucy are fine. This mailing I'm working on goes out today to Idaho voters. Senator Borah of Idaho has been too evasive in his support of the amendment. Alice has served notice that she intends to work for his defeat. Here." She shoved over a stack of folded letters. "Stuff these into the envelopes, will you?"

Laura worked efficiently, inserting the messages with nimble fingers.

"How are Shawn and Joe?" Cassie said in a bantering voice. "Can you keep the cards and flowers separate?"

She paused, wondering if the confusion she felt was evident to Cassie.

"It's not too difficult," Laura said, licking an envelope closed, especially since Joe had sent nothing. "I'm seeing Shawn Saturday. It will be the first time since I had the flu. But he's been sweet and very attentive — calling every day, sending me notes." She paused. "Joe is fine, too. He even braved the flu to visit me, but I don't know, Cassie, he seems more subdued around me. Maybe it's because his mother died. I miss Bertina, too," she said with a catch in her throat, "but it's not the same between Joe and me. He's home now on a five-day furlough before going overseas." She thought of their years of being together and longed for their carefree playfulness with its deep-running vein of friendship beneath. Concentrating on the last few envelopes, she changed the subject. "Michael is coming home in mid-November. The war should be over by then. Did you see today's headlines? The Kaiser has abdicated! I'm so eager to see Michael — any day now he'll be back, depending on the weather and how long his troop ship is detained in New York." She piled up the finished envelopes. "I hope his shoulder will heal without any complications. If I know Michael he'll want to join his architectural firm and immediately begin drawing blueprints!"

"Do you think you'll follow in his footsteps?"

"Not anymore," Laura said slowly. "That was Father's dream, and I always wanted to please him. I know now that being an architect is not for me." She folded her hands in front of her. "I'm not certain, but I think I'll go to law school."

"Really?" Cassie's eyes widened. "Alice Paul is enrolling at American University to pursue a law degree, too. You'll be in good company!"

Laura laughed. "I didn't know *anything* of Alice's plans." She looked at Cassie. "And you?" she asked seriously. "Do you have your future all plotted out?"

Cassie, with a graceful gesture, smoothed back her shiny, waved hair. "I'm not sure. Dad wants me to go into medicine, but I haven't decided."

With affection Laura observed her best friend. "It will be different next year, Cassie, won't it? What will we do without one another? We've been inseparable since the sixth grade!"

"I know," Cassie said wistfully, "but that's part of growing up. We'll keep in touch — always." She chuckled. "If I go into medicine you can defend my malpractice suits."

They both laughed, and Laura rose. "Let's have a cup of tea on that note."

But as she headed for the kitchen, she felt that their close relationship, made even closer by the suffragist cause, would change. They were moving toward a fork in the road and sadly would no longer follow the same path.

Chapter
Twenty-eight

As Laura brushed her hair, letting it fall over her shoulders the way Shawn liked it, she was pleased at her reflection in the full-length mirror. Her pallor had been replaced by a healthy glow, and the finely chiseled lines in her oval face indicated that the last of her baby fat had disappeared. She thought her wide green eyes, as shiny as a new leaf, were her best feature, but Shawn loved her long hair.

She hummed the war tune "Give my Regards to Broadway" and circled around in her black velvet dress. The white lace collar and cuffs made her look almost ladylike, she thought as she grinned impishly. Golden flecks twinkled in her eyes. She couldn't wait to see Shawn!

Suddenly the door burst open, and Sarah

bounded into the room, grabbing Laura's hand and whirling her around.

"Sarah!" Laura laughed. "What's got into you?"

"The war is over!"

Stupefied, Laura stared at her, then let out a whoop. "It's really over?"

"The armistice was signed early this morning in France. Germany surrendered!" They both began to career around the room in a wild circling.

"Stop, stop!" Sarah said breathlessly. Fanning herself with her apron, she sank down on the bed. "Whew! I'm winded." She brushed back a blonde curl, and her round cheeks flamed a hot pink. "There's a big parade down Pennsylvania Avenue this afternoon. Parties everywhere! Mother and I will be leaving in a few minutes for the Red Cross celebration."

Outside in the street Laura glimpsed a young man, perched on the hood of a car with a megaphone in his hand, shouting, "The war is finished! Come to the victory parade at three o'clock — Pennsylvania Avenue."

Sarah moved to the door. "Laura, if Bill Crowley calls, tell him where I am, will you?" She smiled shyly.

"Bill?" Laura said, arching her brows in surprise. "Is he coming today?"

"He might." Sarah flushed. "I don't know when to expect him. I received a letter from

Bill yesterday and he said his discharge from the air force had come through and he should land in New York by the first of November, so, like Michael, it could be any day."

"Rest assured, I'll point Bill in the right direction," Laura said with a grin.

Sarah blushed again, closing the door after her.

Laura lifted her flared skirt and sat by the window, holding back the curtain, watching people begin to come out and to hug one another and to sing. Shawn should be here any minute. Oh, she thought, what a celebration they'd have today and tonight. It had been a long time since she had danced with Shawn. How she was looking forward to it! Thanks to Shawn's expert teaching, she had become a good dancer. She contemplated the last waltz they were dancing when Joe came bursting upon them and pulled her away, telling her Sarah had the flu. Was that only last month? She frowned when she remembered Shawn's kiss. Had he deliberately kissed her when he saw Joe? She sighed. Well, Joe hadn't seemed to notice.

She wondered what it would be like to dance with Joe, then a small smile played about her lips at the memory of Uncle Vito's wedding. She *had* danced with Joe! She had been nine years old when Joe had escorted her to his uncle's wedding. How grown-up and pretty she had felt in her long, ruffled dress among all the adults, many of whom were in Italian costume. Joe had swung her around in a whirlwind dance, the tarantella, and often her feet didn't touch the floor. She'd never forget the merriment, the foot-stomping rhythm, the tables of food, and Joe.

Letting the curtain drop, she wondered why she was always thinking of Joe.

The doorbell rang, interrupting her rev-erie. She flew downstairs to open the door.

There stood Shawn, hat in hand, with a big grin on his face. For an instant they drank in one another's faces, eyes locked. Then Shawn swiftly moved toward her, his fingers lightly caressing her cheek.

"You look gorgeous, sweetness. You have no idea how much I missed you and how much I wanted to see you!"

"Why should you risk the flu, Shawn?" she asked lightly. "That would have been fool-ish." But she remembered what it had meant to her to see Joe's masked face. Dear loyal Joe. He was always there when she needed him — like the wild ride from the jail to school. Little fingers of doubt flitted across her mind when she looked at Shawn. Would he care enough to race to her rescue?

Shawn kissed her gently, then stepped back and chuckled. "What a day we're going to have. First the parade, then dancing." His eyes sparkled, and he pulled her forward again. "I love you, Laura," he said lightly.

Her heart leaped at his words, and everything and everyone, including Joe, were forgotten. All she could see was Shawn's handsome, round face with his crooked smile and blue eyes.

Church bells peeled, and more honking cars went by, with men blaring into megaphones repeating the message that the war was won! Cars choked Cherry Alley, doors banged, and people swarmed everywhere, some clapping trays together like cymbals, and others dancing on rooftops.

"Come on," Shawn said eagerly. "Let's have some fun."

She grabbed her velvet cloak and, happily clasping his hand, followed him, half-skipping and half-running toward Pennsylvania Avenue.

Upon their arrival, crowds were in the street laughing, yelling, weeping, and singing.

Shawn swept her up in his arms, then spun her out and back. Laughing and brimming with health and rejoicing, Laura yearned to leap and cavort like a small girl. She kept repeating to herself, "The war is over. Shawn loves me!" For an instant a pang shot through her heart and her eyes clouded. What was Joe doing? Who was he celebrating with?

"Hey, my beauty!" Shawn said, chucking her under the chin. "No frowns allowed."

A group of soldiers squatted atop a truck,

ringing handbells and blowing horns. Despite the chill November day, the jubilant crowd warmed the air. Policemen were blowing whistles, trying to move the people off the street over to the cordoned sidewalk. As if by magic, flags appeared, fluttering from office buildings and being draped over cars. A miniature flag was thrust in Laura's hand, and she gaily waved it along with everyone else.

All at once the fire engine's siren screamed. The parade was to begin! The flag waving merry-makers crowded together along the wide avenue, and as the Marine band, bugles blaring, drums beating, swung proudly past, lusty cheers broke out. A soldier beside Laura murmured, "God bless this country," and tears rolled unashamedly down his face. First a unit of soldiers and then sailors marched past. An ambulance with an effigy of the Kaiser in the front seat, swathed in bloody bandages, was followed by a coffin with the Kaiser inside.

Government workers, wearing red, white, and blue paper hats, had been given a holiday by order of the president. They had joined hands and were snake-dancing through the honking cars.

Girls ran out to kiss the soldiers and sailors and to press flowers into their hands.

The parade ended with the band striking up the national anthem. Everyone joined hands and sang "The Star Spangled Banner" with verve and pride. Tears stung Laura's eyes. The song had never meant so much to her as at this triumphant moment.

She and Shawn hurried along with the jostling, happy throng to the House of Representatives where President Wilson was to give his speech. The House Chamber was filled to capacity, but they managed to squeeze their way to the front.

Before long, a smiling Woodrow Wilson with his top hat raised walked jauntily to the podium. For all his sixty-one years he appeared almost boyish.

Waving and smiling broadly from the speaker's stand, the President patiently waited for the tumult to die down. Finally the audience hushed, awaiting his address.

He began in a firm voice, "My fellow countrymen, the Armistice was signed this morning. Everything for which America fought has been accomplished. It will now be our fortunate duty to assist by example, by sober, friendly counsel, and by material aid in the establishment of democracy throughout the world."

All this talk of democracy around the world left Laura with a bitter feeling. Everywhere the rights of countries were to be upheld, except right here in America. Women, it seemed, were to be excluded in this victory for democracy!

Interspersed in the crowd were the purple, white, and gold banners of the suffragists, and she wondered if the women holding high these colors shared her same thoughts.

Shawn took her elbow, and they filed out of the chamber and onto Lafayette Square for the fireworks and dancing.

Later in the evening Laura began to tire. "Shawn, I don't know what it is, but I could go to sleep right on the dance floor."

"Nonsense. It's only ten o'clock." He peered more closely at her. "You do look pale. You're not going to get sick on me, are you?"

She laughed shakily. "No, I feel fine, but I think we'd better sit this one out."

By midnight, she asked Shawn to take her home. Although she was exhilarated, she was also exhausted. It hadn't been too long ago that she had gotten up from a sickbed.

As they climbed the stairs to the front stoop she noticed the light in Joe's window. Her glance didn't escape Shawn. He turned to face her. "Don't even think about Joe Menotti with me around," Shawn said firmly, but there were teasing lights in his eyes.

"I'm — I'm not . . ." she lied.

He kissed her on the nose, then wrapped her in his arms, kissing her soundly so that her senses reeled.

Releasing her, he whispered, "Think only of me tonight, and when you dream, dream of Shawn O'Brien."

"I solemnly promise," she said mockingly, "to have dreams only if you're in them!"

He entangled his fingers in her hair, nuzzling her slender neck. "I not only dream of you, dearest Laura, but you're in my every waking thought."

"You'll lose your job that way," she said jokingly.

His eyes were searching, but there was no answering banter. "Good night, my love. I'll call you tomorrow."

For a moment she watched him as his trim figure swung down the moonlit street.

As she undressed she kept thinking of the glorious day. She washed her face, brushed her teeth, and fell into bed. The faint strains of "There's a Long, Long Trail a 'Winding," floated down from Joe's record player. She lay very still, listening. She wondered if the poignant melody reflected Joe's feelings. What was he thinking? Were he and Aldo thinking of Bertina? She doubted if they had celebrated today. And, Laura asked herself, did Joe give her so much as a fleeting thought anymore? Or was his mind turned to new horizons — horizons that didn't include her? She bit her lip to keep the tears back. The wonderful day became tinged with sadness.

Chapter
Twenty-nine

THE next afternoon, as she was about to cut across Lafayette Square, Laura stopped to gaze over its rectangular shape. The impressive rows of stately elms around the square, along with an iron fence, were an appropriate border for the many statues. The large equestrian statue of Andrew Jackson and the many marble groups immortalizing the foreign generals that had helped Washington win the American Revolution dotted the area — Thaddeus Kosciuszko, von Steuben, Comte de Rochambeau, and Comte de Grasse. All of these men fought for freedom to rid the United States of British rule, and as she walked by Kosciuszko's statue, the Polish patriot, she nodded to him, feeling a kinship with this European soldier. She halted, reading the inscription: "And Freedom shrieked as Kosciuszko fell."

Being in the midst of these freedom fighters made her more and more determined to shape her own future in step with the suffragists. Not that she didn't want a home and babies, but that would come later. Shawn loved her, and it was now clear that Joe was no longer interested. Her future lay with Shawn.

She breathed in the crisp November air but thought of the summer when the scent was of heavy lemon from the southern magnolia trees.

When she entered the mansion, she was surrounded by the noise of clacking typewriters, and she knew more heavy mailings would be sent out.

In the tearoom a number of women were sewing at a round table in the corner. Recognizing Rowena Green, Julia Emory, Lucy Burns, and Alice Paul, she went over to greet them.

"Laura!" Lucy exclaimed. "Good to see you looking so radiant. We're stitching new banners. All our signs must be ready by the time Wilson sails for Europe. Every speech he makes in Italy or France will be burned." Lucy threw out her arm toward an empty chair. "Join us! We can use all the help we can get on this project."

The large tricolor was draped over the table, and the purple, gold, and white colors came alive rippling on the heavy satin. Lucy, threading her needle, looked up at Laura and winked, smiling broadly. Her ruddy face seemed lit by an inner fire. "You just missed an interesting delegation, Laura." She glanced at Alice. "Right?"

Alice smiled a rare smile. Her bright eyes fastened on Laura. "Yes, three sailors and one petty officer came to apologize to me for the action of the men in uniform who attacked any suffragist or tore any banners."

"Isn't that a fascinating wrinkle?" Lucy chortled with satisfaction. "We're making an impression, Laura, my girl. When four burly men come in shamefaced at what their compatriots have done, that's progress!" She shifted the heavy cloth folds. "Here," she said, "start hemming."

Dutifully Laura fitted a thimble on her finger and took the offered needle. She enjoyed the camaraderie of these four women.

"Speaking of servicemen," Rowena said. "Here comes a handsome one now!"

Laura glanced up, and her eyes grew round. There was Shawn striding purposefully toward her, without glancing to the right or left, as if he were afraid that this jungle of vipers might attack him.

"Welcome," Alice Paul said dryly, sensing his discomfort. "We can always use another hand."

Shawn did not so much as acknowledge Alice's presence.

"Shawn," Laura began, flustered. "I'd like to introduce you. . . ."

Abruptly he cut her off. "Laura, I need to talk to you."

Flushing to the roots of her hair at his disregard for her friends, and embarrassed at his disrespect for Alice Paul, she frowned. "Shawn," she said, trying to control her anger, "I'm busy."

Lucy's laugh boomed forth. "Run along, Laura. We'll still be here when you return."

Pushing back her chair, she ignored Shawn's hand and moved quickly toward the door. What on earth did he want that couldn't wait until she was home?

"Shawn, what is it?" she demanded impatiently. "Is something wrong?"

"Everything is wonderful." His step was jaunty. "I just had to talk to you."

"Fine," she said curtly. "Let's sit over here and have a cup of tea."

He glanced around disdainfully. "I can't talk in this place. You know I don't approve of suffragists!"

"I realize that," she said coolly. "So why did you come here?"

He grinned at her. "Come on, the car's outside and we'll take a spin down by the river."

"Well," she said hesitantly. "I really should stay and complete what I've started."

He looked deeply into her eyes. "For once in your life put me ahead of the suffragists. This means a lot to me, Laura. I promise I'll have you back within the hour."

"Only for ten minutes," she admonished.

Curious, she went out to the limousine with Shawn.

As they sat in the warm car, overlooking the gray, sluggish river, she faced him. "All right, Shawn, what was so important that it couldn't wait until tonight?"

"I've got my discharge papers," he said simply, his face aglow with a broad smile.

"That's marvelous," she said, catching his boyish enthusiasm and almost clapping her hands. How quickly his mood changed and how quickly he could make her forget their differences.

"I'm leaving next week for New York to see Mom and Dad." He toyed with the steering wheel. "I'll be there for Thanksgiving and Christmas but will take the train back to Washington in time to start the new term at Georgetown University."

"That's so wonderfully quick," she said, "to be released from the army and shed that uniform." She touched the chevron on his sleeve.

"I'm ready to exchange this hat for a bowler," he said lightly, tilting his military hat far back on his head, causing a wavy lock to fall forward. "And to throw away this scratchy wool uniform for white flannels and a boating jacket."

She laughed cheerfully. "You'll make a handsome student — quite the man about campus," she said approvingly.

"And you're quite the most beautiful girl in Washington." He pulled her forward, kissing her lips.

Her eyes closed, fluttering excitement cascading through her veins.

When she opened her eyes, a smile twitched around Shawn's generous mouth. "I've never known anyone like you, Laura." His eyes softened. "You're the only girl for me. University life will be filled with good times. There won't be a dance we'll miss. When I begin my law degree, I want to know that you're waiting for me." His eyes twinkled.

A laugh bubbled up inside as she leaned back against the velour seat. "Shawn," she said teasingly, "I'll wait for you if you'll wait for me!" She gave him a mischievous sidelong glance.

Puzzled, he stared at her, waiting for an explanation.

"You see, Shawn," she said proudly, "I've decided to enroll in law school, too."

"You've decided what?" he said lazily, grinning.

"I'm going to become a lawyer," she said earnestly.

He threw back his head, laughing uproariously. Finally he caught his breath, wiping his eyes. "Laura, tell me you're joking! Not my beautiful doll an attorney-at-law!" He ducked his head forward, peering at her. "You *are* joking, aren't you?"

"I've never been more serious in my life," she answered gravely.

For a long moment the silence was broken only by the oars of a boatman rowing.

Was this what Shawn thought of her? A beautiful doll? Her blood rose, warming her face and touching the tips of her ears. She had known all along that he had disapproved of suffragists. What had he called them? A bunch of cackling old hens. Well, she was a suffragist, but he refused to admit it. He'd said she was meant to keep a man happy and to have a man's arms wrapped around her. She wouldn't listen to this anymore, she thought bitterly. No more would she subject her interests to his. That was what he expected. The memory of his jealousy and the way he provoked a fight with Joe played again in her head. That night of Sarah's illness when Shawn had deliberately kissed her on the dance floor was merely to taunt Joe. It was meant to transmit a message: "Hands off, she's mine!"

Shawn, taking hold of her shoulders, gently turned her to face him. He chuckled. "Why so sober? We'll work this out. After all, you haven't even graduated from high school."

That was his solution, she thought, her heart plummeting. She was only a silly schoolgirl who would be easy to convince to follow his wishes. Tears brimmed, threatening to spill over, but she no longer cared. "I know exactly what my career will be," she said quietly. Shawn had to understand that there wasn't a doubt in her mind and that she wasn't his pawn. "Please," she begged, "take me back to Headquarters."

He moved his head close to hers. "Laura, sweetness. . . ." He ran his hand up her arm.

"Take me back now," she repeated firmly.

He dropped his hand and petulantly ground the car into action, veering toward Jackson Street.

As she jumped out of the car Shawn called, "I'll phone you tonight."

She broke into a run, a sob tearing at her throat. It was over, and Shawn didn't realize it. Tears blinded her as she opened the door, closing it softly behind her. For a few seconds she stood with her back against the door, spirits low, but she determinedly wiped her eyes and moved into the tearoom.

After working two hours sewing banners, fingers flying, and losing herself in conversation, she bade everyone good night and slowly walked home.

As she turned into Cherry Alley she passed the Menottis' store and saw Joe's head bent over the ledgers.

For a moment she stared sadly at him, tears glistening, then walked on.

That night she couldn't sleep. The image of Joe loomed before her. He was the one who respected and loved her. He was the right man for her . . . had been all along.

338

Now it was too late. The love she'd once seen shining in his eyes had long ago disappeared, and she was to blame for extinguishing it.

Restlessly she threw back the covers, pacing the floor. She stopped to stare through the window at the trees. The stark, leafless branches against a dim, moonlit sky were as bleak and barren as her soul. Dejectedly she sat before the window.

It wasn't until hot tears spilled down her face that she realized dawn was breaking. Her recriminations against herself did little good. It was over with Shawn. It was over with Joe. Now she was left with no one, and that served her right. Everything was her own fault and she couldn't blame anyone else — certainly not Shawn. Shakily she drew in a deep breath and rose, her muscles stiff and sore.

A resolve slowly grew in her mind as sunlight poured across the room. She must see Joe and tell him she hadn't meant to hurt him. She hadn't meant to hurt anyone. She smiled bitterly. Perhaps neither Shawn nor Joe were hurt at all. Perhaps they didn't care what Laura Mitchell did. If anyone was hurt, it was herself!

Hastily she brushed her hair. A sleepless night had done little for her appearance, but she wasn't concerned.

With a quickening pulse she dressed and hurried downstairs, knowing what she must do.

Reaching the Menottis' store, she realized it was too early to be open, but if she knew Joe, he would already be there.

With a quick glance through the window she saw him sweeping the floor.

She pounded on the door, each blow matching the hammering of her heart. As she watched breathlessly Joe leaned the broom against the counter and gracefully moved toward her.

Unlocking the door, he held it open, wonderment written all over his face. "Laura!" he said, raising his thick brows. "What are you doing here?"

"Are you so surprised I want to see you, Joe?" she asked softly.

His face was expressionless, except for his gentle black eyes, which never left her face. He shrugged.

She groaned inwardly. Was he so indifferent to her that the only answer to her question was a shrug? Did he no longer care a whit about her?

"I-I've just said good-bye to Shawn," she said, a quiver in her voice, "for good." She gazed at him with trembling lips. Why didn't he say something? Anything?

Digging her nails into her palm, she forced herself to continue. "I've missed you, Joe Menotti." Her voice quavered.

Joe examined her with a faintly amused smile.

She flung out her hands in a helpless ges-

340

ture. "You've been the one all along," she said simply. "You were constantly in my thoughts, even when I was with Shawn."

With a whimper she moved into his arms, hugging him tightly. "Why didn't you tell me what he was like?"

Joe stroked her long hair as she nestled against his shoulder. At last he spoke. "You had to discover what Shawn was like for yourself. No one can tell you what to believe, Laura. You know that."

A hot tear coursed down her cheek. Joe was only comforting her — still the big brother. Why did she always have to ruin things? Joe had loved her once. She knew he had. She lifted her head, gazing into his face, teardrops sparkling on her eyelids.

His lean handsome face and the small smile hovering about that firm mouth was almost more than she could bear.

"I love you, Joe," she said in a voice husky with emotion.

Gently he traced her lips with his slender fingers. "I've waited a long time to hear you say that." Suddenly his dark head lowered and he tenderly kissed her.

"Joe," she whispered against his lips as his arms tightened around her. Once again their lips touched. How could she ever have doubted his love?

"I'm sorry I was such a fool," she admitted, sniffling.

"Laura Mitchell! Do you know what you

just called yourself? A fool!" He grinned, and his even, white teeth flashed in the dim light. "I'm going to savor that phrase because I know I'll never hear it again. Tomorrow you'll be back to being independent Laura — just the way I love you!"

I've wasted all this time, she thought, reproaching herself, but now at last she knew Joe was the only one for her! He had always been here, and she had been blind to his warmth and consideration and love. *I'm so lucky*, she thought, for Joe actually loved her. Her heart thundered as she again nestled within the circle of his arms.

Laughter danced in his eyes, and his arms tightened around her waist. "Laura, darling," he murmured softly in her hair.

She had loved Joe in the past, she loved him now, and she would always love him. She gazed at him solemnly as if pledging this love.

Once more Joe's dark head bent to kiss her.

"Tomorrow night *I'm* the one who is going to take you dancing," Joe said firmly.

Laura moved a little out of his arms. "There's a suffragist rally tomorrow night, Joe. I want to be there. I have to," she said, worried about his reaction.

Joe threw his head back and laughed. "All right, my darling Laura. Then we'll go together. Any objection to that?"

Laura thought she had never been happier in her whole life. "The women will welcome you with open arms, but no one more than I will."

As Joe kissed her, she knew she would love this man forever.

Note: On August 26, 1920, the Nineteenth Amendment was accepted by three-quarters of the states, giving women the right to vote.

An exciting excerpt from the first chapter of EMILY follows.

EMILY

by Candice Ransom

Chapter One

LATE September light fell through the window and across the array of crystal perfume bottles on Emily Blackburn's vanity table. Emily sat before the swivel mirror, dressed in a peacock brocade dressing gown, trapped by the image in the glass. Cherubs trailing golden streamers danced around the gilded frame, but Emily only saw a face without character, reflected as blank as an unwritten page.

Her hands twisted in her lap, and her slender shoulders were stiff. In exactly one hour and forty-five minutes Worth was picking her up for Annabelle's dinner party, but Emily could not move.

Her unwavering reflection stared back at her as she looked beyond the round, blue-green eyes, searching for some sign of life, some reason to get dressed for another party. Feathery brows — "delicate as butterfly antennae," Worth once remarked — arched over pupils the shade of sky and water touched by twilight. Long, spidery lashes, which could flutter coquettishly when Emily put her mind to it, did little to disguise the darkness that clouded her intense gaze. In her misery Emily's eyes were the color of rain showers over the ocean.

"I can't do it," she whispered to her mirrored self. "I just can't."

The door opened and her maid came in, carrying a stack of freshly laundered lingerie.

"Can't do what?" Meg asked, overhearing the last part of Emily's murmurings. "For mercy's sake, Emily. You haven't half-started getting ready. Do you realize what time it is?" The maid deftly tucked Emily's camisoles and slips into satin pouches, careful not to miss the fragile lace trim.

Noticing that Emily still sat like a marble statue, Meg said, "What's the matter, lamb? Can't choose a gown?"

If only that were what was bothering me, Emily thought. She blinked, freeing herself momentarily from the mirror, and turned to her maid.

"Oh, Miggsy." She sighed, lapsing into the use of her affectionate childhood name. "It's not just the gown. It's everything. What's the point?"

"The point is that Mr. Bates will be here in exactly one hour and thirty minutes," Meg said crisply, by now used to handling Emily's recent moods. "It wouldn't be proper to keep him waiting, now, would it?"

"No." Emily's automatic response was barely audible. "You're right, I'd better hurry. Mustn't disgrace the family name by being a minute late. Pick me out a dress, will you, Miggsy?"

The maid finished putting away the satin pouches in the lingerie chest before opening the double doors to Emily's vast closet. Her voice sounded hollow and cavernous as she called to Emily.

"Which gown do you prefer, Emily?"

"It doesn't matter. Anything."

Her maid appeared with several gowns draped over her arm. "How about the silk? You only wore it once last season."

Half-turning on the leather-padded stool, Emily examined the black-and-white dress trimmed in jet that Meg held up, and dismissed it with a shake of her head. "Not that one. It reminds me of funerals."

"What about this one, then? We could fix your hair with feathers."

Emily acknowledged the taffeta gown with a listless flap of her hand. "Fine."

Meg put the other gowns back into the closet, then bustled around, laying out her young lady's lingerie for the evening. Emily stepped into her "combination" — one-piece bloomers and camisole — as though she dressed in the finest batiste undergarments, hand-stitched by old women in Brittany, every day of her life.

Indeed she did. For Emily Blackburn, at age sixteen, was one of the wealthiest girls in New York City in the autumn of 1899 . . . and one of the unhappiest.

Her maid tied the delicate shoulder ribbons of the chemise she had slipped over Emily's head. "You know, I don't think you'll ever be plagued with wearing corsets, Emily. You have no more meat on your ribs than a sparrow. Straighten up and stop looking so mournful. You'd think you were going before the firing squad, instead of Miss Annabelle's party. Guess where Jimmy took me last night?" Jimmy was Meg's latest beau, a hearty blond man who drove a milk wagon.

"I haven't the faintest idea. Where?" Emily studied her maid's familiar freckled face and wide, animated mouth, her interest slightly stirred.

"Now where do you think? Down to one of those restaurants in Chinatown!"

"Really?" Emily had always wanted to dine in exotic Chinatown, but she knew she'd never taste Chinese food any more than she would ever glimpse the dark side of the moon. "What was it like? What did you have?"

"Well, the inside was a lot like the way Mrs. Blackburn decorated the reception room — silk pictures and red wallpaper and so forth. Jimmy ordered for both of us, and I never saw such a conglomeration in all my born days, Emily. At the end of the meal the waiter brought us the nicest pot of tea and fortune cookies. You know, little pieces of paper hidden inside a cookie? Mine said" — Meg pitched her voice lower, so it sounded mysterious — " 'You will meet a tall handsome stranger and cross a large body of water.' I had to laugh. I've already met Jimmy, and everybody knows I'll be going to Europe with you in a few weeks."

At twenty-five her maid enjoyed the best of both worlds, Emily thought. Meg worked in the Blackburn mansion on Fifth Avenue as Emily's personal maid, pleasant work in luxurious surroundings, and was free a few evenings a week to go out with Jimmy to the entertainments barred to Emily.

Last summer Emily listened to endless stories about Meg's jaunts to Coney Island, the greatest amusement park in the world. Emily could almost smell the caramel-coated popcorn on the sea breezes and feel the giddy sensation of riding the scenic railway that dipped thrillingly out over the water. In her mind's eye she was dazzled by the million lights in Luna Park. She envied Meg, who was modern enough to change into a swimming costume at the city bathhouse and go ocean bathing. Coney Island, with its hordes of people laughing and jostling, dangled before Emily, elusive as a mirage. The closest she would ever get to the spectacular park at the end of the trolley line in Brooklyn was tasting the saltwater taffy Meg brought back.

Blackburns did not ride trolley cars or go anywhere near Brooklyn, let alone Coney Island. It simply wasn't done . . . not proper at all.

Emily sighed again. Her maid had more fun than she did. For all the money her father earned "downtown" on Wall Street, Emily often wished she could trade places with Meg for a week, like the two boys in Mr. Twain's novel, *The Prince and the Pauper,* and experience all the forbidden sights of New York.

"Your mother is talking of redoing this floor again," Meg remarked, smoothing the folds of the gown Emily had chosen.

"Oh, no! I like my rooms just the way they are. Why can't Mother leave things alone?"

"Emily Blackburn!" Meg's brown eyes were wide. "That's no way for a young lady about to come out to talk."

Defensively, Emily said, "I'm not coming out till late next summer. Mother has her hands full with Annabelle's debut."

Mrs. Vanderbilt must be redecorating

again, Emily thought. Now everyone in town will be yanking down drapes and getting rid of furniture that had scarcely been sat on.

Or was there another reason? Why the sudden interest in Emily's suite of rooms? Could it be that her mother was feeling guilty again for neglecting her daughter? The only time Harriet Blackburn visited this end of the second floor was to make sure the maids were cleaning properly or to criticize the lack of starch in the lace curtains that hung between the drapes.

Whatever the cause, Emily hated to see her bedroom changed. She had picked out the hand-printed wallpaper herself and loved its pattern of alternating violet nosegays and strewn daisies. Her favorite color, purple, was in the satin draperies and the tufted bedspread. Violet-sprigged satin skirted her vanity table, and lavender-fringed shades covered the gas globes, softening the harsh glare.

"Ready?" Meg held up the silk taffeta gown.

While Meg dropped the gown over her head, Emily hung onto one slender pencil post of her rosewood bed.

"Turn around," Meg said, buttoning the last loop of Emily's gown. "It looks perfect. Sit down and I'll put your hair up." Taking a silver-backed brush, the maid deftly brushed Emily's hair, sweeping the champagne-colored strands into a Psyche knot on top of her head, puffing the sides and front into a soft pompadour. She pulled wisps to curl over Emily's forehead and lie sweetly on the nape of her neck.

Emily stared at her reflection in the mirror. The hairstyle was becoming, flattering her high cheekbones and long, graceful neck. Once Emily's silvery beige horsetail-straight hair reached her knees. She used to climb up on a chair to see it all in the mirror. But her nurse, a starchy English nanny, complained that the child's hair was unmanageable and was making her vain besides. Vanity, of course, was not proper, so Mrs. Blackburn had Emily's hair cut when she was nine. From then on, Emily's hair grazed her shoulder blades but was never allowed to grow longer.

She held her head still while Meg pinned a trio of rosy feathers to one side of her head, then the maid fastened a pearl choker around her neck and slipped matching earrings into Emily's pierced ears.

A dawn-colored scarf, silver evening bag, and silk elbow gloves completed her outfit.

"There," Meg said with the satisfaction of a job well done. "You're a regular Gibson girl, Emily. You'll knock 'em dead tonight."

Emily stood. Her gown was an exquisite creation of changeable moiré taffeta; the delicate pinks and grays of a pigeon's throat suited her fair complexion. The box-pleated skirt fell from the Empire waist, the full leg-of-mutton sleeves narrowed to wrist-cinching bands, trimmed with irridescent beads like tiny soap bubbles.

Yes, Emily agreed silently. *From head to toe I'm the perfect Gibson girl. Except for my eyes.* The empty, metallic cast had crept into her eyes again, her expression lifeless.

The mirror darkened as the pale evening light ebbed, and when Emily looked past her reflected image, she saw nothing.

If anyone will look like the perfect Gibson girl, it'll be Annabelle, Emily decided as Worth's carriage pulled up before Walter Blackburn's three-story brownstone. Her uncle's house was lit top to bottom, and a liveried footman assisted guests from their carriages.

Headstrong Annabelle, she knew, could always play whatever part she chose. Tonight Annabelle was acting as hostess for the first time. This evening should be quite a triumph for her seventeen-year-old cousin.

"Annabelle has been campaigning for months to hostess this dinner party," Emily said to Worth. "She even got my mother to appeal to Uncle Walter —"

"Who gave in as usual." Worth adjusted his snowy cuffs, causing the sapphire studs to sparkle in the light slanting through the carriage window. Even though she couldn't see his face in the semidarkness, Emily suspected that Worth had raised one sandy eyebrow in sardonic amusement. "Can anyone ever resist the charming Miss Annabelle Blackburn?"

Worthington Bates III, better known as Worth, gave Emily's arm an affectionate squeeze to let her know that he found her every bit as charming as her cousin. Emily was tempted to swat him the way she did when they were younger.

Two years older than Emily, Worth used to take advantage of his seniority by teasing her, sometimes unmercifully. But now at eighteen, Worth stepped into the role of polished escort with ease.

Emily, Annabelle, and Worth had grown up in each other's company, linked by their fathers' business. The Blackburn family firm, owned by Emily's father Gifford and her Uncle Walter, took in a third partner before Emily was born, Worth's father.

"We're a triumvirate," eleven-year-old Worth had declared when their tutor assigned them *Julius Caesar*. "Like the rulers of ancient Rome. Without each other we are nothing." Annabelle had thought his notion a little farfetched, especially since she struggled with Shakespeare's play. But Emily adored the idea.

"Mother and Papa just pulled up behind us," Emily remarked now, glancing out the back window. "We can get out now."

The footman sprang forward to open the carriage door, helping Emily alight. When

Harriet and Gifford Blackburn were assisted from their carriage, the two couples were ready to enter together.

"Carry your train, dear," Harriet instructed her daughter after studying Emily critically on the flagstone walk. "Don't let it drag."

Emily picked up the circle of taffeta, slipping the fingerloop over her index finger. As always, her mother was resplendent, if a little plump, in a gold Pacquin evening gown, topped with an ivory satin opera cloak.

"Let's get this going," Gifford Blackburn said, tapping his cane on the walk. "Emily, you're holding up the parade."

Stifling a giggle at her father's flip remarks, Emily led the way into her uncle's marbled entrance hall.

Leave it to Annabelle to stage a scene, she thought when she first saw her cousin.

Posed dramatically under a full-length portrait of herself, Annabelle Blackburn graciously greeted guests into her father's home. The painting was compelling; Emily felt herself being drawn into the knowing blue eyes.

But tonight Annabelle managed to look even more beautiful than her portrait. Her blonde hair, more golden than Emily's, was upswept in swirls on top of her head. A solitary ostrich plume tucked into the curls made her appear haughty and older than her seventeen years. She wore a chiffon gown in that new shade of green, belted with gold mesh, which whittled her waist to fashionable nothingness.

Almond-shaped, china-blue eyes, tipped slightly upward, coolly appraised Emily and Worth as they approached. "Good evening." Annabelle's voice was as melodious as the swan fountain that stood nearby, banked with pots of white lilies and trickling scented water. Another prop in a well-staged setting, Emily thought.

Worth bowed gallantly over Annabelle's extended hand. "Mr. Gibson would be so proud. You certainly do his drawings justice."

"Don't spoil this for me, Worthington." Annabelle spoke through gritted teeth, although her smile never faltered. "Emily, don't you look sweet. And your mother let you put your hair up tonight. It looks wonderful. Good evening, Aunt Harriet, Uncle Gifford. So glad you could come."

Emily's cheeks flamed as the reception line moved down the hall. Harrison, Uncle Walter's butler, took Emily's velvet wrap and the coat Worth wore flung over his shoulders. She could have killed Annabelle! Imagine mentioning that her mother "let" Emily put her hair up, in front of all these people. Just because Annabelle would be presented next summer, she acted as though she were years older than Emily, instead of the scant nine months that separated them. Everyone knew that young ladies usually wore their hair loose or tied back with ribbons until their debut, after which they put their hair up, signifying their entry into womanhood. Annabelle had been wearing her hair up for months now. Uncle Walter, who had always spoiled his only child, gave in to his daughter's wheedling, and Annabelle had lorded it over Emily ever since. Because this evening was special, Harriet permitted Emily to dress her hair in a Gibson-style pompadour.

The Gibson look. Every girl in New York coveted and imitated the style made famous by popular illustrator Charles Dana Gibson, whose drawings depicted his ideal of American beauty: "shatteringly pretty," with a wasp waist, swirls of hair, long eyelids, and a slightly tragic air, like Juliet.

Except for the latter, Annabelle could have stepped out of a Gibson drawing. Already several admirers clustered around her, hoping to capture her attention in the moments before dinner.

"She certainly has changed in the last year," Worth commented, following Emily's gaze.

When the butler announced dinner, Worth offered his elbow to Emily, and they followed the other guests into the dining room.

"Annabelle's first party seems to be a success," Emily said, waving to her Uncle Walter, who was across the room.

"Did you expect anything less?"

"No, I suppose not." Emily turned slightly

away from him, feeling the shadow of her vivacious cousin looming over her.

As Emily took her place a footman shook out the tulip-folded damask napkin and laid it across her lap.

Annabelle took her seat at one end of the long table, signaling the waiters to begin serving.

Worth lifted his water goblet in a mock salute to Emily. "To the new century."

"Don't say that too loud," Emily warned. "You'll start an argument, and Annabelle will be furious."

"I don't care if 1900 marks the new century or not. Just so I go on my grand tour." Worth was looking forward to the traditional journey young men made, traveling the Continent for a year or more, before settling into the gentlemanly pursuit of making money. Emily dreaded the prospect of Worth's grand tour — he'd be gone so long!

The dinner was a long, tedious affair, lightened only by Worth's whispered witticisms.

As the soup course was removed and replaced with Virginia ham in champagne sauce, the inevitable occurred: the conversation veered to the coming turn of the century.

"December thirty-first only marks the end of ninety-nine years," an old man was stating emphatically to Emily's mother. "These anxious young pups have the date reckoned wrong. It takes a full one hundred years to make a century and that won't happen until December thirty-first, 1901."

Who cares? Emily thought, dipping her fingers into the rose-petaled fingerbowl that preceded the dessert course. *Whether the next year is 1900 or 1999, I'll be just as miserable.*

Looking over the centerpiece of hothouse orchids, she glanced at her cousin, who was enthralling the senator's son on her right. Annabelle will debut and get married. Worth will go to Europe. And what did she have to look forward to?

Nothing . . . nothing at all, since that awful day of discovery last summer.

SUNFIRE®

Read all about the fascinating young women who lived and loved during America's most turbulent times!

☐ 32774-7		**AMANDA** Candice F. Ransom	$2.95
☐ 33064-0		**SUSANNAH** Candice F. Ransom	$2.95
☐ 33156-6		**DANIELLE** Vivian Schurfranz	$2.95
☐ 33241-4	#5	**JOANNA** Jane Claypool Miner	$2.95
☐ 33242-2	#6	**JESSICA** Mary Francis Shura	$2.95
☐ 33239-2	#7	**CAROLINE** Willo Davis Roberts	$2.95
☐ 33688-6	#14	**CASSIE** Vivian Schurfranz	$2.95
☐ 33686-X	#15	**ROXANNE** Jane Claypool Miner	$2.95
☐ 41468-2	#16	**MEGAN** Vivian Schurfranz	$2.75
☐ 41438-0	#17	**SABRINA** Candice F. Ransom	$2.75
☐ 33933-8	#18	**VERONICA** Jane Claypool Miner	$2.25
☐ 40049-5	#19	**NICOLE** Candice F. Ransom	$2.25
☐ 40268-4	#20	**JULIE** Vivian Schurfranz	$2.25
☐ 40394-X	#21	**RACHEL** Vivian Schurfranz	$2.50
☐ 40395-8	#22	**COREY** Jane Claypool Miner	$2.50
☐ 40717-1	#23	**HEATHER** Vivian Schurfranz	$2.50
☐ 40716-3	#24	**GABRIELLE** Mary Francis Shura	$2.50
☐ 41000-8	#25	**MERRIE** Vivian Schurfranz	$2.75
☐ 41012-1	#26	**NORA** Jeffie Ross Gordon	$2.75
☐ 41191-8	#27	**MARGARET** Jane Claypool Miner	$2.75

Complete series available wherever you buy books.

Scholastic Inc.
P.O. Box 7502, 2932 East McCarty Street, Jefferson City, MO 65102

Please send me the books I have checked above. I am enclosing $_____
(please add $1.00 to cover shipping and handling). Send check or money order--no cash or C.O.D.'s please.

Name_____

Address_____

City_____ State/Zip_____

Please allow four to six weeks for delivery. Offer good in U.S.A. only. Sorry, mail order not available to residents of Canada. Prices subject to change.

SUN987

point®

Other books you will enjoy,
about real kids like you!

- ☐ 40708-2 **Acts of Love** Maureen Daly
- ☐ 40545-4 **A Band of Angels** Julian F. Thompson
- ☐ 41289-2 **The Changeover: A Supernatural Romance**
  Margaret Mahy
- ☐ 40251-X **Don't Care High** Gordon Korman
- ☐ 40969-7 **How Do You Lose Those Ninth Grade Blues?**
  Barthe DeClements
- ☐ 40935-2 **Last Dance** Caroline B. Cooney
- ☐ 40548-9 **A Royal Pain** Ellen Conford
- ☐ 41115-2 **Seventeen and In-Between**
  Barthe DeClements
- ☐ 33254-6 **Three Sisters** Norma Fox Mazer
- ☐ 40832-1 **Twisted** R.L. Stine
- ☐ 40383-4 **When the Phone Rang** Harry Mazer
- ☐ 40205-6 **Yearbook** Melissa Davis

**Available wherever you buy books...
or use the coupon below. $2.50 each**